RETURN
OF THE
DRAGON

RETURN
OF THE
DRAGON

ALEX J. WEBSTER

Shazbaar Press

Fonts used with permission from Microsoft.

Cover Design: Rob Williams - C5 Designs

Printed in the United States of America
First Printing, 2016
ISBN 978-0-9969880-0-1

Shazbaar Press

For Mina,

"Ah, that wonderful Madam Mina! She has man's brain, a brain that a man should have were he much gifted, and a woman's heart. The good God fashioned her for a purpose, believe me, when He made that so good combination."

Prologue

Trail of Blood

Dearest Mary,   **Oct. 4th, 1897**

11:00 AM- I was greatly refreshed to spend my fleeting days on land with you and it pains me to be departed from you. Indeed, my heart aches knowing we must be apart these many weeks. I pray that when I return from Varna that I may convince your father that I would indeed be a fine husband for his daughter!

I have decided, when expedient, to write to you in this journal. The thought of conversing with you through these entries warms me. For though they be mere words on the page, the act of writing transports me to your Father's sitting room where we spent many a night laughing and enjoying sweet fellowship. It is my hope that through this journal that you can begin to understand what my life on board the *Czarina Catherine* consists. Through them, I pray you will be armed with knowledge to entreat your father on my behalf to bring me into the family business and that I may leave the life of the sea. A life that I would happily leave to others!

5:30 PM- We brought on a passenger late this afternoon. He carried himself as a gentleman. Count De Ville is his name. It is amazing what doors open when presented with a full money purse! Although we carry only cargo in our holds and have no accommodations for passengers, our guest prevailed himself to ride along with his cargo. I gather from his accent, he is from Varna. I am not sure if he is representative of his race, but he seemed frail and undernourished. He was introduced to Captain Donelson's foul mouth. The captain's vocabulary has been so overladen with expletives that he has seen fit to supplement it with expletives from other tongues. He is a veritable "Tower of Babel" of curse words! The crew delights listening to his harangues. I must carry his shame for him since he seems to have no use for it. His continued ranting against the French is tiresome and one would think we are still in the middle of the Napoleonic Wars! I pray that you may never have to bear his presence.

6:30 PM- At sundown, Count De Ville returned with a horse and cart with his cargo in a great box. The men from the Eastern lands must be of hearty stock; for, he single-handedly removed the crate from the cart. I would have dismissed the account had I not seen it with my own eyes! It required 4 men to load it into the ship's hold! The stranger did not come aboard but said he had other business to attend to which sent Captain Donelson to cursing him, threatening to leave without him once high tide arrived.

7:00 PM- The tide is rising, but a sudden mist has risen from the river. It was strange how quickly it thickened and enveloped the ship. I disembarked to retrieve some additional dry goods for the ship's cook and to my surprise the fog seemed to blanket only the *Czarina Catherine*! I pray this is not an omen of bad seas ahead.

7:30 PM- Count De Ville returned and once he was assured his cargo was secured; the fog quickly dissipated. We will be able to embark on the ebb tide. Captain Donelson is silent and the men prepare to get underway. May God have mercy on us.

Dearest Mary,   **Oct. 5th, 1897**

8:30 AM- I rose early today and went to retrieve the Count for breakfast, but he was nowhere to be found. I inquired with the crew and none had seen him since the previous evening. The *Czarina Catherine* is not a large ship. I pray nothing ill has befallen him.

10:30 AM- Still no sign of the Count. We fear he may have fallen overboard.

2:00 PM- I overheard some of the crew debating whether the cargo which the Count loaded was of any worth. The Count's insistence on traveling with it has convinced some that it must be of great value. They are convinced that they will all be rich once it is distributed among themselves. I broke up the conversation by insisting that the cargo was going to arrive in Varna with or without the Count. It is very unnerving to stand up to this rough crew. Some of them are twice my age and their disdain for me can barely be hidden. I shall speak to the captain about the matter.

5:30 PM- The weather has taken a turn for the worse. The sky filled up with angry clouds and a stiff wind has picked up from the Southwest. The clouds obscure all attempts at finding our bearings. I believe we may be nearing Dieppe but is hard to say. The rate which this storm is strengthening is frightening.

7:00 PM- I must take a break from the storm to write what I have just witnessed. As the crew and I struggled to keep the ship on course, I saw the Count standing at the bow of the ship. He stood as hardened flint against the howling storm and seemed at perfect peace. As the crew was buffeted from port to starboard, he was rigid as a mast! I went to him to entreat him to find shelter below and the look on the Count's face shall haunt me forever. He had the countenance of a demon! His eyes glared a hellfire red and the grin of on his face was that of a sneering wolf. It shook me that I forgot the storm raging around me and had to retreat. I will keep my distance from him. He is not as he appears. An evil cloud follows him.

11:30 PM- The ferocity of the storm has passed. The ship has been terribly damaged; we have 2 crew unaccounted for. Must rest. More later...

Dearest Mary,   **Oct 6ᵗʰ, 1897**

7:30 AM- It has been less than two days since our departure and yet this must be the longest journey I have ever undertaken. From the bearings we have taken we seem to be have been blown north. Captain Donelson has stated that Calais will be the closest port.

9:00- Sad news. We are missing another crewman. I know I saw him after the storm and I have my suspicions; I dare not voice them.

9:30 AM- I believe I am going mad. I saw the Count while below deck and he appeared to be 20 years younger!

12:00 Noon- Nearing Calais. Count De Ville seemed greatly agitated. I overheard him speaking of a Dutchman. This Dutchman must be formidable to cause him such distress.

2:00 PM- We are done with Count De Ville. He insisted that his cargo be unloaded at Calais. He could not disembark fast enough. I pray that the remainder of our journey will be uneventful.

~ FIELD DISPATCH ~

FROM: Captain James Willard, MD

Medical Corps

1st. Battalion, Dorset Regiment.

TO: Major John Appleby, MD

Medical Corps

1st. Battalion, Dorset Regiment.

DATE: 27 May 1915

LOCATION: Bellewaarde Ridge, east of Ypres, Belgium.

*****

Sir,

I trust that you are recovering from your injuries and that you will soon be released from the hospital.

As requested, I submit my report on the aftermath of the Second Battle of Ypres, with specific reference to the assistance of the wounded on and around Bellewaarde Ridge, after the German retreat of 25th May 1915.

It appears that losses to Allied forces could have been even greater than they have been, had not the Germans begun to run short of munitions, supplies, and manpower. Having said that, the casualties for this battle are estimated at close to 70 000 souls, including 10 000 French losses.

It has been a disastrous tragedy of epic proportions, I'm afraid to inform you.

The enemy's first use of poisonous chlorine gas, in the late afternoon of 22nd April, took everyone by complete surprise and caused devastation amongst the French 45th and 87th Divisions at Gravenstafel Ridge.

This cowardly attack opened up an 8 000 yard gap in the Allied lines and the 1st Canadian Division of the Second British Army fought bravely to counter the German occupation of the breached area.

As you know, they again launched a gas attack on 24th April in an effort to take St. Julien, just before you suffered your shrapnel wound. There was another gas attack on 1st May, near Hill 60, but the enemy was beaten back by a force which included many of our own battalion. It made me very proud to be a part of the 1st Battalion, Dorset Regiment.

Now, as to the details of the aftermath:

As you are well aware, the no-man's land, between Bellewaarde Ridge, and running eastwards towards the German trenches, was a complete slaughterhouse.

Every time we sent men over the top, the majority were mown down by the German machine guns before they got more than a hundred yards. You are well aware of the carnage, and the wounded we have treated together bear testimony to man's inhumanity to man.

As with every other attempt to rescue the wounded from that dread killing-field, the Germans had left snipers behind when they started retreating and we were hampered in our efforts to a great extent by them. Eventually, it was decided to postpone the rescue attempts until after dark on 25th May, so that our men did not become mere additions to the toll.

You would hardly recognize that field now, sir. Instead of the verdant trees and grass, the terrain is just a quagmire of mud and shell holes, with scarce a blade of grass or vegetation visible anywhere, such was the artillery barrage we sustained during that month of hell. So it was a wonderful relief to see the German forces retreating after such a long time.

As to the unearthly conditions in those trenches, it breaks my heart to recall and relate them, but this I must certainly do. Every day, men were dying around us. The trenches became mud-bedecked and rain-soaked breeding grounds for all sorts of pests, from fleas to clouds of flies, maggots, and mosquitoes which tormented us beyond a reasonable man's tolerance.

But the very worst were the rats!

These demons from Hades would actually feast on the dead bodies of our men; any open wound was an invitation to a banquet for the horrific beasts. The soldiers, exhausted and hungry themselves, would bayonet and bludgeon the rats so that hundreds of dead rodent carcasses lay strewn all along the trenches, being trodden underfoot until they disappeared into the general muck and mud.

And still, the rats came. Now, they were emboldened to attack even the living, and I have treated men who had suffered the most horrendous maulings as they fell into fitful sleep.

A severely wounded infantryman lay sprawled on the trench floor while a rat burrowed its way into the eyeball he'd taken a bullet in. By the time his companions could get him to our field hospital, not a hundred yards along that same trench, the man's brain had been eaten half away and he had succumbed. This plague of rats is almost as terrifying, sir, as the bombardment. And I lived in fear of a pandemic amongst the troops as to wipe out as many souls as the accursed enemy had done.

So to the night of 25th May, when the enemy had finally gone, leaving just the snipers to guard the killing-field . . .

I was assigned a group of ten sappers from the Engineers to help me and took along three medics I thought I could spare from hospital duty. The fourteen of us went over the top with not much attention from the snipers and almost immediately ran into a pile of dead humanity, not twenty meters from the lip of the trench. The poor buggers had been mown down in the last push we made over the top; a totally wasted effort in hindsight, sir.

There was not a man alive amongst this first batch, but we found many wounded and dying a little further into that field. The sappers were extremely helpful to us and they made numerous trips back to the field hospital supporting and carrying the soldiers we had treated and bandaged up. They worked like men possessed and I have the names of those who assisted us - that is, the names of the eight who survived. Two were shot dead in their tracks by a German sniper as they carried a litter.

In passing, sir, there was a strange and eerie occurrence on that night.

It was getting towards dawn and I was convinced that we could do no more to help. The two engineers had just died and I feared that if we tarried any longer, the sniper fire would be the death of us all. We could neither see nor hear any more survivors, and we had to call an end to the search.

And then we saw it - the biggest wolf imaginable, sir, not fifty yards to our right. I remember wondering how it could have survived the huge bombardments – and what indeed, it was doing here at all. It was feeding on something, and I fear it may have been a human corpse.

Suddenly it looked up, eyes gleaming red, blood smeared across its jowls, and started loping towards us.

Well! The men split in all directions, some back to the trenches, but I, two of my medics and a single sapper took off towards the stream, further into no-man's land.

The beast bore down on us in a flash. My men and I made it to the stream and waded into its rushing torrent. We crossed over to the other side, forgetful of snipers and all other dangers but this ferocious-looking beast. It came to the opposite bank and stopped, eyeing us malevolently. I wondered why it should hesitate so, but then it trotted away to the south - and we saw it no more.

*****

Case Number: TG-061019290130

Date: 6 October 1929

Reporting Officer: F. Albrecht

Prepared By: C. Kasper

Incident Type: Homicide

Address of Occurrence: Tiergarten, Western sector near Neuer See

Victim Name: Sofie Klein [Identity confirmed]

Cause of Death: Undetermined. Awaiting autopsy

Weapon/Objects Used: Undetermined

Witnesses:

Jan Bergmann

Lukas Fuchs

Evidence: Purse

Contents: Silhouette matchbook

25 Deutsch Marks

Coin purse

Keyring (3 keys)

ID card

Lipstick case

Compact

Crime Scene

On 6 October 1929, at approximately 0045, Jan Bergmann and Lukas Fuchs, both from the Agricolastrasse and Jagowstrasse block, entered Tiergarten from the southwest entrance. As they walked along the bank of the Neuer See, they spotted victim lying in the grass. The witnesses approached victim to render assistance and found her unresponsive. Call to the station was logged at 0105. Witnesses claim to have no relationship with the victim.

The victim was laying in a prone position with arms to her side. Her legs were together. There was no sign of a struggle. Body placement may indicate murder occurred in a different location. No indication of sexual assault. No blood present at the scene. Wound discovery found no significant wounds. Two small puncture wounds found on victim's neck. Puncture wounds seemed significant enough for blood loss. No blood present. The precision of the wounds and absence of struggle may point to use of general anesthesia, perhaps pointing to someone with medical experience. At this point in the investigation, this is merely speculation.

Victim's purse was found intact. Robbery does not seem to be motive due to the presence of 25 Deutsch Marks in purse. For a complete inventory of contents, see attached list. A matchbook from the Silhouette cabaret on the corner of Geisbergstrasse and Kulmbachstrasse was also present.

Inquiries at the Silhouette indicate the victim was a frequent patron. From all accounts, the victim was well-liked at the establishment. She was last seen leaving The Silhouette alone on October 5th at approximately 2300.

A search of victim's flat uncovered address book and various correspondences. Officer Albrecht is following up on leads produced through a search of victim's flat.

Case Number: CH-121019290630

Date: 12 October 1929

Reporting Officer: G. Vogel

Prepared By: C. Kasper

Incident Type: Homicide

Address of Occurrence: 9-10 Fasanenstrasse

Victim Name: Unknown

Cause of Death: Trauma to throat [See attached report]

Weapon/Objects Used: Unknown

Witnesses:

William Fitzpatrick [American citizen]

Gretchen Bauer

Evidence: None

Crime Scene

On 12 October 1929 at approximately 0130, witnesses William Fitzpatrick and Gretchen Bauer left the Delphi Palace Dance Hall on Kantstrasse. Herr Fitzpatrick and Fraulein Bauer were guests at the Savoy Berlin on 9-10 Fasanenstrasse in Charlottenburg borough. Witnesses entered alley adjacent to the Savoy to enter through the back entrance. Upon entering the alley, witnesses observed body lying between two rubbish bins. The call was logged at the station at 0145.

The victim appears to be a 20 YO male. The body was splayed on the pavement with the head facing toward the sky. Legs were separated and arms were positioned overhead of the victim. The victim's forearms had three-pronged slash wounds which extended the length of the forearm. The victim's throat had been mutilated. Despite the severity of the wounds, there was little blood on the scene.

Observation: Lack of blood on scene may indicate that murder occurred in a different location. Similarities with case # TG-061019290130. Both victims appear to have been exsanguinated. Both murders are a short distance from the Bahnhof Zoo Station. I will consult with Officer Albrecht.

Case Number: CH-121919290345

Date: 19 October 1929

Reporting Officer: G. Vogel

Prepared By: C. Kasper

Incident Type: Homicide

Address of Occurrence: 12-13 Kurfürstendamm

Victim Name: Unknown

Cause of Death: [See attached report]

Weapon/Objects Used: Undetermined

Witnesses:

Emmerich Neumann

Reinhold Beck

Adelaide Beck

Crime Scene

On 19 October 1929, the witnesses left their place of employment at the Gloria Palace on Auguste –Viktoria –Platz at approximately 0200. Witnesses recall seeing the silhouette of a man kneeling in Plaza. The man seemed startled by witnesses' approach and walked at a swift pace toward the Kaiser Wilhelm Memorial Church. It was at this point that the witnesses observed the victim's body in the plaza. The witnesses crossed the Kurfürstendamm near the Kaiser Wilhelm Memorial Church to render assistance. The 2 male witnesses pursued the suspect but were unable to see any trace of the suspect. Call to the station was logged at 0215.

The victim appears to be a 40 YO female. She was found in a fetal position. The body had no identification. She was fully clothed with no evidence of sexual assault. Wound discovery found no major wounds. 2 symmetrical puncture wounds found on the neck. A significant amount of blood found on victim's blouse and overcoat. Wounds from the neck do not seem to be the source of blood. The source of blood is undetermined.

Evidence discovery found a trail of bloodied footprints leading away from crime scene. Footprints disappeared in the middle of plaza. The footprints measured 28 cm in length.

22 April 1938

Hauptmann Schröder,

I am reporting that our occupation of the Krieger Gut located on the banks Schwabach River has been a success. Our original assessment that the manor house was vacant turned out to be inaccurate. The main building was heavily guarded by twenty-five (25) gypsies. They appeared to have taken up residence and were very protective of the grounds; not giving up any ground without direct engagement. Their ferocity in defending the manor was surprising when you take into account their race is one known for being nomadic. Unfortunately, we sustained more casualties than our projections estimated. To gain positive control of the house, and the surrounding area without damaging the structural integrity of the manor itself I was forced to call upon the assistance of the Einsatzkommandos. The storm troopers were able to clear the entire building in a matter of hours while my platoon secured the small houses within a twenty-kilometer radius. The specialty soldiers have vacated the position and my own platoon has set a base of operations as well as roaming patrols of the parameter. I would like to assure you that upon your arrival you shall find the accommodations to meet or even surpass your expectations. We have a clear line of sight in nearly every direction with little to no cover which should prove an advantage should the enemy attempt an ambush. We have placed sandbag bunkers and reinforced the outlying structures, as well as the main house. We currently number sixty-three strong including myself, with seven losses and three wounded during the initial occupation process. I will report with updates and any status changes.

-Oberleutnant Stockhauson, Jans

25 April 1938

Oberleutnant Stockhauson,

I am pleased to receive word of your success. The Krieger Gut position is one of tactical importance. If we are called upon to come to the defense of our brothers in the Sudetenland, we will be well placed to come to their aid. Since Krieger Gut lies only fifty kilometers from where the Schwabach River meets the Rednitz, it will be crucial in maintaining a steady supply route. The outlying farmland is plentiful in the spring time, and the storehouses should still be close to full at this time and we have a long campaign ahead of us. I intend to accompany the Garrison commander to your position before summer's end; however; our cause does not permit me the luxury of a visit for inspection at the present time. My current duties are of critical importance and I am unable to discuss such matters through correspondence. I look forward to receiving your status reports as well as a full supply inventory of the newly established outpost.

-Hauptmann Schröder, Alrich

27 April 1938

Hauptmann Schröder,

It is with great excitement that I report to you the fruits of our exploration of this area. The store houses seem nearly untouched with supplies, and the moment we obtain water transport, a steady supply line should be easily established. My men are well fed and well rested. I do however wish to inform you that our wounded are not fairing as well as they should be. Medical supplies are abundant and our medic competent, yet recovery has made little progress for the three wounded. The medics have told me they complain hearing a pig at odd hours of the night. As detailed within my supply ledgers, there is an absence of any livestock on the premises, which initially led me to believe the men were simply feverish. Upon his examinations, the medic informed that the wounds that were sustained are nowhere near fatal, and no fever has set upon any of them; yet they grow frail and weak with each passing day. Last evening, soon after nightfall one young private was in a state near panic, clawing at his ears and begging for us to silence the bell tower. I dispatched a squad to search the parameter, and they confirmed the lack of any structures containing a belfry. Under normal circumstances, I wouldn't concern you with such a trivial matter, yet word has spread amongst the platoon. Some of the men are speaking of witchcraft, or curses placed upon us by the previous occupants. I seek your guidance on how to properly handle the matter and maintain the high level of morale we currently enjoy. I have attached a ledger of the current supply list and request three to four watercraft to properly establish a supply line to and from our outpost.

- Oberleutnant Stockhauson

29 April 1938

Oberleutnant Stockhauson,

I have reviewed the enclosed ledgers and I am quite pleased with your report. I will have my staff procure the requested watercraft to establish a steady supply line. Unfortunately, I cannot give you an accurate arrival time due to the majority of the resources at my disposal being dedicated elsewhere to support more critical missions. Do not be discouraged, your post is very much necessary and our ability to maintain a holding on the position may later prove to be a key component in the success of the upcoming campaign. As for the issue with the wounded soldiers, you have mentioned. I must say that I am rather disappointed in your inability to properly handle the matter. I expect more critical thinking from my officers, and would encourage you to solve such insignificant issues at a much lower echelon. Were it me in your situation, my actions would be to quarantine the wounded, and allow minimal contact with the other soldiers. This would include reducing, or even eliminating non-medical personnel from having any contact with the wounded until their madness ceases to be. However, should this issue begin to grow beyond your control you have my permission, as well as that of the Garrison Command to evacuate, or, if necessary, dispatch the wounded as you see fit to maintain proper health and morale for the rest of your unit. Should you choose the latter option, I would highly recommend doing so with utmost discretion and ensure the official record reflects they have each died of their wounds. I trust that you shall take appropriate action and will no longer concern me with such petty matters.

-Hauptmann Schröder, Alrich

6 May 1938

Hauptmann Schröder,

I apologize in advance for the mixture of good and bad news contained within this report. The roaming patrol has reported an absence of enemy activity, and all has remained quiet. We have received two of the requested watercraft, and I greatly appreciate the additional personnel you have granted me. This brings our numbers to seventy-six (76) not to include the crew members of each craft which I assume are only there for transport. Although the physical conditioning and training of the men has been a continuous effort, an illness has begun to develop amongst my platoon. It has been affecting some of the junior enlisted amongst us and has incapacitated nearly half of the third squad. It began but three days past when Bravo Team returned from roaming patrol. The report was insignificant, containing the same terrain features with zero enemies sighted. The team leader, Oberschütze Reiser, reported an odd occurrence which took place soon after nightfall. The team was returning to the post, when they spotted a roaming pig, followed closely by a woman in white. The woman did not acknowledge him when he hailed her and showed no intention of responding to any of his inquiries. As the men approached the woman seemed to drift away and vanish into the darkness, following the grunting sounds from the pig she accompanied. Upon their return, the parameter guards denied spotting anything out of the ordinary, be it human or animal. To promote a speedy recovery, the returning patrol would be permitted sleep in the common room of the main house until proper barracks have been constructed. All appeared to be in order until the morning after when the entire fire team was found tightly bound in their bedrolls. None, to include Unteroffizier Lutz Schacht, the team leader would rise from their resting places upon the floor. When probed to arise, he only curled up like a child and began to mutter about the shadow that consumed his men, stealing the very warmth from their blood. The rest of the team was sluggish, and none seemed to have their wits about them, simply speaking of the grunting shadow in the night. The squad has been removed from the patrol rotation and relocated to a quarantined tent away from the main force, and our medic has assigned rotating guards to ensure no one else enter the tent but him and myself. He hopes to prevent whatever illness they may have contracted from spreading throughout the post, yet, I fear that may be an impossible task. The afflicted men can be heard screaming from their tent each night as the sun sets, and I fear that small talk of curses and witchery has become an epidemic amongst the men. Of the three wounded men, I regret to inform you that only one remains alive if the state he is in can be called such. Oberschütze Reiser, who was suffering from a broken leg during the initial assault, has fallen into a state of madness. He has been found each morning clawing at the floorboards of the small room we have been using as a detainment area in the main house. He has been heard muttering about the sound of bells, and he has even once been found unconscious with scratches across his abdomen and gashes covering his arms. The medic assumes these wounds were most likely self-inflicted as he attempted to move about the room without the aid of crutches, of which we still have none. The other two were burned last night, as the ground is too frozen and solid so any attempt at digging would only be a waste of fuel and manpower.

I have enclosed the identification tags of the deceased with this report. Tomorrow morning I shall have the main house inspected, and the medic shall perform full examinations of the remaining men. I pray we find the cause of this illness before it spreads any further.

- Oberleutnant Stockhauson

8 May 1938

Oberleutnant Stockhauson

 I agree your current situation is unfortunate, yet far from dire. I would like to encourage you to send your deceased home via the waterway if possible as well as those who are unfit for duty beyond your medic's ability to properly treat. I regret that I am not able to provide you with any additional troops for the time being. However, I plan to arrive shortly with a fresh garrison to reinforce, or replace you and your men if the need be. The supply exchanges are running smoothly, and correspondence time has been cut by a great margin. I expect you to take every measure to improve your conditions, and I have faith that you will find the source of this illness and eradicate it before my arrival. The Garrison Commander has informed me that this outpost will be under my complete control, and, therefore, I will no longer accompany him, but instead shall be present upon his arrival. I intend to arrive before the commander and will conduct a thorough inspection to assure that all is fit for occupation. I am still unable to provide you with a hard time, yet I am still confident that I shall be arriving before the year's end.

-Hauptmann Schröder, Alrich

12 May 1938

Hauptmann Schröder,

I would like to formally request additional troops and a swift evacuation of those in my unit who have taken ill. Our numbers have been decimated and the barn which had previously been used as barracks is now serving as the new infirmary. The men who report hearing these scratches during the night now outnumber those of us who hear nothing and rest somewhat peacefully. This situation grows more severe each passing night. Some of the men in the outlying bunkers have been heard firing upon the empty fields at some sort of invisible enemy. Members of the Third Squad Bravo team have been ranting about whispers in the dead of night, keeping them awake. An entire bunker had engaged in what had sounded like an intense firefight. The first incident took place only two nights ago when rifles, as well as grenades, could be heard on the parameter, and it awoke me in the dead of night. As I arrived with a fresh squad in an attempt to gain fire superiority, I was shocked to find the two men huddled together screaming and firing into the darkness. It took nearly an hour before I was able to safely detain the two and they were immediately escorted to the main house where I interrogated the two. When asked what events had taken place, the response I was given still has me skeptical, yet chills me to the very bone. They had heard the sound of a pig grunting in the darkness, soon after the sounds ceased a tall, pale man in a tattered suit appeared close to the parameter. He had ignored any commands to halt, and approached with his arms outstretched, as he was reaching for the two. The men panicked as he drew near and opened fire. The rounds expended seemed to have no effect on the man and they resorted to throwing grenades. As he approached, he stood tall, blocking out the moonlight, and both men claim that as his shadow enveloped the two of them, they could feel their blood freezing, and their bodies grow weak. He medic's examination proved useless, as there were no wounds, and both appeared to be of sound mind. Soon afterward more men claimed to have seen the very same figure stalking about the parameter, sometimes accompanied by a silent woman following. Others complain of the sound of bells ringing after the sun sets at night. My most recent head count inspection resulted in forty-six men afflicted with such madness, twelve of which are so weak and frail they are no longer considered to be fit for duty. Five more are now deceased the remains of which have accompanied the most recent supply shipment. I have reviewed the numbers, and taken multiple counts yet I still have seven personnel unaccounted for. I sent out an additional patrol to scout the surrounding area, yet they found no traces of any passer-by to include the mysterious woman in white, or the dark figure. Our location is bereft of any cover, concealment, or shelter as far as the eye can see and no traces of any means of travel have been found. Many of the men are speaking of demons as if this were the cause of all these mysterious vanishings. My every attempt to quell these rumors has fallen upon deaf ears as our once strong morale has been shattered into near nothingness. The few remaining men of sound mind grow weary and some have even begun to speak of desertion yet remain only for fear of what lies further out. I fear without a personnel rotation this outpost is doomed to collapse upon itself. The medic himself has been overtaken by this madness claiming he hears a chewing sound whenever he is alone in his quarters. The recent ailments have been greatly hindered him in any attempts made at treating the rest of the platoon. I once again must formally request reinforcements and replacements before the situation worsens.

- Oberleutnant Stockhauson

13 May 1938

Oberleutnant Stockhauson,

I am beginning to doubt your leadership abilities. After reviewing your report, doctors have confirmed that your men are experiencing what is known as cabin fever. They have been restricted to a small enclosed area, due to being confined to such a small area with idle hands. Your inability to control this situation has become an embarrassment to our fatherland, and I have no choice but to make arrangements but to send a replacement to ensure operations are correctly established before my arrival. I expected many a great deed from you Oberleutnant, yet as I reply the disappointment causes my resolve to waiver. Our great nation needs little from cowards and incompetent officers such as yourself and you will rejoice to hear that you will soon be rid of this burden. I can only hope that you find your courage and strengthen your resolve before my arrival, be expecting a replacement in eleven days.

-Hauptmann Schröder, Alrich

15 May 1938

Hauptmann Schröder,

Upon receiving your correspondence, it pains me to inform you that the situation has grown to catastrophic proportions. The men have far surpassed a simple cabin fever as you so mildly worded it. They have fallen into some form of all-consuming madness. I have been unable to conduct a proper headcount inspection, yet our numbers have grown thin. Some of the men have taken the idea to slay themselves before nightfall. The crew members of the watercraft refused to disembark, nor would they transport the deceased for fear that the madness should spread amongst them all. The outpost is a chaotic mess, men clawing their faces, some digging at the frozen earth with their hands or helmets. Others have continued to fire upon the invisible enemy occupying the vast empty fields. No man is brave enough to set foot within the main house aside from myself, Stabsfeldwebel Hettinger, and Unterfeldwebel Wilhelm Jentzsch. The rest have all been afflicted with this curse, or sickness whichever it truly is I no longer know. I no longer have control over those who occupy this outpost, and men speak of bells or grunting sounds haunting them each night. I know not what to make of the situation, nor am I able to coordinate any movement should we be attacked before the day's end. I know only that as the night falls, the three of us shall remain within the study which has served as our communications room, and pray that we survive the bombardment of insanity which has overtaken this place. The madmen tear at the floorboards, ranting about the evil haunting them and how it lies beneath the ground. I pray that you are able to see beyond your initial assessment and see the situation as it truly is.

- Oberleutnant Stockhauson

30 May 1938

Oberleutnant Stockhauson,

Please send an updated status of your situation. I have not received any communications from you in two (2) weeks. Oberleutnant Schiebau's squad has been delayed from full deployment, but they are now in the process of finalizing the details of their departure.

-Hauptmann Schröder, Alrich

5 June 1938

Hauptmann Schröder,

I am pleased to inform you of the safe arrival of myself as well as my squad; however, we were under the assumption that this outpost was fully operational. The area is large and spreads out over a wide clear area. Upon inspection of the grounds, my squad and I found sandbag bunkers, as well as an established parameter. All of the small houses as well as the barn had been converted and would likely hold a large number of troops. We found tents set up within the parameter, yet everything was deserted. The supply houses were nearly full, and enough gear to properly equip an entire platoon has been left behind neatly stored as if awaiting an inspection. Aside from the lack of personnel, there were some other discoveries we found unsettling. Scattered about there were areas where the ground had been dug up as if someone had spent their days trying to dig without the proper tools. The bunkers were found with casings of expended ammunition as if there were multiple skirmishes fought in every direction. The area around the main house was littered with empty casings as well, accompanied by small craters which looked as if grenades had been thrown about. Yet we found no traces of blood, and there were no signs that dead or wounded had been carried off. Outside the parameter, there was only a single trail which led back towards the outpost as if someone had sent out a patrol. The house itself was untouched on the outside, yet the inside we found in a state of complete disarray. In some places, the floorboards had been torn up to reveal the cold earth below. Doors were found in splinters, some still hanging, most in pieces upon the floors and scattered down the halls. The staircase had been nearly destroyed and the ceiling had collapsed in most places as if those who resided on the second floor had tried to dig their way into the ground floor. There was one door which took us much effort to open. Obergefreiter Bornhof had to pry apart the hinges and we removed it only to find that furniture had been piled up against it barring any entry. As we cleared away the debris, we found what looked to be a communications center. I must make a formal request that you send additional troops to establish a functional outpost. My squad contains only ten men to include myself, and I fear that we are not adequate in number to hold such a large area successfully. In the meantime, my squad and I will attempt to secure the rest of the parameter, and repair the damages as best we can.

-Oberleutnant Schiebau, Einhart

March 21, 1944

Night Patrols Slain at Posts

Residents of Prague 2 reported gunfire and explosions late in the night yesterday. The bodies of three patrolmen were found along their assigned routes through the Vyšehrad. The body of a fourth member of the patrol unit is still missing. Occurring between 12 PM and 1 AM, the battle between the soldiers and their assailants was short but catastrophic. Adjacent buildings were riddled with bullets and, at least, one hand grenade was detonated, causing significant structural damage to nearby houses. Fortunately, no civilians were killed.

Government authorities have been actively searching for the fourth patrolman and clues to the identity of the attackers. Given the kidnapping of a soldier, it has been widely speculated that the Czech Resistance is behind these brazen attacks. Given the swift and decisive response to the assassination of the Deputy Protector Reinhard Heydrich, it is surprising that continued resistance exists. The first action has been to systematically target the hideouts and safe houses of known sympathizers to the Czech resistance. The list of suspects grows by the hour and the government has made quick work of processing the details of the night.

The crackdown on the rebels has already begun and our servicemen will not have given their lives in vain. It is only a matter of time until the perpetrators of these murders and reckless endangerment of Czech citizens are brought to light. Confronted with the full force of the law, these rebels will very soon regret the day that they tried to smear the honorable campaign of the Reich.

March 24, 1944

Czech Resistance Brought to Justice

The villainous traitors of the Czech Resistance have been caught. Standing accused of the murders of four servicemen, two high-ranking resistance fighters have faced the courts today and suffered a significant defeat. Both men have repeatedly claimed their innocence, despite signing confessions that clearly outline their criminal actions on the night in question. They face the death penalty for treason with a pending execution date.

After uncovering an elaborate plot to sabotage military outposts and government agencies, the government authorities have been able to prevent significant damage to the unity and functionality of the Republic. The rebels' plan was months in the making and only days from being enacted. Using the cover of night to hide their insidious actions from other Czech citizens and the authorities, the resistance movement had plans to surreptitiously destabilize important points of control across Prague by cutting communications lines, damaging electrical transformers, and knocking out much of the government's operational capacities by damaging administrative transport and buildings. Because of these plans and the high degree of unrest still present in Prague, the city council has approved new curfew laws to protect the citizenry.

Taking effect immediately, public curfew hours are now set to 9 PM. All citizens must be within their residences by this time or else suffer harsh penalties to their civil liberties. The number of patrol units has been increased dramatically so enforcement will be strict. The new curfew will remain in effect until further notice. During this time, the city government will be working diligently to remove the threat of the Czech Resistance. There have been many significant leads generated through the round-up of notable resistance fighters after their counterparts' heinous murders, so take heart in your leaders' swift actions. If you have any information regarding the rebels, it will be greatly helpful to society overall if you report it to the authorities. The sooner we are all safe and united in our ideals, the sooner the curfew will be lifted.

March 26, 1944

Dear Sir,

I am writing to you regarding the loss of two of our patrol units. A cowardly ambush was sprung in the dead of night and four men lost their lives. We have been unable to locate one of the men's bodies, so we have sent notice to his family that it was destroyed in an explosion during the firefight. It is beyond obvious that the patrolmen posed a threat to the underground movement of the Czech Resistance, perhaps because they had stumbled onto a significant plot to undermine the Reich. Local witnesses from the scene had incomplete and conflicting reports on the exact occurrences of the night, so it has not been difficult to create a believable narrative to distribute to the public.

It has also been incredibly easy to detain a large group of suspects that were already established as rebel sympathizers. From this body of riffraff and degenerates, we have a wide selection of criminals to put before the Czech courts. Besides this, the murders have given us the justification we have needed to continue our monitoring policies on the public. New curfew laws have further increased our stock of known sympathizers, although we have less leverage in the courts against most of these suspects. Regardless, our new rules will make it much easier to suppress future uprisings.

All in all, we have lost four servicemen but gained a much tighter grip on the public at large. I have reassigned three new units to the patrol route where the rebel fighters were engaged. This should make them think twice about opening fire on our soldiers. Other patrols routes have been updated on this incident and been provided with adequate resources to deal with any future incidents throughout Prague.

Please give Deputy Protector Frick our assurances that this matter is under control.

Sincerely,

Stabsfeldwebel Werner

March 30, 1944

Stabsfeldwebel Werner,

Your report on this incident has some glaring omissions. I am troubled by the existence of so many witnesses to the events. Do you believe they will remain silent in the face of your provided narrative? Have you considered they will seek out the Czech Resistance for help to publish their first-hand accounts of the incident?

I have personal knowledge of one of these eyewitness accounts and I believe it foolish to ignore such a subversive story for the sake of convenience. From the court documents, I've learned that one witness has many more details about the night than you have. We have no witnesses on our side! This simple man has stated the facts so plainly that it seems impossible to discredit him without our own first-hand accounts. But the absurdity of his tale! I cannot fathom that he is sane; though this may work to our benefit should we be forced to remove his voice from the public arena.

According to his account, he saw only one assailant confront our patrolmen. He claimed that the man was tall, too large to be a normal man. He was so large that he could reach the street lamps, which he was systematically breaking. That would make him nearly 5 meters tall. When confronted by our patrolmen, this giant vanished into the shadows. One of our soldiers was taken down by a blow to the head and the battle erupted. This man carried no weapons and yet he killed all four men. The part that chills me to my soul is the final moments. According to this witness, the fourth soldier's body – the missing one – was dragged from the scene after the fight ended.

I do not know if anyone will believe this story. But I do know that it will be a significant setback to our management of the incident if the Czechs find out that it was our soldiers that caused all of the collateral damage from that night. Do whatever it takes to silence this witness and do not let this fictional giant cause any more problems for our public reception. Whether or not he is real, the threat he poses is large enough to undo us.

It is my recommendation that any action you undertake proceed with extreme caution. We are in a very precarious situation. We cannot afford the same level of force we displayed when avenging the assassination of Deputy Protector Heydrich

Regards,
  Leutnant Becker

April 6, 1944

Dear Sir,

I apologize for my incomplete response to the incident. You are correct, this witness account is very troubling. However, from all accounts, it appears the man was recounting an old Jewish myth about a Golem which arises to protect the people. I am reassured by the fantastic nature of this man's tale and believe it will be a straightforward task to label him an alcoholic and buffoon. We can explain the street lamps as collateral damage from the firefight though I was not made aware of their disrepair until your letter. I agree that discretion is necessary in this matter. I will personally locate the witness you have mentioned and see to it that his story does not reach any more ears than it already has. Thank you for your guidance and insight.

In regards to the safety of our patrolmen, I have decided to suspend all additional patrols in the Vyšehrad area during the night. Whether or not the monster from our witness's story is real, I will not risk more lives and the exposure of our cover up to prove it a farce. We will release those we have arrested as a goodwill gesture. I can assure you there is no one remaining in the area that is willing to subvert our orders. The curfew has been accepted with only a few hitches so less oversight of one neighborhood may be adequate.

As for the Czech Resistance, they will not be providing assistance to anyone soon. Their numbers have been significantly culled by our sweep of known hide-outs and the curfew has made it clear to the rest of the Czechs that obedience is more fruitful than petty nationalism.

Sincerely,

Stabsfeldwebel Werner

Dacă aveți de gând pentru a trage regelui, nu ratați.

If you plan to shoot the King, don't miss.

Good Communists

"Want to hear a joke?" Gheorghe asked. The buzz of the overhead light filled the silence.

The man across the table blankly stared back. His lips quivered on his sweat glazed face.

Gheorghe returned his stare, "Hmm? How about a joke? Everyone likes a good joke."

"Okay," he whispered.

"Why do Militiamen travel in groups of three?" The joke sent the man's eyes to the table, fixing a nervous gaze on his clasped hands. He started biting his lips as he struggled to speak.

"I have it on good authority that you know the punchline to this joke. Isn't that right, comrade..." he looked at the dossier to confirm, "Claudiu Gabor?"

Claudiu murmured, "Yes," without looking up, "It is just a joke."

"Regardless, the attitude the joke represents, undermines public order and erodes the civic spirit that the People's Republic is attempting to foster. Do you understand?"

"Yes, comrade," he said in a half-whisper.

"However, your choice of humor is not why we have ordered you in for an interview," Gheorghe flipped through the files, "Do you know Ecaterina Ardelean?"

"No."

"Well, she remembers you," Gheorghe continued, "She is a cashier at the food store on Strada Sucevei. Last Tuesday night, she was taking the daily deposit to the Central Deposit office and was savagely attacked and robbed. Does any of this ring a bell, comrade Gabor?"

"No, it doesn't," he swallowed.

"So, if we were to search your home, we would not find the 6,500 Lei that was in her possession?"

He nervously glanced up, "No."

"Comrade, you may have been able to play games with the police but..." He paused to ensure he had his attention, "the militia is different. It would be in your best interest if you fully cooperated. Do you understand?"

"Yes, comrade."

"Do you stand by your story?"

"Yes, comrade."

Gheorghe heaved a deep sigh as he slammed the folder shut, "Okay, my work is done here. Let me introduce you to a fellow comrade," his head tilted to the door behind him as his voice punched the silence, "Comrade Bălan!"

A metallic click rang through the sparse room and the door scraped on its hinges. Bălan lumbered into the interrogation room with a broad smile. Before Gheorghe could turn to speak, he was hovering over him. Gheorghe sprang from the chair, trying to avoid the fog of body odor enveloping Bălan. As Gheorghe jetted for the door, he pivoted back to Bălan, "I'll be back in thirty minutes."

Bălan scrutinized the trembling prisoner, "I should be finished in twenty." Gheorghe flashed a thin smile and bolted out the door.

Gheorghe burst out of the Militia substation onto the sidewalk. With closed eyes, he drew in a deep breath. *I can't do this anymore,* he thought. *This is not who I am.* His cheeks deflated as he slowly exhaled. Raking his fingers through his hair, He glanced at the empty sidewalks and walked. Walking helped clear his mind. He remembered walking these streets with his mother. For all the destruction and upheaval the war brought, Oradea's old quarter survived intact. *Oradea is the Vienna of Eastern Europe*, he remembered her saying. He did not appreciate it as a boy. But, now he concluded: *Beauty is wasted on the young.* How else could he explain the beautiful buildings which he grew up seeing every day? Yet, as he made his way through the streets lined with buildings with intricate vining edifices and windows entwined with sprays of vibrant color, it was as if he was seeing them for the first time. These buildings would make the buildings in the new quarters of Oradea bow their heads in embarrassment. He had never been to Vienna, but he imagined this must be close to what it would feel like. The smell of coffee brewing in the cafes and the poses people struck at the tables completed the Viennese illusion. However, the beauty of the city contrasted with the ugliness behind the interrogation room doors of Militia Substation 17.

What would she think of me now? The thought caused his chin to buckle. He did not venture far from the station. *I don't want to give Bălan too much time*, he thought. But his thoughts kept him longer than he had intended. He ran back to the interrogation room.

An empty chair greeted him when he entered the room. A soft moan rose from the far corner of the room. Comrade Gabor lay crumpled on the floor. Gheorghe knelt to help him to his feet. At his touch, he recoiled, "No, no, no please."

"Shh..." Gheorghe soothed, "Let me help you back to your cell." The blood oozing from his forehead mingled with his tears forming a macabre tapestry on his face. When he saw Gheorghe's face, he tried speaking but tripped over his shallow breaths. Finally, he choked out, "I understand, I understand." Gheorghe whispered, "I know. Just relax. Once you have recovered, we will talk again. Okay?" Gabor clung to Gheorghe's words, "Okay, okay." Gheorghe guided him through the halls to the cells.

The cell door squeaked open and Gabor entered without protest. A man slowly rose from the edge of the bunk and retrieved Gabor from Gheorghe's grasp. "This is Radu Baboescu," Gheorghe announced, "He is your cellmate."

"Comrade Baboescu," he declared, "tend to comrade Gabor." Baboescu gave Gheorghe a slight grin and a wink, "Yes, comrade."

◌੩੬◌

Walking the banks of the Crişul Repede River always gave Gheorghe a sense of sophistication. After the spring rains, the river became pregnant with rushing water. Gheorghe never tired of his walk home. It was strange how the architecture revitalized his sense of hope and creativity. Intermingled within swirling, stucco moldings, and stained glass was the drive to create and dream. It was not until he reached the outer quarters did the gloom of his life return. As he left the old quarter, the buildings abruptly changed into jagged, colorless brutes. If the old quarter reminded him of his mother, then the new quarter was a reminder of his father. The buildings of the new quarter sat there humorless, wondering why you were there with them. Very efficient and coldly calculated, they were immune to your aspirations.

Planted in this grotesque garden of former villages, most of which had been razed to the ground, were apartment blocks. Entire villages had been uprooted for the sake of efficiency and supplanted with monstrous buildings which pummeled the former countryside like brass knuckles. The earthy four-story concrete block buildings seemed to emerge overnight as if a nauseous earth had rejected them and spewed them out onto the Romanian landscape.

Gheorghe entered the belly of his apartment block. A plum tree ornamented courtyard was encircled by apartment blocks which hovered over it like playground bullies closing in on their prey. Gheorghe passed through the courtyard to reach his flat.

"How are you today?" he asked the elderly tenants who flocked to the courtyard for the breezes. "Good," they said as they turned away, avoiding his gaze. Before the purges, he was simply a police detective. Since he survived the purges and became a member of the militia, Gheorghe fell under suspicion.

"Looks like the plums are coming in beautifully," he tried to reassure them.

"Yes they are," said one of his neighbors with rigid indifference. A distinct murmuring followed behind as he passed their bench. Before the rise of the communists, the air would have been filled with animated conversations and roaring laughter; now, nervous whispers and oblique comments hung like fog.

Bunicuta Alexandrescu stood at the top of the stoop leading into the building. Her gaze fixed on Gheorghe.

"My window is jammed," her eyes glared, demanding an answer.

"Bunicuta-"

"I need my window opened. When the afternoon sun hits, it is a furnace."

"Bunicuta-"

"It is stifling in there. Do you want to come up and see for yourself?"

"Bunicuta, I believe you, but you should contact the housing cooperative. They should be able to fix it."

She flung her head to the sky, gave a heavy sigh. "You and the cooperative are trying to kill me."

"I will open it for you again, but you need to contact the cooperative."

"Thank you, my son," Bunicuta's head dropped as if in prayer.

When they assigned Gheorghe his flat, it was believed having a militiaman on the bottom floor near the entrance would deter criminal elements. Gheorghe found that it was more a deterrent to his own privacy and sleep.

Gheorghe's standard answer: *I do not manage the building. I am a militiaman*, began to take on the sound of a recording and his replies to Bunicuta's constant requests varied little each day.

With the radical changes in Romania, it was unclear who was ruling. For Gheorghe it was crystal clear; two divisions of Soviet troops removed all doubt. However, they could not be called upon to unclog a toilet. That was Gheorghe's unofficial duty. He entered the building with resignation and a deep sigh.

The metallic echoes of the hallway elevator doors closing reminded Gheorghe of prison doors. Gheorghe could not shake the thought that coming home was reporting back to his cell. Ten families lived in the cooperative and their interaction was just as utilitarian as their flats. Most of the families were placed in the cooperatives with no knowledge of who would be their neighbors. Which seemed strange to Gheorghe since Oradea was a fairly small town. Stranger still was for all the grand rhetoric about the virtues of communal living, collectivism seemed like a lonely pursuit. It could not be helped. These days bred suspicion. Even an innocent inquiry would bring a narrowing of the eyes as they inconspicuously pulled away. He entered his flat and set down his things from work.

Forty years of life was now distilled into the small confines of a small flat specifically designed for widows or bachelors. Gheorghe had filled it with family mementos and now it was a shrine to his past. An otherwise Spartan flat was adorned with ornate furniture which contrasted with the austere setting. Other than these few items Gheorghe was indifferent to his flat. The large, sun-soaked rooms of his youth were constricted into the utilitarian blandness of a Soviet housing cooperative.

After a glass of water, Gheorghe collapsed onto the divan and quickly fell asleep. Sleep came easily to him. Gheorghe had vivid dreams as a child, but even his dreams had succumbed to his surroundings. Most of the time, his sleep was dreamless. As if his life were paused for a brief moment to give him the energy to make it through another day. When he did dream, his dreams were typically filled with endless mazes of drab hallways with distant screaming or pitiful crying.

But on occasion, his dreams transported him back to his childhood and his grandfather's farm. These dreams were welcomed, but a tinge of sadness accompanied them. The ghosts of his dreams stayed with him during his waking hours. The love of his youth, Camelia, untouched by time, entered his mind and blocked out the realities of his day. In his dreams, Camelia instinctively knew he was witty, wise, and loving, qualities that would shock his neighbors and colleagues to witness in the present. She clung to his every word and playfully teased him under his grandfather's large oak tree. This was what he missed: living in peace with loved ones close at hand. As he lay under the tree with Camelia, suddenly the tree was engulfed in billows of smoke. The expansive branches swelled by an invisible fire. The smoke did not rise but collapsed into itself and fed the cloud, increasing its size and volume exponentially.

Gheorghe, please put the fire out! Camelia pleaded to him with terror-filled eyes.

His vision of the dream was fading and he reached out to her. *I don't see* - he halted. Gheorghe was suddenly seized by a burning in his lungs which gave way to spasms of coughing.

Gheorghe rolled over and waved away a veil of acrid cigarette smoke. Radu's face emerged from the cloud of smoke with narrowed eyes and a smirk.

"You need an alarm clock," Radu said.

Gheorghe bolted up from the divan in a spasm of coughing. "Radu," he said through clenched teeth, "how did you get in?"

"My friend, you disappoint me. Do you think my lock picking skills have diminished to the point that I would be reduced to knocking?"

Gheorghe mustered a weak smile as he pulled himself up from the divan. "Of course, the consummate militiaman."

"Thank you, finally, someone who acknowledges my skill and value."

"Don't get ahead of yourself."

Radu burst into laughter. "Besides, they gave me a key."

"Oh."

"Don't sound so disappointed. How long did you think you were going to live here by yourself before they assigned you a roommate? Be glad it wasn't Captain Codreanu."

"He is married."

"So there you have the solution to your problem. If you want to be rid of me, you will need to find yourself a wife."

"I will double my efforts tomorrow," Gheorghe scrubbed his face, "Any luck with comrade Gabor?"

"Oh, yes." Radu said with a grin, "Gabor was a hard one, but Bălan worked his magic. Gabor sang like a baby. He buried the money in his barn."

"Hmmm..." Gheorghe sighed.

Radu examined him, "What?"

"What do you mean, *what*?" Gheorghe deflected.

"I know you Gheorghe. What is wrong?"

Gheorghe refused to look Radu in the face. Instead, he studied the rug.

"Gheorghe-," Radu barked, "What is wrong?"

"Well," he glanced up, "Doesn't bother you how the militia operates?"

"Gheorghe," Radu protested, "Gabor nearly beat that poor woman's brains out. He deserved what he got."

"When we were police detectives, we would have never done that."

"Is that what it is?" Radu snickered, "You're afraid to get your hands dirty? As long as Bălan the Baboon is here, you won't have to worry about that."

Gheorghe gently shook his head. "It is ironic..." he murmured.

"What is?"

"For a country named The People's Republic of Romania," he stood and started toward the bathroom, "They sure seem to hate people."

Radu belted out a laugh, "Your right. You better hope our flat isn't bugged."

"I doubt it, that would be too expensive," he popped his head from the bathroom, "that is what you are here for."

Another laugh, "No worries, old friend."

Radu drifted around the apartment. Dark stained furniture crowded the walls of the apartment. "We would have more room if you got rid of all this furniture." Radu leaned back to catch

Gheorghe's eye. "Why do you keep all this stuff? It is very bourgeois, comrade," his smile broadened.

"It belonged to my mother," Gheorghe said flatly.

"There is no room for sentimentality in the new Romania, my friend." Radu's fingers groped a green glass vase with an iridescent sheen. He clumsily held it up to the light. "What use is this?"

In an instant, Gheorghe snatched it from his hands. "You are beginning to sound like a good communist," Gheorghe deflected with dismissive laughter.

"Relax," Radu assured, "I was kidding. You know me better than that."

"I'm sorry Radu. These are interesting times and you should be careful what you say."

"Gheorghe, you have nothing to worry about. The Russians' failure to grasp sarcasm has served me well."

"Perhaps," Gheorghe replied, "but as long as Captain Codreanu is Chief Inspector, he will translate your humor for them."

"Chief Prosecutor Nicholae Codreanu," Radu said broadly, "I knew people like him growing up; little men who would worm themselves into a crowd and ruin good conversation by their incessant yammering. It is so obvious that he is groveling for power. Don't the Russians see that? I think he sees himself being the head of the Securitate someday. I guess they tolerate him."

"And Codreanu will destroy anyone who gets in his way," Gheorghe added. His thoughts drifted to his old friends. There were many men that valued life more than death because they had seen the atrocities of war. These were leaders that had fought beside Gheorghe with courage and honor. They earned their positions through personal sacrifice, not the sacrifice of others. As political opponents, they were quickly swept from power in a landslide of deceit and backstabbing, enacted by men that were younger and unsatisfied with the stagnancy of peace. Codreanu masterminded these political assassinations, but blame fell through the cracks he created. Gheorghe was happy to keep his head down and maintain an unassuming position with the militia. His motto was simple: *Invisible is alive.*

"Don't think that being a member of the communist party makes you immune. You should be more careful."

"I should take your advice, but irritating people comes naturally," Radu said lightly through the bathroom door to Gheorghe.

Radu was right. Gheorghe had nothing to fear from Radu. Radu's problem was not that he spoke his mind but that his mouth seldom lets the mind intervene. It was difficult for Gheorghe to be angry with Radu because he was his only remaining friend. Gheorghe had the luxury of witnessing Radu's antics and their fallout with little of the consequences. Gheorghe savored them since he agreed with many of his views. Sarcasm and humor were how Radu coped with these turbulent times. Others stood up valiantly and bravely for their convictions. *Strong convictions have a way of shortening your life span,* Gheorghe concluded. He kept his mouth shut and avoided politics.

Gheorghe finished in the bathroom and surveyed the shared room upon his return. Radu was right. If two grown men were going to live in this apartment, then some of the furniture would have to go. The designated 10 square meters per person not only seemed unreasonable, but abusive.

"Do you think the comrade who devised this living arrangement has the same problems with space that we do?" Gheorghe asked.

Radu laughed. "Are you kidding me? They probably came up with this while eating on King Michael's banquet table."

"Yes, some people are more equal than others."

"Hey, that is funny! Did you come up with that yourself?"

"No, I read it somewhere."

"Where?"

"I don't remember. Maybe in a newspaper article," Gheorghe lied. Books banned as subversive were not to be quoted, even to your best friend.

Gheorghe scanned the room once more and gave a deep sigh.

"We will make the best of it, Gheorghe," Radu reassured.

Gheorghe mulled in his mind how they might be able to circumvent their living arrangement. A tight smile stretched across his face and he patted his friend on the back conclusively. "Well, we don't have much to work with."

Little Men and Big Offices

The small box windows reluctantly gave up the morning sun as Gheorghe awoke to Radu's heavy breathing which was interrupted by an occasional snort. Gheorghe wrestled with the windows to let in the morning breezes. Even with open windows, the air would lie stagnant giving the flat a musty smell. He quietly got dressed. As Radu lay there unresponsive to the morning light, Gheorghe began making noise to stir Radu from his slumber. When a book slammed on the table did not faze him, Gheorghe surrendered and resorted to shaking him from his slumber.

Once they arrived at the bus stop, to Radu's distress, Gheorghe kept walking. "Where are you going?"

"I prefer to walk," Gheorghe called back.

Radu stood his ground surrendering only when Gheorghe kept walking. "Is this why you woke me up so early? So you could walk? If we took the bus," Radu gasped as he caught up to Gheorghe, "we could get more sleep."

"It helps clear my mind. Besides, I need the exercise."

"Well, I will let you walk. I am empty-headed and don't need exercise. I need sleep."

Gheorghe looked at Radu's pained expression, "Are you really that out of shape?"

"What makes you think I'm out of shape?" Radu said with a face glazed with sweat.

"Well," Gheorghe started as he examined him, "You..."

Radu stared awaiting a response, "Yes?"

"Let me just say that you are not as quick on your feet as you use to be."

"You've noticed that too? Well, you have discovered my little secret. I decided I needed to slow down to give the ladies an opportunity to catch me."

Gheorghe decided to show him mercy, "We'll get on the bus at the next stop,"

"No, we'll walk today and ride tomorrow," Radu conceded, "I have never understood why you like walking so much."

"I guess it is a habit I picked up from my mother."

"She was a free spirit."

"Yes, she told me as a child she would travel with her family and be gone months at a time."

"Where would they go?"

"Everywhere but she really loved Paris and Vienna. My uncles thought she was strange because she preferred the cities. I think that is why she liked Oradea, it reminded her of Paris."

Crossing over the Crişul Repede River, they leaned on the railing watching the river swirl beneath them. On the broad banks, the wispy branches of the willows dredged the surface of the water. The river lulled Gheorghe away and quickly his thoughts sunk beneath the fast-moving current. He drew a long, contented breathe, "I hope to go to Paris someday."

"Не мочиться в реке!" cracked a booming voice. A chorus of bawdy laughter rolled down from the bank of the river. Gheorghe and Radu glanced to see disheveled Russian soldiers reclining on the grass as one acted out what appeared to be an episode from the previous night.

Radu shook his head turning his back to them, "I'll be glad when our liberators get the hell out of here."

"I guess we aren't quite liberated enough."

Radu composed himself and turned back to face the river, "Well, your family's gypsy ways are over." He flashed a grin, "for now."

"I hope you are right."

They crossed over the river and entered the park. Gheorghe turned heading toward the substation, but Radu kept going straight.

"Where are you going?"

"Let's go to the Green Tree Inn and get some coffee. I'm still trying to get the taste of yours out of my mouth."

Gheorghe's feet failed him as he faltered and stopped.

Radu turned, "You coming?"

The broad tree-lined paths emptied into what Gheorghe saw as a forgotten, unsolved crime scene. Gheorghe brooded over why no one seemed concerned about all that happened here. However, the rapid changes throughout the country did not give people the luxury of introspection. The expansive park, once open and inviting, now had the stain of melancholy to Gheorghe. The park was mostly unchanged from his youth yet the statue and trees seemed to stand a silent watch, waiting to reveal the secrets they had witnessed.

Radu became distant; his voice muffled and entwined in Gheorghe's thoughts.

"Gheorghe," Radu broke his trance, "What's wrong?" He followed Gheorghe's gaze to a large building outside the park.

As a child, while climbing the trees and chasing his big brother, Ulmann Palace kept watch over the south entrance of the park. Its topmost rounded windows peered over the treetops. Its cupola in the center of the roof became the crow's nest of a pirate ship in the imagination of a child. Gheorghe had not noticed until recently that the bowed bay windows were banded with a frieze of two muscular lions guarding a menorah. A hollow feeling overcame him and tears began to rim his eyes.

A brusque Radu grabbed him by the shoulder, "Gheorghe, it's over. It is in the past. Let it go."

"I wish it were that easy," he shook his head, "I should have done more to save her."

"Gheorghe, she was dead the moment she married your father."

"I was a coward."

"It was insanity. You did what you needed to survive."

"Is that supposed to make me feel better? I saved myself?"

Radu blankly stared at Gheorghe. Gheorghe gave a slight smile, "Ah, Radu the Speechless."

"You need to get out of this town," Radu deflected, "Perhaps Codreanu will banish you to Paris."

Gheorghe patted him on the back as they exited the park, "Perhaps I could liberate a young Parisian?"

Radu shook his head, "My friend, If they saw you coming, they would refuse to be taken alive," a smile crept onto his face, "the base of the Eiffel Tower would be littered with their bodies."

Gheorghe's cheeks bubbled up into a smile, "I have no doubt."

Militia substation 17 was the center of Gheorghe's world. He reported here every morning and returned here after fanning out through the city investigating his cases. When he entered the substation, Bălan greeted them with a snarl, "Ianculescu. Baboescu. Comrade Codreanu has been looking for you. He wants you to report to his office."

They pivoted out of the substation and back to the street. As they continued to City Hall, Gheorghe confessed, "Every time we are called into Codreanu's office I always expect the worst."

Radu waved his hand dismissively, "You shouldn't worry so much. We were kept because they need us."

"That is what worries me. What do they need us for? I think Codreanu is saving us to sacrifice us. It is not the first time Codreanu has done something like that. Ever heard the proverb, *Keep your friends close but hold your enemies closer?*"

Radu fell silent mulling Gheorghe's words. "Well, I think I was kept because of my superior deductive mind, but you-" he stopped in his tracks. A smile popped onto his face, "you were kept because you are a proletarian slob." He exploded with laughter, slapping Gheorghe on the back.

Gheorghe did not laugh. "I do not understand how you can be so careless about what is going on around you."

City Hall lay in the heart of the city. The steep pitch of the red tiled roof was visible from most parts of the city. As they entered the cavernous marble foyer, their footfalls ricocheted off the columns.

"What do you think this bootlicker wants?"

"Radu, please," Gheorghe quietly pleaded. "Watch what you say."

They sat in ornate overstuffed chairs in a brightly lit office. The morning sun reflected off the walls and gave a golden hue to the room. The walls leading to Chief Prosecutor Codreanu's office were lined with framed pictures of his predecessors. They hung like tombstones in gilded frames. Gheorghe examined the portraits and his chest began to ache. The last three Captains had been personal friends of Gheorghe, but these portraits were the only traces of their previous status. He quickly turned away from the portraits to avoid their piercing stares.

"If he needed to see us," Radu shifted in his seat, "Why does he make us wait?"

"Don't you know that your importance is tied to how long you make people wait?"

Radu squirted out a laugh, "You can be funny when you want. You should try it more often."

"I will leave that to you. I don't want to be misunderstood."

"What do you mean by that?"

"Humor is telling the truth and it can be costly these days."

Radu gave a snort and shook his head. They both fell silent. The portraits caught Radu's attention, "I wonder what old Captain Stanescu would think of all this?"

Gheorghe's eyes joined Radu's at Captain Stanescu's portrait. Gheorghe gave a weak smile, "He was a good man."

Radu nodded, "Yes, he did not deserve what Codreanu did to him."

"Who deserves that kind of treatment?"

"Other than Codreanu," Radu smiled, "I can't think of a single person."

Gheorghe gave a stifled laugh, "It is amazing how Codreanu has been able to survive all these years."

"You're right. His treachery is legendary. He has slithered his way to the top by pitting people against each other. Do you think he really is a Communist?"

Gheorghe gave Radu a flat stare, "Do you think he was a Nazi when he betrayed Captain Antonescu?"

"No"

"Then He wasn't Communist when he betrayed Stanescu."

The room fell silent. The portraits continued their silent vigil. The silence caused Radu to fidget, "What amazes me," he continued, filling the silence, "is how he has been able to stay in power."

"Yes," Gheorghe pondered, "I guess he is useful to the Russians."

"Useful to the Russians," Radu brooded over Gheorghe's comment, "Maybe the Russians know your proverb too, Gheorghe." With a burst of contempt, he spit out, "We should do our best to put his picture on this wall."

Gheorghe leaned into Radu, "Shh...not so loud! I know there are many who hate Codreanu as well, but their fear of the communists tempers any thoughts of revenge."

"I think he will be Chief Prosecutor for a long time," Radu concluded.

Gheorghe flashed his eyes toward Radu, "Do you think he is content to be Chief Prosecutor?"

"True, he is probably scanning the horizon looking for the next back to stab."

Gheorghe laughed.

Codreanu's door opened and his voice beckoned them in. As Gheorghe and Radu entered his office, Gheorghe's jaw flexed and stiffened at the sight him.

Captain Codreanu sat wedged behind a huge desk of carved wood with intricate patterns chiseled into its hard frame. He peered over the desk like a small child, his pudgy, boyish face pinched at the neck by a suit which seemed two sizes too small. His office was well-decorated with mahogany walls, gilded fixtures, and rich, red carpets. This beautiful lion's den was not meant for such a petty, little man. Codreanu moistened his thin lips with his reptilian tongue.

"Gheorghe. Radu. Please come in and sit for a moment," Codreanu said. His eyes followed them as they sat. "How are the new living arrangements?" His eyes drifted back to his paperwork.

"Thank you for asking comrade! I appreciate your concern for our well-being. I always tell everyone how magnanimous you are comrade Codreanu," Radu blurted, cutting off Gheorghe.

Codreanu slowly looked up and blankly stared at Radu, "Thank you." Now he spoke as if he had just awakened. "Listen, Major Shalberov from the Brigada Mobilă was at the café on Republicii and he brought to my attention that you two seem to be spending too much time together."

"It is funny you should mention him," Radu smiled, "because it turns out the only time I see Major Shalberov is when he is at the café. Perhaps he should get off his fat ass and find other places to drink his damn coffee."

Codreanu's face burst into a hot crimson.

Gheorghe glared at Radu and intercepted Codreanu's rage. "Yes, comrade. We recognize how improper it must appear. We will address the problem."

"Lieutenant Baboescu. You are one of my best Inspectors. I would hate to lose you due to your rashness. Your peers have been sent to Făgăraş penitentiary for much less or perhaps you prefer we find you employment at the Băiţa mine?" Codreanu's gaze drilled into Radu's eyes and he waited for a reaction. "I cannot stress enough the precariousness of your situation. Do you understand?"

"Yes, comrade," Radu grasped his hands and limply bowed his head, "I understand." As Codreanu broke his gaze, a small, covert smile crept onto Radu's face and met Gheorghe with a wink.

Codreanu quickly recovered his composure. "The party officials in Borş have requested our assistance. There have been three child abductions and they are making the people nervous. We need a quick resolution on this matter. You could amend your past behavior with an arrest," he stabbed his finger in the air toward

Radu. "Gheorghe, we have some leads on black market activity we want you to follow up on. Now both of you get out of here."

When Radu stepped out, Codreanu stopped Gheorghe and motioned for him to sit.

"I want to speak to you in private," Codreanu said.

Gheorghe's stomach rolled as he anticipated what Codreanu would say next.

Codreanu rested his clasped hands on the desk and leaned forward.

"How long have you known Radu?"

"Over twenty years comrade, we both served in the same unit during our compulsory army service."

"Why do you cover for him so much?"

"Loyalty, I suppose. We have been through a lot together,"

Codreanu smiled, "That is very nice Gheorghe. However, I would be careful who you associate with. You are well liked by many people and you may have a future with the Securitate."

Gheorghe's stomach fell. "The Securitate?"

"I know you are uneasy about the Brigada Mobilă, but they are only trying to streamline the security services in Romania. They set up the Securitate to ensure the safety of the People's Republic from external enemies. I find the work of the Securitate much more interesting than the Militia. Now, don't misunderstand me, both are important to the ongoing security of our fragile Republic. If you want a part in the future of Romania, you should join," with eyes flashing with child-like giddiness, "Imagine the respect you could gain. We need men like you to help Romania solidify it's standing with the Soviets. There are many rewards for success."

As Codreanu spoke, Gheorghe refused to look him in the eye, unwilling to imagine being a member of the Securitate. Opportunities would open for him. Perhaps he could get a larger apartment. People would respect him. However, his neighbors already thought he was a member and they could barely conceal their contempt for him. Their opinion of him was closer to fear than respect. Codreanu viewed fear and respect as synonymous, but Gheorghe knew better. Gheorghe had seen over 10 years of brutality and the thought that he was being invited to participate made him nauseous.

"It is an honor to be considered," Gheorghe said.

"If you like, I can arrange a meeting with Major Shalberov," Codreanu offered.

A disingenuous smile crept onto Gheorghe's face while he sought the right words to refuse without disrespect. The entire room seemed to shrink as Codreanu waited for a reply.

"Well..." He became aware of the silence as Codreanu's stare intensified. "Once I follow up on these black market leads, we can sit down and discuss it with him."

"Excellent, I will let him know."

Gheorghe drew a deep breath, having placated him with his answer. The high volume of black market activity guaranteed that Gheorghe would remain busy for a long time. Perhaps the topic would never arise again. Gheorghe could only hope that he would be forgotten again.

"By the way, if you happen to find any watches," Codreanu's eyebrows darted up with his boyish smirk, "Shalberov is looking for a new watch."

Radu greeted Gheorghe as he came into the hallway, "What did he want?"

Gheorghe hastily moved away from the door, "Shalberov wants a new watch."

"Why do Russians have such a fascination with watches?"

Gheorghe grabbed him by the arm and scurried down the stairs. "Are you Romanian? Or do you think you are an American cowboy?" Gheorghe asked.

"What are you talking about?"

"What was that display in there? You are going to get us both shot. You cannot speak about Shalberov like that. He will hear about this..."

"Gheorghe, he's an ass," Radu shrugged, "Everyone knows Shalberov is an ass."

"You do not know..." Gheorghe could not believe he was defending him.

"Listen, if one person calls you an ass, that person may be having a bad day. On the other hand, if fifteen people call you an ass chances are good you're an ass."

Gheorghe telegraphed a withering gaze, "Were you not with me when he shipped our friends to Făgăraș penitentiary? Radu, you are not invincible. I would take his threats of sending you to the Băiţa mine very seriously."

"A quartz mine?" Radu fell silent and looked into space as if figuring an equation, "I don't see myself being a miner."

"No one who works in that mine ever saw themselves as miners," Gheorghe stopped Radu in his tracks grabbing him by the shoulders, "Radu, listen. I have no idea what is going on there, but I have heard rumors that many people have died."

Radu waved him off, "You heard him. He said I was one of his best investigators." Gheorghe looked to the ceiling and blew a long breath and closed his eyes as in prayer. "Please just keep quiet."

"I will try my best," Radu skipped down the front steps and reaching the bottom turned. "If I need any help with the abductions in Borş, I will let you know."

They parted ways, each heading to their separate assignments.

CR80

Gheorghe arrived at the stake-out where they were to capture the black market traders. They were waiting in an industrial warehouse supply yard, surrounded by ghosts of dead industry. The outer skin of the warehouses had collapsed exposing the inner ribs of the frame which protruded through the tangle of steel and glass. The evening rain glazed the ruins with an oily sheen.

"Do you think they will come tonight, sir?" Officer Dobrescu asked. He was a young cadet with a bright stare and too much enthusiasm. He had more questions than answers, as usual.

Gheorghe pondered, *How much do I tell him?* "They always seem to come on cue, Officer Dobrescu."

"We have good Intelligence as to their movements?"

"The best, there is an Informer in the convoy."

"He works for us?"

"No, he probably was promised a cut from the plunder." The rookie looked disappointed. "Not very noble, don't you think?" Gheorghe asked.

"A cut with whom?"

"Let's drop it. Sometimes ignorance is the best defense." It seemed impossible that Dobrescu could be unaware of the dirty dealings of his superiors, but the young were known for their hopefulness.

The sound of clucking cargo trucks mercifully brought the line of questioning to an end. They roared through the smashed gates of the old petroleum warehouse and skidded to a stop in a clearing. The passengers spilled out and quickly began unloading the cargo. On cue, the parameter of the clearing was lit up with the sound of militiamen, "Militia! Militia! Put your hands up!" Enough force was applied that no resistance was offered. As the marketers were hauled away, the militiamen began rifling through the merchandise.

"Don't we need to secure this as evidence?"

Gheorghe looked at Officer Dobrescu's earnest face. "We will, but the department likes to do a complete inventory of the contents." His words lost some of their weight as they observed the militiamen filling their pockets with whatever would fit. As he inspected the crates, he came across a ruby encrusted Bulova watch and remembered what Codreanu had said. Even if they were illegal goods, they would become dirtier in the hands of such filthy crooks as his superiors. Gheorghe was happy to have a simpler task than Radu. He left the watch where it lay.

The Fine Line between Mischief and Rebellion

Gheorghe was awakened by a pounding at his door. He quickly got dressed. As he was going to the door, he noticed that Radu had not returned from Borş. He had been away for almost a week and it was out of character to not hear from him.

He must have found some solid leads, Gheorghe convinced himself.

When he opened the door, he was greeted by Officer Dobrescu. "Captain Codreanu needs you at his office as soon as possible. He told me to bring you myself. "

The car ride was silent as Gheorghe went through a litany of possible scenarios in his head. It was uncharacteristic to be fetched by car. He could not but think that Codreanu was up to something.

Dobrescu's eyes kept darting over to Gheorghe. He fidgeted and scanned his surroundings, "This driver must have learned to drive without using brakes," His weak smile gave way to a weak laugh which lasted too long for the occasion. Gheorghe's blank gaze was fixed on the driver's hat, "Yes, perhaps."

"Have you heard from Radu?"

Gheorghe's trance was broken, "No, have you?"

"Oh no, no…" Dobrescu stumbled over himself, "Just curious."

A normally curious Dobrescu was now embarrassed to ask questions. Gheorghe became suspicious of the young militiaman. What did he know?

"Is this about Radu?" Gheorghe asked.

Dobrescu's eyes fluttered with a pasted smile, "I really can't say."

Gheorghe returned his gaze to the driver's hat, *What has he done now?*

ᏣᏰᏠ

When Gheorghe entered Codreanu's office, the smell of alcohol and cigars hung in the air. Shalberov stood behind Codreanu with his oily hair swept back over his head and his large mustache hovering over his lips. Shalberov was the Russian liaison between the Securitate and the Soviets. His uniform squared the shoulders and disguised an overweight undercarriage. He rested his hand on the back of Codreanu's seat, like a smug puppet master.

His puppet sat at the desk with a stern look. "Deputy Chief Inspector Ianculescu," using Gheorghe's last name did not bode well. "You know Major Shalberov, do you not?"

"Yes, good morning comrade," Gheorghe felt his chest tighten and his breathing begin to wane.

To this Shalberov mumbled something in Russian which was met with ugly laughter from Codreanu. The smoke from their cigars swirled around their loud laughs.

Gheorghe knew a smattering of Russian, but not enough to understand their inside joke. Gheorghe's eyes darted to see Shalberov rock back and forth on his jackboots and give a great sigh, as he checked the time on a ruby encrusted watch. Gheorghe's throat tightened.

"Have you heard from your brother?" Codreanu asked. His face full of contempt, daring Gheorghe to answer.

"No comrade. I have not heard from him in over six years."

"Last I heard," Codreanu cocked his head back to explain to Shalberov, "He was in the Carpathians rutting in the dirt with the Iron Guard." Codreanu was playing with Gheorghe like a bully torturing a turtle struggling on its back.

"I believe that is correct, comrade." Gheorghe began to squirm as he struggled to understand where this questioning was leading. Any answer could be twisted to mean whatever they wanted. As soon as words left his mouth, they were diluted and ambiguous in the swirling cigar smoke.

"Those fascists will soon be extinct," Shalberov said.

Gheorghe seized upon his proclamation, "Yes, I am optimistic that the Securitate will root out the remaining subversive elements which undermine the great plans of the People's Republic."

Codreanu rolled his eyes. "So you are familiar with the various terrorist groups within our borders? Are there any more that you have intimate knowledge of?"

"I know of the Iron Guard, but the smaller ones have already been crushed."

Shalberov lumbered to the edge of the desk. "It has come to our attention that a new insurgent group may be forming," he said.

Gheorghe began to relax. "Really? Where?"

"We do not have many details at the moment, but we suspect that they are aligned with King Michael. From what we have heard, we suspect the group calls themselves the Order of the Dragon."

"King Michael abdicated his throne and is in exile," Gheorghe said.

"Yes, but he has already proven himself capable of leading a coup when he conspired against the Nazis. He did it once, he could do it again. He has already repudiated his abdication saying it was done by force. We cannot discount him as a threat yet."

"Well…" Gheorghe processed this in his mind, "I find it hard-"

"Listen, comrade, there are still many who would love him back on the throne. The priests would wet themselves to see him riding in a gilded carriage in the streets of Bucharest. That is why we called you in," Codreanu's face softened, "You seem to be a magnet for rebels."

Gheorghe felt his face go flush. "If you are saying that I am a subversive…"

"It seems Nazism runs in your family."

"I may be my father's son, but I am not my brother," his words spilled out in disgust and he could not contain his growing anger. "I find the Nazis repugnant."

"Relax lieutenant. You have sufficiently repudiated your family. You are not on trial. We are only saying that you may have more knowledge into their thinking."

"I have not spoken to my brother in years and I do not know if my father is still alive."

Codreanu gave a broad smile. "But Radu, on the other hand…"

"What does Radu have to do with all this?"

"Radu has betrayed the People's Republic and has aligned himself with these new rebels and other criminal elements who seek to bring King Michael back to power," Shalberov announced.

On any other occasion, Gheorghe would be inclined to laugh. *Radu the Usurper is a stretch,* he thought. Radu was more inclined to perch on a rooftop and belittle both sides of a fight and never bother himself with taking a side. That was why he had survived longer than Gheorghe's other friends.

"Are you sure?" Gheorghe asked.

"Absolutely, he has been placed in preventative detention and we want you to talk to him and see if you can gather any additional information about this 'Order of the Dragon' I believe that addressing this threat early will show the competence of the Militia and demonstrate our loyalty to the Soviets. There can be no challengers to the will of the people or our collective authority and we must prove this."

Gheorghe was looking for an exit. "Isn't this a job for the Securitate?"

"Yes, it is comrade," Shalberov extended his nicotine stained hand with a broad smile, "Congratulations."

Gheorghe drew an astonished breath and inhaled a cloud of second-hand smoke. He became sick to his stomach and spoke no more. He shook the clammy hand that was offered to him, gave a quick salute and left the room, heading straight to the bathroom to throw up.

CRSD

Gheorghe arrived at the Militia holding cells and entered the interrogation room. The room had a pungent, earthy smell which reminded Gheorghe of his grandfather's root cellar. The passers-by heels clicked on the cobblestones as they went past the small barred window. A small wooden table groaned under the weight of a large reel-to-reel recorder. They gave Gheorghe a quick lesson on how to use it while he waited for the guards to bring Radu. Officer Dobrescu slipped in through the door.

"Sorry, I'm late."

"Late?"

"Captain Codreanu did not tell you I would be here?"

"No."

"He wanted a witness."

"To what?"

Dobrescu quickly went to the recorder. "I haven't seen a recorder like this before," he inspected it. "Do you know how to operate it?"

"Yes," Gheorghe fixed his stare on the rookie.

"I still prefer pencil and paper," Dobrescu fumbled out with an awkward laugh.

"How old are you, Dobrescu?"

"Twenty-five, sir."

"Did you see any combat during the war?"

"No, I was in a support Battalion. That is where I met Captain Codreanu."

"He helped you get this job?"

"Oh, yes. If it weren't for him, I would be back in my village."

"You must be very grateful to him."

"Definitely."

That was all Gheorghe needed to hear. "Sit in the corner and keep quiet," he ordered.

Gheorghe was about to open the door on Militia work he desperately wanted to avoid. He turned to Dobrescu, "Do you know if comrade Bălan will be joining us?" "No, he is assisting on another case."

Damn.

Most of his cases involved theft or an occasional murder. If force was needed, Bălan had always been there to apply it. The Securitate would usually handle political interrogations and their techniques had low survival rates. They always seemed to get the information they needed. It may not be accurate information, but it was the information they required. His instructions to 'talk' to Radu were sufficiently vague. *Do they expect Radu to pour out the grand designs of the "Order of the Dragon" because we are friends?* He thought. The prospect of torturing his best friend made him feel sick again.

The metallic echoes down the long stone hallways gave way to muffled voices. The door scraped on its metal hinges and Radu was tossed into the room. Radu's appearance caught Gheorghe by surprise. His swollen face looked like an over-ripened plum rotting on the tree. His face cradled two eye sockets which had swollen to grotesque proportions. He winced with each step as he hopped on his toes. When he sat, he heaved a great sigh.

Gheorghe squirmed in his seat while trying to keep his gaze firmly on Radu. He tried to mask his disgust though he desperately wanted to divert his eyes. "Radu?"

At the sound of his name he tilted his head back to fix his swollen eyes on Gheorghe. "Gheorghe, my friend," he attempted a smile through cracked lips. "You just missed Bălan. I want to post a formal protest. The room service is terrible."

"I'll see what I can do," Gheorghe forced a weak smile.

"Thank you," Radu said. The exertion of keeping his head aloft finally collapsed with a thud on the table.

Officer Dobrescu leaned over and switched on the recorder.

Gheorghe's eyes flashed a quiet fury as Dobrescu sat back down. Everything from this point on would be on the official records and their unofficial banter had been wasted on jokes. The rookie had no idea what was at stake for the two men, only that he had to follow orders from the highest powers.

The whirling recorder brought Radu back upright. He sat silently and listened to the recorder as the device's wheels clicked in rhythmic time.

"Officer Radu Baboescu, you were sent to Borș to investigate a string of child abductions and you return a traitor to the People's Republic of Romania-" Gheorghe began.

A snorting laugh interrupted, "sounds pretty accurate."

Gheorghe's eyes widened as he struggled to maintain his composure. "Are saying it is true?"

"Gloriously true, my friend! And it is only fitting that his Highness should return through Oradea and join the royalty which is buried here."

"Are you stating that there are plans to smuggle King Michael back into Romania over the Hungarian border through Oradea?"

"It is much bigger," Radu regained his energy. "These are the plans of the immortals!" He burst into a wild fit of laughter. "It will be beautiful."

"What can you tell me about the 'Order of the Dragon'?" Gheorghe asked.

"I have already told them..."

"Radu," Gheorghe pleaded. "Please."

"The 'Order of the Dragon' was a brotherhood of like-minded warriors who swore an oath to expel any foreign invaders from Romanian soil. He did it to the Turks and he can do it again."

"The Turks? Radu that does not make sense."

"It will, my friend," tears oozed from the corners of his eyes. He caught a shallow breath. "When you meet him it will all be clear to you."

Gheorghe cleared his throat. "Meet who?"

"The Master. I have told him all about you," Radu said.

Gheorghe suddenly noticed that Officer Dobrescu was feverishly taking notes on a small pad of paper. A wave of panic rushed through him as he felt he was losing control of the interrogation. The recorder continued its rhythmic clicking.

Radu became more and more agitated, "We both want the damn Russians out of our country!" His voice was reaching a feverish pitch. "He drove out the Turks, he will drive out the Russians! There is no human that can oppose him!"

"We have been free from the Turks since the War of Independence over 70 years ago."

Radu raked his fingers through his hair, "I'm not talking about that. There was a time when the Turks ravaged our lands and destroyed everything in their path. Our Master drove them out and made them pay for their savagery."

"He is not *my* Master," Gheorghe snapped, "The Turks haven't been in these lands for over three hundred years. Radu, calm down. You are speaking nonsense."

"We are of the same mind. We can prevail over-"

Gheorghe snapped the recorder off. He punched the air with his finger, face red with rage. "You do not speak for me," he seethed. He turned to Dobrescu, "He doesn't speak for me."

"The Master will come to you," Radu assured, "Then you will understand."

Gheorghe stood and looked down at Radu. "You have gone mad."

"We should continue with our questioning," Dobrescu darted up from the corner.

"It is clear to me that Lieutenant Baboescu's previous interrogations have left him with impaired thinking," Gheorghe declared. He wanted to distance himself from Radu, who seemed intent on dragging him into whatever he was involved in. He had never seen Radu so passionate about anything before. He must have been beaten into insanity.

"What should I tell Codreanu?" Dobrescu asked with a note of anxiety in his voice.

"Tell him that we are going to let Radu's wounds heal and try again in a few days."

"Make sure he gets proper rest," Gheorghe called to the guards.

As Radu shuffled out the door, he turned to Gheorghe, his turgid face slowly blossoming into a grin, "Aren't you going to ask me about the Borş abductions?"

"Yes, what did you uncover?"

He leaned into Gheorghe and whispered, "Find the teacher and you will find the children."

"Where can I find her?"

"Find the children and you find the teacher."

Gheorghe sighed. "Radu, you are delusional. Does the teacher live in Borş?"

Radu began to titter with laughter as if hearing a silent joke. "She use to..."

Pursuing the Reports of Mad Men

Codreanu drummed his pen on the desk and refused to acknowledge Gheorghe's presence. He held Gheorghe frozen until he slowly looked up with an annoyed sigh, "So Inspector," pointing to the chair, "Did you enjoy your visit with your old friend?"

Gheorghe shifted in the chair unable to relax, "I do not think 'enjoy' is the word I would use."

"I was reviewing the interrogation transcript," as he scanned the document on his desk, "I was very disappointed. In the future, I can supply a list of questions and required answers."

Did I just hear him correctly? This is crazy, Gheorghe thought. "Well, he seemed-"

"However," he blurted with an intentional stare, "Officer Dobrescu has submitted his notes and observations. They were revealing enough for the time being."

Gheorghe swallowed. "Well, I am sure we will find a resolution-"

"Meanwhile, we still have a problem in Borş. While your friend was planning a revolution, there has been another disappearance. I need you to take over the Borş case. I need you to be vigorous and imaginative in your investigation. It is upsetting the villagers. An unsettled worker is an unproductive worker and the Borş' Collective wheat quota has been increased to meet Soviet expectations."

"I understand," Gheorghe said as he rose from the chair.

"I cannot stress enough the importance of coming to a solution in this matter," Codreanu declared. "The party does not like loose ends. I would like this wrapped up neatly and buried. "

CRSO

In the middle of vast tracts of wheat fields, three country roads converged to create the small village of Borş. Even though it lay eleven kilometers west of Oradea, it was hundreds of years removed from modern sensibilities. Gheorghe had to restrain his frustration when he became wedged between a horse-drawn wagon and a tractor on the narrow road leading into Borş. The pungent, grassy manure mingling with the diesel fumes only added to Gheorghe's irritation. The only major street was shared by cars, tractors, and horse-drawn wagons. The small village was a bustle of activity with the rumble of tractors filling the streets. As soon as he arrived, Gheorghe felt the collective gaze of the villagers pouring over him. The mistrust of outsiders was palpable on the occasions when Gheorghe visited Borş. A man pushing a cart laden with decrepit farming tools stopped when he saw Gheorghe, waiting for him to pass without a word. With dirty face, simple clothes, and an icy stare, He stared down Gheorghe with unblinking eyes. His stance stiffened as Gheorghe passed by; Gheorghe tried to assuage him with a quick differential nod.

Gheorghe had been directed to the party officials in Borş, but past experience had taught him the most knowledgeable person in town was usually the village priest. Radu had taught him that trick and he had found it to be accurate. Making his way down the street, he did his best to ignore the eyes of villagers locking onto him. Gheorghe spotted the black cassock of a priest leaving a vegetable stand. He broke into a trot to intercept him.

"Excuse me!" He called out as he approached.

The priest turned to face him. His furrowed face was draped with a snowy, scraggly beard. His eyes seemed tired and Gheorghe's voice seemed to have pulled him from distant thoughts. He carried a bundle of produce under his arm.

"My name is Deputy Chief Prosecutor Gheorghe Ianculescu from Oradea-"

"Hello, I'm Father Petre. Do you work with the other militiaman?"

"Yes, he is my partner."

"Where is he?" His manner stiffened, "He was helping us with the disappearances and then he disappeared himself. Since he left, we've had another abduction two nights ago."

"Yes, I am sorry but Lieutenant Baboescu has fallen ill. I am here to resume the investigation."

"What kind of illness? I will say a prayer for him. Sickness has consumed Borş."

"It's unclear, but I am sure he would appreciate that Father," Gheorghe pulled out his notebook. "Lieutenant Baboescu mentioned in his debriefing a school teacher but did not state her name-"

"Tatiana?"

"Yes, Tatiana. I need to speak to her."

"You can't. She died two months ago."

"Died?" Gheorghe looked up from his notebook.

"Yes, it was very sad. She faded before our very eyes. She was full of life and such a joy to everyone. The children especially loved her. She would be shocked if she knew her students were being abducted."

"All the missing children were her students?"

"Yes but this is a small village."

"How did she die?"

Father Petre did not answer immediately, weighing Gheorghe with his stare.

"The villagers believe she died of anemia. She had never before shown signs of the illness, but she began to lose her color and grew weaker. By the end, she could barely get out of her bed. When she finally died, she was white as a sheet." The priest fixed his gaze into the sky then slowly brought them to meet Gheorghe's. "It was an unnatural death."

"What do you mean?" Gheorghe asked.

Gheorghe felt a flush creep across his face. He should not have taken the tip from Radu to find the teacher. Now he was getting worse clues from a second madman.

"Tatiana loved her students as if they were her own children. The children miss her terribly and even say she comes to them in their dreams. With all the disappearances, they must find comfort that she has come to protect them."

"I would like to interview the missing children's parents. Could you arrange that for me?"

"Lieutenant Baboescu has already spoken to them, but I can help you."

Gheorghe followed Father Petre as he plodded out of Borş and up a muddy side road that gently arched around a stand of fir trees. The wind filtered through the woods which insulated Gheorghe's ears from the noise of Borş. The further they walked up the rutted lane, the more the vestiges of Borş were left behind. In its place were the rushing breezes through the firs whose resonance mimicked rushing water.

Father Petre stooped down, hands on knees. "I am getting too old for this," he said with a shallow breath. "I am sorry."

"You don't need to apologize. Take your time." Gheorghe stood on the side of road letting the bucolic scenery encompass him. He closed his eyes and let the breeze wash over his face. "This reminds me of my grandfather's farm."

Father Petre stood using Gheorghe to steady himself. He surveyed the summer landscape, "It is beautiful. We used to have a simple life, but the wars have complicated everything," He fell silent as his focus glazed over and he seemed transported to another place, "They say we priests are becoming obsolete. I am old and I cannot fight anymore. I pray for the day when Paradise will be restored and people will share what God has given them not what they have taken from others. The people are taught the virtues of envy and discontentment! Perhaps they are right; I am obsolete. There is no more room for faith or good deeds. It has made us vulnerable to an increasing number of evils. But I am so tired and cannot fight anymore," with a great weary sigh his craggy face sank, "Tatiana was one of our brightest stars. I failed her and her family. I have failed the entire village." A preternatural shroud seized Father Petre as he seemed to age right before Gheorghe's eyes.

Gheorghe blankly nodded as he searched for a word of encouragement, "Well," He scanned the horizon and surrendered a weak smile, "Let's keep moving, Father."

They continued until they reached another section of the village. A low pitched thatch roof capped a humble plaster house with small, deep-set windows which gazed down on the fields below. Approaching the house, Gheorghe and Father Petre went through a gauntlet of four massive hay bales which attracted every farm animal and ensured they did not wander to far from the farmhouse. The door was opened by a woman who, if it were not for the heartbreaking appearance, would have been beautiful. The hard life of farming had hardened it and the loss of her child had shattered it. They stooped into the low hung door to enter. The room was thick with spicy smoke which hung heavy in the one room house. On a small table was placed a photograph of the missing child framed with candles.

"Why do you mourn for the dead, Elena? Have you received any news?" Father Petre asked.

"My little *puiule* has passed over. His star has passed through the heavens," Elena's voice fluttered as she tried to breathe.

"Who told you this?"

"Tatiana has come to me and told me that my boy is now safe with her," she said in a mournful, singsong voice.

"You have spoken to Tatiana?" Gheorghe had a sudden rush of adrenaline.

"Yes, she comes to me in my dreams."

Unfazed by her answer, Gheorghe continued. "What was she wearing?"

"She was wearing her funeral dress. She looked prettier than ever. Full of life. She said that my boy would come to me soon."

"Was your son close to Tatiana?"

"Oh yes, she was like a big sister to my son. He was sad when she died. After she died, he would get visits from her at night."

"How-"

"-in his dreams," she finished.

"Did your son tell you what Tatiana said in his dreams?"

"She would reassure him that she was fine and wanted him to come outside to play,"

"How often did he dream about her?"

"He dreamt of her almost every night."

Perhaps Radu and the priest are not mad after all, Gheorghe thought.

As they made their way back to the road, Gheorghe mused out loud with Father Petre.

"Father, for a dead woman, Tatiana sure does get around a lot. Do you see anything in common in everyone's accounts?"

Father Petre squinted as he thought through Gheorghe's question.

"Tatiana visited them all before they disappeared," Gheorghe said.

Father Petre was nodding along with Gheorghe's train of thought.

"Are you sure Tatiana is dead?"

"She is certainly dead. I was there with her family when she breathed her last breath. I stood by her graveside and performed the memorial service. I saw her coffin lowered into the earth." Father Petre said no more, his hand on his chin again.

"I want to speak with Tatiana's parents," Gheorghe said.

CRESO

The smoke tracing its path from the chimney of Tatiana's parents' farmhouse lay low over the knoll. The smoke lingered over the entire farmyard. As they navigated through the fog of smoke, no animals greeted them. A profound silence seemed to have descended on the house.

Surveying the scene, Gheorghe was uncertain they were in the right place.

"Are you sure they still live here?" he asked.

Father Petre seemed puzzled by the weeds choking the garden. "Andrei is usually a very conscientious farmer. Tatiana's death has taken a toll on them."

When they entered the home, Father Petre made the sign of the cross.

"Andrei, what has happened here?" he asked.

"Father," he sighed with red tear-stained eyes.

"Where is all your livestock?"

"Dead or gone."

"What happened?"

The gaunt man shook his head and wrapped his weathered hands into his face. "My animals started dying off and finally, the rest ran off." He looked over his shoulder anxiously, as if a demon dwelt inside his home. "Father, this house is cursed. Ever since Tatiana died everything has gone against us. The Devil has visited this home."

"Where is Dorotthea?"

Andrei's words were intercepted by trembling lips which refused to form the words. He slowly pointed to a darkened corner. The darkness had veiled her presence. As they approached her, they could hear faint breathing under mounds of quilts. Her pale, hollowed out face slept with quick involuntary spasms. "How long has she been like this?"

"About three weeks, Father."

Father Petre pulled back the covers and gave out a loud gasp. He stumbled back and made the sign of the cross again. He darted to the kitchen and started rifling through the pantry with an urgency Gheorghe had not seen before. As he went through the kitchen, Gheorghe looked down at the withered form wrapped in quilts. Two angry puncture wounds adorned her throat. Father Petre returned with a fist of garlic buds. "Andrei, I will return later tonight. Meanwhile, I want you to make these into a necklace and put it around Dorotthea's neck."

Father Petre tumbled out into the sunlight and gave out pained wince, "No, No," he droned with increasing intensity, "No!" He fell to his knees leaning against a moldering hay bale. His shaking, crumpled form, muttered, "Lord have mercy! Christ have mercy! Spirit have mercy!"

Gheorghe knelt next to him, "Father, what is wrong?"

"I have failed."

"Failed at what?"

"We were warned of this long ago but I dismissed it. I was so focused on the evil I could see that I have let the invisible evil grow unchecked. The shepherd has neglected his flock."

"Father, what are you talking about?"

A catatonic silence fell over the priest. His furrowed face relaxed as he began to speak silently to himself, "Yes, it is clear," his head slowly began to nod, "Yes, I know now what needs to be done."

As he rose to the ground, he swatted Gheorghe away who was trying to help him to his feet. His stooped shoulders drew back and gaze hardened into steel. "Inspector Ianculescu, you must go to Alexandru's house tonight. Take my crucifix," he said in a steady, low voice.

"Who is Alexandru?"

"…One of Tatiana's students."

"Why do I need a crucifix?"

Father Petre's face became electrified, his tired eyes wide and awake. "Tatiana is a strigoica!"

"A what?" Gheorghe squinted in confusion.

The priest stopped in his tracks. "A vampire. Tatiana is a vampire!"

Father Petre barreled down the windswept lane with new, uncharacteristic energy. He stopped to catch his breath, but the excitement kept him barking out orders. "Remember," as he gasped for air, "A vampire can only enter a home after it is invited. You must never let a vampire into the home for then they can come and go as they please."

"Father, please," Gheorghe inserted. "There must be another explanation-"

"There is no other explanation! I should have seen the signs all along!"

Gheorghe saw the entire investigation spinning out of control by the force of the priest's convictions. Like his interrogation with Radu, this fanatic was taking him on a wild ride completely divorced from reality. Codreanu would not accept vampirism as a cause of death and he had already wasted an entire day with this old priest. There were real consequences for any failures here.

"Father," Gheorghe said in a slow, deliberate tone, "the simplest explanation is that Tatiana is alive and behind all the abductions. I've been trying to tell you all along."

The priest stopped in mid-stride sensing the condescension.

"Laugh if you like Inspector, but in 1815, the Archbishop Nectarie sent a circular to the clergy exhorting them to be watchful for the presence of vampires. When our First Parents fell in the Garden, we lost our native righteousness and became like senseless animals. To become a vampire is to yet fall once more and become like the demons. I would not be fulfilling my duties as a shepherd if I did not guard against the wolves who seek to destroy the Lord's sheep. "

Gheorghe gave a deep sigh.

"Ok, I will go to Alexandru's house tonight and you can return to Tatiana's parent's house."

"Very good and tomorrow we must exhume Tatiana's body-"

"Father that seems unnecessary," Gheorghe said with a pinched face.

"I did not take you as a dimwit. Have you understood anything I have told you?"

"Father-"

"We unearth her body tomorrow. The most reliable gauge of vampirism is the state of her decomposition."

"If we find any evidence for your claims, we will exhume her grave tomorrow," Gheorghe said dismissively. It seemed like a perfect solution. An evening to mull over the day's events would bring the priest back to reality and his notions of vampires would burn away with the morning mist. For now, it seemed a suitable compromise: Gheorghe could continue his investigation with Alexandru and Father Petre could chase his monsters.

"Very good, I have one more thing for you before you leave," the priest proclaimed. They went into the small domed church that was the priest's office in Borș. In the church narthex stood a simple brass font on an ornately painted stand. "I keep Holy water available for anyone who would like to take some home," he explained as he began filling a stash of small bottles. He handed two to Gheorghe. "We will meet back here in the morning," he grabbed Gheorghe's arm. "Stay alert."

Unholy Unrest

The trees' shadows were stretched by the setting sun. The purple and orange sky announced the end of another day and a reprieve from the summer heat. Gheorghe knocked on the door and as the door opened, he was greeted with the smell of roast and potatoes. The odor reminded him that he had not eaten and suddenly hunger pummeled him in the stomach.

"Good evening, I am Inspector Gheorghe Ianculescu. Father Petre gave me your name. I am investigating the child disappearances. I had a few questions for your son, Alexandru."

"Please come in, I am Violeta, Alexandru's mother," she directed him to a chair, "have you eaten yet? Would you care to join us?"

He sank into the chair, "That would be wonderful. Thank you." She disappeared into the kitchen, leaving Gheorghe alone. The house was larger than the other houses. It was more refined than the previous houses; yet, it had a fading refinement due to negligence.

A man bolted out of the kitchen. When he saw Gheorghe, he skid to an abrupt stop. "Hello, can I help you?" His face was wound in a coil of worry. Gheorghe stood to introduce himself. Violeta intercepted his greeting, "He is looking into the children who have disappeared." "Oh...", A wave of relief washed over him, "Please sit down. My name is Iulian. How is the investigation going?"

"I believe we are making progress," Gheorghe said.

"Good, good..." he muttered. Once he had taken a seat across from Gheorghe, he rubbed his hands down his pants leg. He continued rubbing his hands until, becoming self-conscious, he willed himself to quit. Once he brought his hands under control, his knees began a nervous bounce. Both simmered in an awkward silence.

Gheorghe cut the silence, "What do you do for work?"

"Farming," came the blunt response. "We are all farmers here."

"What did you do before the war?"

Iulian sighed, "I had a vineyard. I made the finest wine in the Crişana Region," as his eyes rimmed with tears, his face deflated at the thought, "They ripped out my vineyards and told me to plant wheat." He sat with a blank stare, mourning his loss.

Gheorghe began to squirm in the clumsy silence. "You have a nice home," he offered.

"Thank you, We shall see if the party allows me to keep it. I have heard they have begun seizing people's property."

"Yes, the collectivization has started to the east and to the south."

Iulian gave a deep sigh of resignation, "So, it is just a matter of time, huh?"

"I'm afraid so," he said in a conciliatory voice. At the news, Iulian retreated back into his fog of melancholy.

"I have heard that it takes five people to run a collective farm," Gheorghe blurted.

"Really?"

Gheorghe could not contain his laughter, "Yes, three plows and two briefcases." Iulian's initial chuckle slowly boiled in a full laugh. "I believe you are probably right."

Violeta ushered in the meal, followed by Alexandru. He came armed with dishes and utensils. "Alexandru," his mother announced, "This man is looking for your friends. Can you say hello?" He filed past Gheorghe darting a bashful glance as he started setting the dinner table.

"Hello, Alexandru," Gheorghe said trying to put him at ease.

"He is shy; He will need to warm up to you."

"I understand," he said as he took his seat.

The table was cleared of all but the necessities. The tablecloth was stripped off revealing the rough-hewn surface. "We did not want to appear too bourgeoisie," Iulian explained. There were great parcels of unused table space which once held flower arrangements and an abundance of dishes. "I am sorry," Violeta looked down at her plate, "We do not have much to offer you...." Her voice tapered to silence. Gheorghe's appetite vanished as every subsequent bite felt like an act of robbery. "Everything is wonderful. Thank you for having me," he assured.

Alexandru blurted out, "Were you in the war?"

"Alexandru-," his mother protested.

"That is alright," Gheorghe reassured, "no, I was a little too old but I did my part."

"We all did our part," interjected his father.

"Let's change the subject, the war is over," concluded the mother.

Gheorghe ate the remainder of his dinner as the awkward silence returned to the table. "It seems that the whole village is still mourning the death of your teacher."

"Yes, we all loved her."

"You must miss her very much."

Alexandru's parents' eyes darted to meet each other.

"I did until she started coming to visit me-"

"In your dreams," Gheorghe finished

"Yes, how did you know?"

"It seems she has been visiting all her students. What is she wearing in your dreams?"

"She always wears the same white dress."

"Does she seem well or sickly?

"Oh, she is beautiful. She gets more beautiful every night."

"What does she talk to you about?"

"She talks about how wonderful it is where she lives. She wants to show it to me. She said she was going to bring her puppy to show me tonight."

"She said she was coming tonight?"

"Yes, and my classmates are coming too."

"Did she say your classmates live with her?"

"Yes. And the Master."

The trapdoor under Gheorghe's stomach dropped.

"The Master? Did she say who 'the Master' is?" he asked.

"No," he trailed off as he lost interest in the conversation.

Gheorghe motioned to the door with his head, "May I speak to you privately?"

Once they were out of earshot, Gheorghe turned a serious face on the parents.

"We believe that Tatiana is behind the disappearances of Alexandru's friends. Would it be agreeable to you if I stayed the night in Alexandru's room and monitor what goes on during the night?" A wave of relief washed over the parents' face. "Yes, please. We have been terribly worried. Ever since Tatiana died, there has been a cloud over the whole village."

CR&SO

Alexandru's bedroom was a converted sunroom in the back of the house. The walls were boarded up to allow privacy but the center section, which contained the doors, was left intact. The large glass doors allowed access to the backyard. Thick hedges boxed in the backyard. Alexandru's bed lay next to a large wardrobe with full-length mirrors. Gheorghe dragged a large wing back chair into the room placing it facing the wardrobe. While sitting in the chair, he could still have an unobstructed view of the glass door and be fairly hidden in the dark.

When Alexandru settled into bed, he resumed his questions about the war, "Did you ever see planes?"

"Yes, many planes," Gheorghe replied.

"Did you see any bombers?"

"No, they came at night but you could hear them."

"Have you ever seen a dead body?"

"Yes," Gheorghe yawned, "How many more questions do you have?"

Alexandru grinned, "I don't know."

"I will probably run out of answers before you run out of questions."

Alexandru laughed through a yawn, "You're funny."

The questions became fewer and were punctuated with increasing periods of silence. The silence was filled with the metronomic tick of a clock in the next room. As Alexandru fell into a deeper sleep, Gheorghe watched the moon finally overcome the clouds which held back its light. The darkened room was filled with the blanched light of the moon. The brightness cast shadows which enveloped the chair and hid Gheorghe deep within the chair.

"This is perfect, I can see everything and she won't be able to see me."

Gheorghe looked at Alexandru as he slept. The moon gave him the appearance of a china doll. The rhythmic breathing became deeper and sustained as he fell further into a deep sleep. Gheorghe adjusted himself in the chair. The ticking clock began to direct Gheorghe's eyelids.

Tick-open Tock- close Tick-open Tock-close

Gheorghe's bobbing head finally surrendered and rested itself on the chair. Gheorghe bolted awake when the clock struck one. Waking suddenly was disorienting and the chiming clock did not help.

Is it 12:30, 1:00 or perhaps 1:30?

Gheorghe looked in the mirror to see the hedges outside gently swaying in the moonlight. The house was now completely silent all had gone to bed and the clock finally lulled Gheorghe back to sleep. He surrendered and fell into a troubled sleep.

The cold evening air pricked Gheorghe awake. He slowly opened his eyes to see his warm breath billow from his mouth into the frigid room. He pulled his jacket together to keep his body heat from escaping. He then realized that it was too cold for a July evening. He slowly turned to face Alexandru. His ruffled sheets were splayed open revealing an empty bed. A rush of adrenaline rushed through Gheorghe. Through the mirror, the moonlight clearly revealed Alexandru sitting crossed leg in front of the glass door. His inaudible whispering was answered by a raspy laugh, "Yes, Alexandru, we have one for you too."

Gheorghe squinted to see if he could see where the voice was coming from, "This puppy is for you. If you open the door, we can all play together." Gheorghe slowly wheeled his head around the side of the chair to face the disembodied voice.

Gheorghe gave out a gasp as he faced a hideous figure crouched down in front of Alexandru. Gheorghe slipped and fell to the floor. He looked back into the mirror to confirm what he had seen, but the mirror did not comply. Looking closely at the glass he saw cockroaches skittering over the glass.

The throaty voice cloyingly said, "His fur is soft. Come outside and I will give him to you."

Gheorghe drew in a deep breath and turned to face Tatiana.

Tatiana squatted on the ground like a putrid reptile. Her once white dress was now tattered with smeared mud and grass. Her long hair dangled around her face like wet yarn as she held out her hand as if holding a puppy, "Come and play," her voice slowed to a hypnotic cadence, "Come... and... play."

Gheorghe bolted up and desperately frisked himself looking for Father Petre's crucifix. He patted himself as if trying to extinguish invisible flames. He fumbled it out of his breast pocket and jumped to his feet. He held the crucifix rigidly in front of him and slowly walked toward her, "Tatiana."

As he approached her, a low guttural growl rolled from her throat. She did not acknowledge Gheorghe but focused on Alexandru. As Gheorghe circled to the foot of the bed, Tatiana's hunched form was framed by four sets of red flaming eyes. Faint tiny voices were calling out, "Come Alexandru."

Gheorghe crept slowly forward with the crucifix extended as far as his arm would allow. His heart beating wildly, he could barely squeak out, "Tatiana." She slowly turned her gaze to Gheorghe. Her blazing red eyes fixed on Gheorghe. Waves of nausea overcame him as his legs buckled and he fell to his knees. His movements slowed as his body felt as if he was submerged under a great weight.

Her blood stained mouth opened to reveal the fanged mouth of a wolf, "Who are you?"

A leaden weight on Gheorghe's chest, "Tatiana," he gasped, "You must-"

Her gravelly voice shrieked, "Leave us alone!"

Her scream shook Gheorghe from his paralysis and he slowly returned to his feet. He continued toward her and her growl transformed into a searing howl when she saw the crucifix. "Alexandru," she pleaded, "Help me!" As he closed in on her, she seemed to wither back into hedges to rejoin her hellish progeny.

As she withdrew, Gheorghe gained more confidence.

"He is hurting me, Alexandru," she wailed. "Help me!"

Alexandru burst to his feet, "Leave her alone!" He rushed Gheorghe and pushed him with an unnatural strength. He launched Gheorghe headlong into the glass door. The shards of glass sliced into his hands and impaled him as he hit the ground. Tatiana trounced him instantly. He was greeted by her broad hungry mouth which reeked of decaying flesh. The rancid smell gagged Gheorghe as he tried to catch his breath. When rolled over on his back, tiny dead hands began pawing at his sleeves pulling him into the hedges. The dead little eyes flamed with a malicious hunger as they descended on Gheorghe. He began flailing his arms in desperation and the crucifix grazed Tatiana's cheek. She gave a pained shriek as she pulled back. The brood of children withdrew into the hedges as Tatiana lunged toward Gheorghe. He raised the crucifix over his head and brought it down to intercept Tatiana's attack. The crucifix seared her dead flesh. She howled in pain and retreated in the hedges. Gheorghe scrambled back into the room. Leaning against the foot of the bed, Tatiana and her children called to Alexandru.

The struggle awakened Alexandru's parents who burst into the room. They seized him before he could slide through the hole in the door. Gheorghe lay on the floor bloodied and shocked at what had transpired. He fainted suddenly, overwhelmed by the sights and sounds of his struggle.

ରୋଚ୍ଚ

Gheorghe opened his eyes again. The stabbing pain in his hands and side confirmed he had not dreamt the previous night. The terrified family huddled next to the fireplace as the sun mercifully arose. Gheorghe struggled to his feet, "I must go see Father." Gheorghe cleaned his wounds and straggled back to town.

Father Petre met him at the door of the church. "Nothing happen-" Father Petre stopped at the sight of Gheorghe's injuries. "What happened to you?"

"We need shovels."

"...and stakes," Father Petre finished.

୧୫୫୬

The windswept hilltop was dotted with headstones which stood at the head of grave plots that had been cordoned off with decorative stone edgings. Gheorghe and Father Petre shuffled through the high grass to get to the newer portion of the graveyard. Tombstones jutted out at odd angles, some lay broken on the ground. Gheorghe tripped over one which was submerged in the grass. Tatiana's grave was not difficult to find. Amassed on top of the grave was a pyre of fir limbs decorated with faded ribbons. Their vitality drained from them, they turned a brittle brown and the weathered ribbons flipped in the morning air. The top of the tree had been placed at the head of the grave.

As they started to clear away the branches, Gheorghe's hands were pricked by the crumbling needles. He winced as he pulled back his hands. "Why do they put all these branches on the grave?"

"This tree represents Tatiana's Wedding fir-tree. There is a funeral song the old women sing where the fir tree laments that it will never be used to build her house but must be left to wither and rot at the head of her grave," Father Petre answered.

"I did not know..." Gheorghe trailed off.

Uncovering the grave revealed the ground had sunken about two hand-breadths.

"Looks like a sinkhole," Gheorghe said.

The sunken ground had wrenched the stone edgings from where they rested and was pulling them into the hole. The shovels chewed into the soil easily. As the spades pierced the soil, areas of the grave collapsed into hollow pockets where the soil appeared to have been excavated from below. The ground gave way under Gheorghe's leg and it collapsed into a deep hole. The tip of his foot touched something fleshy. Gheorghe recoiled and grasped for Father Petre.

"Get me out of here!" The old man helped him out of the hole and he sat on the ground shaking, trying to regain his composure.

Father Petre continued the excavation with gusto as Gheorghe rested his head on his knees blankly staring at the ground. It was like the old man had been recharged, transformed into a young man by his supernatural beliefs. The grass, the sun, and the breeze were real. Gheorghe could see them but Tatiana and her brood were but a dream in his imagination. The light of day made everything seem improbable and would prove that all Gheorghe had witnessed was false. Maybe Father Petre's fanatic spell had worked on him and it was finally wearing off now.

"Inspector!"

Gheorghe's reassurances were broken. He rose to his feet and peered into the grave. The coffin was framed with holes which disappeared into the earth. They opened the coffin and were greeted by the corpse of Tatiana.

"The saints of Heaven!" Father Petre gasped. He made the sign of the cross as he once again laid eyes on the girl he had buried two months earlier.

Her once white funeral dress was now a soiled bronze with dark rust splatters of dried blood. Her alabaster skin was kissed with blood red lips. Her once innocent face was desecrated with a debased smirk. The coffin sides had been ripped out and the earth burrowed out to make room for her progeny. The children, dressed in their pajamas, clung tightly to her.

"Hand me my bag," Father Petre called to Gheorghe as he slid down into the grave. His movements had no impact on Tatiana. She lay motionless with not even a flutter of the eyes. Her chest gave no sign of breathing. Tatiana was dead. As he fished through his bag, Tatiana suddenly grabbed his ankle and gave a serpent's hiss. Her dead eyes opened, but the sunlight weakened her from overpowering the priest. He pulled out his crucifix.

"Lay back in your grave, you defiled witch!" he cried.

At the sight of the crucifix, Tatiana snarled like a wild animal and obeyed him.

"Keep her down," Father Petre barked. "I need to send this demon back to Hell."

Gheorghe placed the crucifix around his neck and stood at the head of the grave. When he knelt down to hold down her shoulders, the crucifix dangled in front of Tatiana's face. Her dead, marbled eyes spewed out hatred as Gheorghe tried to avert his eyes from her gaze. The dull thud of the mallet was met with the horrible scream which first sounded demonic but then morphed into the cries of a human. Tatiana's twisted face instantaneously unraveled into a peaceful countenance as the stake pierced through her heart. Her struggling ceased and her former beauty and innocence were restored. Gheorghe jumped to the edge of the grave and lay down in the grass. A wave of relief washed over him. The clouds skirted across the sky as he lay there collecting his thoughts.

"You must finish," an exhausted voice sighed. "I am getting to old for this." Father Petre was wiping his bloodied hands off and cleaning the stake. "Once you drive the stake in their hearts, you must decapitate them." He was bent and gray again, his youthful spark drained by the gruesome work. There were tears in his eyes as he looked upon the defiled grave.

"Who?"

"The children."

Gheorghe recoiled. "The children? I have to do the children?"

Father Petre grabbed Gheorghe by the shoulders. "Do not look at them as children; they are now vipers."

Gheorghe took the bag from Father Petre's hands.

They worked the rest of the morning reburying Tatiana and the children. Both were somber as they put the grave back in order. Gheorghe broke the silence.

"What do we tell the parents?" he asked.

Father Petre remained silent. Gheorghe wondered if he had heard him. He was about to repeat the question when Father Petre froze in mid-stride, "We tell them nothing. Let them remember them as they were. They are gone and will never be seen again."

"Yes, that seems best," Gheorghe nodded.

They straggled back into Borş immersed in their thoughts.

"Father," Gheorghe began, "how did Tatiana become a vampire?"

"I have been trying to answer that question myself since yesterday. Becoming a vampire is not like catching a cold. There is only one way to become a vampire. It is the one idea that even I cannot bring myself to accept.

"What is it?"

"Something far more powerful and sinister is at work here. What, I do not know."

Gheorghe scanned the horizon. "Have you ever heard of 'The Order of the Dragon?"

"Yes, why?" Father Petre as he stroked his chin.

"Inspector Baboescu mentioned it. Also, both he and Tatiana spoke of 'The Master'. Perhaps the two are related. Could this 'master' be behind this?"

"Order of the Dragon...the Master..." the priest's face scrunched as his thoughts became more labored. "The 'Order of the Dragon' was a medieval order formed to defend the Christian lands against the Ottoman Turks."

Gheorghe's face lit up, "Lieutenant Baboescu mentioned that this 'Master' had driven out the Turks."

"If that is true," Father Petre stopped in his tracks, "we are facing a three hundred-year-old vampire. It is worse than I feared – a great evil has returned!"

Deals with Devils

When Gheorghe entered Codreanu's office, his presence went unacknowledged. He stood there like a grade-schooler before his headmaster. Gheorghe's heart raced at the silent confrontation. He refused to look downcast and forced himself to look directly at Codreanu. A slurry of contempt and fear roiled within him as he waited for Codreanu to acknowledge him. The longer Gheorghe was ignored, the more his thoughts steadied, his breathing slowed and sounds of the city replaced the sound of his heartbeat in his ears. Codreanu's preferred tactic helped Gheorghe regain his composure.

He looked up from his desk and dismissively returned to his paperwork.

"Excuse me, sir-," Gheorghe began.

"Comrade," his eyes shot up, "Call me comrade."

"Excuse me, comrade. We have had success in Borș..." Gheorghe paused when he heard the door open behind him and sensed two people enter the room. He turned to see Shalberov and Dobrescu enter the room. Gheorghe's heart fluttered in his throat.

Codreanu looked up and through a smirk said, "You were saying, Inspector?"

Tripping over his words, Gheorghe continued. "We have had a successful conclusion to the situation in Borș."

Codreanu blankly stared him down, "Ah, yes. An overly zealous school teacher?"

A ripple of laughter came from behind Gheorghe. "Well, yes-."

"In the larger picture the children are inconsequential," Codreanu said with a wave of his hand. "Do you think the teacher was a member of the 'Order of the Dragon'?"

"She seemed to be answering to a leader, referred to as 'The Master.'"

The booming voice of Shalberov interjected.

"Yes, and Lieutenant Baboescu has stated that this 'Master' is coming to see you." Shalberov turned to Dobrescu. "Is that not what the transcript of the interrogation says, Officer Dobrescu?"

"Yes, Comrade," he snapped.

The room began to shrink as Gheorghe sensed he was being interrogated. His heart pounding in his chest, the saliva drained from his mouth leaving it parched. He moistened his mouth as he tried to counter the subliminal accusations. "I think there must be a misunderstanding-."

"About what, comrade? We have made no allegations," Codreanu smiled.

"I do not think you should take the ramblings of a disturbed man seriously."

"And yet, there seems to be something to what he says. Don't you agree Inspector Dobrescu?"

"Yes, Comrade."

Shalberov's boots clicked as he approached Gheorghe. "We have heard that you and the priest of Borş have become fast friends."

"Father Petre?" Gheorghe's eyes darted toward Shalberov.

"Oh, you are on a first-name basis with him?" Codreanu laughed.

A chorus of laughs surrounded Gheorghe. They triangulated around Gheorghe and fenced him away from the door and the chair.

Shalberov's musty odor, like mothballs and cigars, crept into Gheorghe's nostrils as he neared. "Most priests report to the Securitate. We find them useful."

"Except for your priest, I don't trust him," Codreanu announced.

"Why? I have found him to be trustworthy and loyal to his people," Gheorghe fumbled out.

"And who are 'his' people?" Codreanu sniffed. "You have an odd choice of friends Inspector and now you seem to have found yourself in the middle of an elaborate plot to bring King Michael back to power. This compromises the security of the People's Republic and I am delighted to have a chance to crush that meddling tyrant's throat with my boot. We are going to cut the head off this 'Dragon' and you are either with us or against us. Do you understand?"

"Whoever disrupts this plot certainly will be looked upon favorably within the Securitate," Shalberov added, patting Codreanu on the back as if the deed were already done.

Codreanu's eyes lit up. "I will be the one to destroy this brood of snakes and their 'Dragon,'" he fixed his fiery gaze on Gheorghe, "at any cost."

Gheorghe felt a noose tightening around his neck. He felt that he would be sacrificed on the altar of Codreanu's ambition.

"What do you want me to do next?" Gheorghe deflected.

"Use your contacts to find the ringleader – this 'Master' as he likes to be called. Once you have relevant information, do not act without my permission. Understood?"

"Yes, Comrade," Gheorghe said.

"Good. I want you to visit Radu again, see what you can get out of him. You might find that he is much more agreeable, now that he has had some time to acclimate to his life in prison," Codreanu smirked at Shalberov.

Gheorghe gave a quick nod and tried to make eye contact with Dobrescu, who stubbornly stared at the carpet. The massive door slammed shut sending echoes down the vaulted corridor. Gheorghe found himself alone in the hallway. Gheorghe's mind raced and his senses heightened by the meeting. He heard the faint murmurs of Shalberov and Dobrescu huddled around Codreanu's desk, laughing and shaking each other's hands with satisfaction. He stood for a moment in the hallway, consoling himself knowing that King Michael was not the head of the Order of the Dragon. Codreanu's casual dismissiveness of Tatiana brought a cynical smile to Gheorghe. While Codreanu's Dragon was a scheming royalist; the dragon whom Tatiana and Radu served was something far more sinister. Codreanu refused to depart from the narrative he had conjured in his own mind. He was determined to slay his dragon, riding it to greater glory within the Securitate. The disconnect between Codreanu's Dragon and Tatiana's was irreconcilable. Codreanu's declaration, "I will cut the head of this Dragon," caused a spontaneous sputter of laughter. *If he only knew,* he thought. He was pulled from his thoughts by the opening of the office door.

Dobrescu greeted him quickly, his eyes darting back down to his notebook.

"The Captain wants us to get a move on,"

His feeble orders brought a heat flushing through Gheorghe's body. He flashed a withering gaze at Dobrescu and an awkward silence fell between them.

"Is something wrong, Inspector?", he asked weakly.

Gheorghe slowly exhaled his contempt through his nose and pasted a smile on his face. "No, I am just tired."

"I see," Dobrescu said tentatively, "We should probably go ahead and interview Radu."

It appeared that sycophants bred lesser sycophants. Gheorghe felt his lips pursing together in disgust but suppressed the feeling. He walked off down the hallway to leave upper floors of the militia station without answering the young Inspector. They walked in silence to the holding cells in the station's basement, greeted by the smell of mildew and body odor. They gave brief nods to the attending guard and signed the visitation sheet.

As they approached Radu's cell, Gheorghe called through the metal bars to wake him. Radu sat on his metal cot, leaning against the stark, gray wall of his room. They entered the cell without ceremony. He awoke with a start when he heard his name. His face was healing. The bulbous swelling had receded but been replaced with a pale complexion with spidery veins lacing the skin. Gheorghe reached out to shake his hand and clutched a limp, clammy hand.

"Are you well, Radu?"

Though the swelling was gone, Radu squinted against the light of the small windows lining the basement walls of the holding area around them.

"Yes, but the light hurts my eyes."

Gheorghe pulled up a chair. "Radu, I need to ask you about the Master-."

"Ah, yes. You will know more very soon. I will let him speak to you. I was told you met Tatiana," a smile spread across his face.

A sudden coldness spread through Gheorghe. "How did you know?"

"Master shares everything with me, just as I share everything with him."

"Did your 'Master' tell you I met Tatiana?"

"No, I saw everything through his eyes," he began laughing. "I even saw the little brat push you through the door and you squealing like a little school girl."

Gheorghe looked into space as he struggled to formulate a question: "How?"

"After he fed on my blood, he allowed me to drink his blood. We have been united by a bond of blood. My blood flows through him and his through mine," Radu began to cry. "We are one!"

"You see what he sees?"

"Yes, when I sleep I am with my Master, as I was just a moment ago before you arrived. He has seen your resilience. He needs someone like you."

"Why do you say that?"

"He once had the gypsies to help him but they are scattered and few now."

Gheorghe's face suddenly clouded over, "Yes, The Nazis were ruthless..."

Radu seized on the sorrow he saw in Gheorghe's face. "He could help you find your father, and then you could repay that bastard for what he did to your mother."

Gheorghe shook his head as if waking from a daydream. "Radu, my father is probably dead. Besides, that is in the past."

"Believe me, he knows what it is like to see loved ones taken away. He fought for his land and people against those who wanted to take them away from him. As Voivode over the Transylvanian lands, he drew on all the dark arts to expel the Turks from our lands. His bravery and ruthless pursuit of the Turks earned him admission into that great fraternity of the Dragon." Radu leaned in closer. "He can give you the power to avenge your mother."

"So, this leader of yours was lord of Transylvania?" Gheorghe asked, ignoring the offer.

"He was, is, and will always be Lord of Transylvania, and when the people rally to his side, he will be Lord of all Romania. The 'Order of the Dragon' will return and drive out the Communists."

"He told you this?" Gheorghe said in an unimpressed voice.

Radu rolled his eyes. "No, but he has the power to do it."

"You have big plans for him. You never struck me as someone who cared much about politics," Gheorghe said through a smile.

Radu bit his lower lip as he lowered his head. "You should not dismiss me so easily." He caressed his temples as he closed his eyes. He lifted his head and his eyes opened as if the sun had broken through the clouds. His eyes pierced Gheorghe with uncharacteristic conviction, "Gheorghe," His gaze seized Gheorghe, "One thing I have learned is that cynicism is easy. If I stayed as I was, always scoffing and dismissive, nothing would change. Cynicism does not require sacrifice. Master has shown me that now is the time to choose a side. Don't be like I was, Gheorghe. With the Master's return, everything has changed. Change is coming. Believe me, it will happen. Do you not want Romania to be freed from its oppressors? The Dragon is the symbol of freedom and strength; don't you want Romania to be free and strong?"

"Is your Master King Michael?"

Radu's blank stare bore through Gheorghe as if an incomprehensible joke fluttered past him. He leaned into Gheorghe's face, "Do you think I would sell my soul to King Michael?" Radu burst into laughter as if he now understood the joke, "They have tried to break me, Gheorghe," He straightened his back to show his resolve, "but, it has made me stronger."

"Radu," Gheorghe said through clenched teeth. "You are putting me in a difficult situation."

"Then let Master help you find your way out! Your fortunes are about to change. He is coming to see you tonight."

An unexpected wave of panic rushed over Gheorghe. With his experience with Tatiana still fresh in his mind and his wounds still fresh, He began to shake. He imagined the terrible face of a monster, even more, powerful than the filthy pallor of the one he had barely overpowered.

Dobrescu's feverish scribbling on his notepad brought Gheorghe's thoughts back to the room. His panic now had the added burden of Codreanu's political schemes. The constriction of competing aspirations wrung his stomach as he caught himself squirming in his seat.

"Can I bring my friends?" Gheorghe deflected, nodding over his shoulder at Dobrescu.

Radu turned a derisive gaze to Dobrescu. "You can't fool me Gheorghe. We both know that I am your only friend. Master will find you when you are alone. He is much more convincing than me," Radu began to laugh again.

"That is because I'm not convinced by mad men," Gheorghe said. He turned to Dobrescu, who was still furiously scribbling notes. "And neither should you. We are done here."

Gheorghe turned to face his old friend before departing. Gheorghe and Radu had been friends for over twenty years and now a wave of sadness descended on Gheorghe as he thought of what awaited his old friend. It seemed there was no returning from his present madness.

"Radu," he whispered, "I have loved you as a brother. I am afraid this may be the last time we see each other."

Radu offered a weak smile, "Do not worry friend. We will see each other again. Master has opened my eyes to mysteries which I cannot even begin to understand. He is the Lord of a realm into which we all must pass. Ultimately, we will all bow to him, for death waits for all of us. He is the Lord of death and I no longer fear it."

They left the holding cell and waited for the guard to lead them back down the hall. Radu's laughter echoed behind them and followed them out of the building.

"So, it's not King Michael we're after, is it?" Dobrescu asked.

"I cannot say with any certainty," Gheorghe obfuscated.

"What was he talking about in there? What happened in Borş?"

"I should give you a copy of my report but take what Radu said lightly. He has lost his mind."

"Do you believe what he said?" Dobrescu asked.

"About what?"

"Do you think the Order is going to contact you tonight?"

"I do not think so. Madmen should not be trusted in these types of investigations. This was a bad lead."

"Don't you think you should go along with it to see if it was a legitimate lead?"

"Perhaps, but I believe the priest in Borş is a better lead. He seemed familiar with 'The Order'. Perhaps I need to press him more on the subject."

"We should explain this to Codreanu. Do you think you could interview the priest and return in time to meet Radu's contact?" Dobrescu's eyes gleamed and a restrained excitement covered his face. "I will do anything I can to help!"

"Perhaps that could work." He was happy to, at least, have Dobrescu's trust though the idea was ill-founded. They had no idea of the evil they were pursuing. His heart began to speed up again, knowing that all the military in the world could not protect him from what he had seen.

They left the dingy lower floors of the station and headed back upstairs. Dobrescu now led the way, brimming with the excitement of a new lead. Together, they entered Codreanu's office. Gheorghe remained quiet while Dobrescu gave his report.

"Well, Gheorghe, what do you think?" Codreanu asked.

"I think we should be pursuing other leads."

"Dobrescu, I want you to stay with Gheorghe tonight since his old roommate has moved out."

"With your permission, comrade, may I follow up on my contact in Borş?" Gheorghe asked.

"The priest? Why?" Codreanu leaned back in his chair, eyeing Gheorghe suspiciously.

"He said he knows of the Order. You may not trust him, but he has proven his loyalty to me. I will be back before nightfall so that you can still monitor my meeting with the leader of the Order. If the priest has any valuable leads, I will report them to you immediately."

Codreanu pursed his lips in thought, weighing Gheorghe with his eyes. He looked at Dobrescu, whose smile had still not faded. He stood from his chair and walked around from his desk. A full head shorter than both men, he held his chin high to speak down to Gheorghe.

"How has this priest proven his loyalty to you?" Codreanu asked.

"He was integral in solving the case of the child abductions. He is a wise man."

"His loyalty to the Republic is far more important than his ability to make your life easier. We already have what we need from Radu, and soon, we will have a direct connection to the Order. You are not permitted to visit the priest."

Gheorghe stared at the floor.

"Captain, if I may," Dobrescu piped up. "Inspector Baboescu was clearly out of his mind. I think it is a good idea to build our case from as many sources as possible. Who can trust such a desperate man?"

Codreanu returned to his desk and sat.

"You make a valid point, Dobrescu. Radu is not quite desperate enough to trust which is why I have decided to transfer Inspector Baboescu to Piteşti prison. We will send him off for re-education immediately. Piteşti strips the falsities out of a man and replaces them with the truth. Radu will no longer have the ability to tell a lie," a slow smirk emerged from Codreanu's face, declaring, "It is Gheorghe here that I do not trust."

Chills went down Gheorghe's spine. He had heard of the Piteşti experiments.

"Father Petre has become a friend to me. I want to seek his help again. I am being honest," Gheorghe said. "He is a holy man serving the Republic. You have nothing to fear, comrade."

Codreanu's eyes bulged at the insinuation. "Fear? Believe me, I do not fear the priest." He drubbed his fingers on the desk as he held Gheorghe with his gaze. "Gheorghe, I've heard enough of your begging. You may pursue your lead in Borş. Give Dobrescu the keys to your apartment. Dobrescu, I expect a detailed report in the morning." He dismissed them with a wave.

Gheorghe handed his keys over to Dobrescu. "Mrs. Alexandrescu may need help with her window this evening," Gheorghe added.

With that, he hurried to the bus station and boarded the next bus to Borş.

Seeking Immunity

Gheorghe arrived in Borş and walked with purposeful speed. It was still early in the afternoon and the townspeople were going about their business as usual. However, as he brushed past them, many of the people gave him nods and smiles. Gheorghe was surprised by the reception. Though the children were not returned, and most of the villagers had no idea what he had done to them to release them from their misery, a measure of peace had returned. It dawned on Gheorghe how much Tatiana's presence had affected the village. He continued to the church to find Father Petre.

"Inspector!" someone yelled.

Gheorghe stopped and turned. It was Andrei, Tatiana's father. They shook hands.

"I..." Andrei looked down at his feet. "I wanted to thank you for helping my family. For helping my daughter. I don't know what happened that night," Andrei trailed off.

"It was nothing," Gheorghe said, "If that's all, I must be going."

"Wait." Now Andrei looked him dead in the eye. "I don't know what happened, but I know that you removed our curse. My wife is getting better and the fog that haunted our home has left. I went to my daughter's grave..."

Gheorghe became uneasy with the pause.

"She is at rest again. I replaced the fir branches with new ones. It is against tradition, but you gave her a second chance to rest in peace," Andrei's eyes softened. "You've helped my family and the entire village, even if they won't say it to you. Thank you." He shook Gheorghe's hand and walked away without any more words.

Gheorghe pressed on through the village center, arriving at the small domed church. In the afternoon light, the black stones seemed to radiate heat and the air around the building shimmered. The sight of this aura froze Gheorghe. He would stay here tonight, even if it meant Codreanu would have him put in Pitești tomorrow. He hurried inside and closed the large wooden doors behind him. He was greeted by overwhelming darkness until his eyes adjusted.

The air inside the church was cool and calm. Sunlight streamed in through windows on either side of the altar and motes of dust idly lilted through the empty space. Gheorghe immediately saw Father Petre, kneeling before the altar with his back to Gheorghe.

"Father!" Gheorghe called out.

There was no response.

Gheorghe approached the old man slowly. As he passed through the beams of light and up the aisle of pews, his temperature alternated cool and hot. The motes swirled around him like the indifferent villagers outside. He walked up to the old man and studied his face. The serenity he observed made him calmer than he had been for many days.

Father Petre stared vacantly ahead with his chin lifted high. His eyes were unfocused and seemed either to be looking at the altar itself or out the large window behind it. The slanting columns of sunlight illuminated his face giving it a warm glow.

Gheorghe knelt next to him and slowly leaned into him. "Father Petre?"

Father Petre blinked suddenly and rapidly, leaving his trance. "Gheorghe?"

"I need your help, Father. I spoke with Inspector Baboescu again and was told that the Master is coming to visit me tonight. I cannot face him. Please, let me stay here in the church tonight."

Father Petre did not respond immediately, instead rubbing his eyes and clearing his throat. He moved slowly off his knees with several cracking and popping noises of his joints.

"Inspector Baboescu? So his sickness is unnatural?"

"Yes."

"It is as I thought," he rose to his feet and did not address Gheorghe. He went to the baptismal font propping his arms against it as if he were holding it to the floor. He looked deeply into the shallow bowl as if it were a mirror. "How far along is Inspector Baboescu in his transformation? Has he feasted on the blood of innocents?"

"He said he had drunk the blood of his Master, but it is impossible for him to leave his cell. He has not harmed anyone to my knowledge."

Father Petre turned suddenly.

"He has tasted the blood of the undead?" he asked urgently.

"Yes, but there is no way for him to get –"

"The time has come!" Father Petre cut him off. He walked quickly and unsteadily on stiff legs. He entered a small room and left the door open behind him.

Gheorghe followed.

"Listen to me, Father! I need your help!"

"No Gheorghe. It is my people who need my help."

"But –"

"And yours as well! We cannot let his evil spread any further! I have been praying for many days that Tatiana was the only one cursed with his plague. The news of Inspector Baboescu is troubling. Who knows how many more he will take under his wing? We must destroy him now."

"I-," Gheorghe stopped and corrected himself. "We have never faced anything like this before. What makes you think we have the slightest chance of success? He will destroy both of us,"

Father Petre stopped rummaging through the desk drawer that occupied him. He did not say anything, but his eyes bore heavily into Gheorghe.

"Did you hear me, Father? He is coming for me tonight! You must help me!" Gheorghe was becoming frustrated and the volume of his own voice startled him as it reverberated off the stark walls.

Father Petre stood silently and let the echoes of Gheorghe's protests fade. "Do you think if he wanted to kill you, he would announce his coming?"

"Father-."

"Do you?", he split Gheorghe's thought in half.

Gheorghe drew a deep breath. "No."

"Obviously, he needs you for some purpose that Radu and Tatiana could not fulfill. We may find that whatever he requires of you may also be a weakness we can exploit."

Gheorghe suddenly felt his vitality drain from him like water in a broken vase. His head swirled as a wave of exhaustion flooded over him. He needed relief. The sympathetic priest he had hoped would shelter him had turned against him. He closed his eyes, hoping for a different outcome. "Father-."

"You cannot stay here," Father Petre said abruptly. He continued rummaging. He pulled out a piece of paper, the object of his search. He sat at his desk and began to flatten the aged parchment by rubbing his hand over it many times. He read through the lines of text quickly with his finger and stopped when he found what he sought. He rose again and went to an overloaded bookcase along the wall, taking the paper with him. He scanned the shelves and pulled a large tome out. He slammed it onto his desk and filled the dark room with more dust motes.

"Why can't I stay here?" Gheorghe asked.

A broad smile spread across his face. "We have work to do." He opened the book and turned to Gheorghe. "This old volume contains the circular sent by Archbishop Nectare in 1810 to his protopopes to determine which districts were having problems with vampires. The Archbishop gave instructions on the how the church was to properly dispose of them. However, he also revealed several accounts of how vampires could regain their powers." Father Petre was deeply immersed in the yellowed pages of the book, speaking almost to himself.

Gheorghe approached the desk looking over the old man's shoulder.

"We live in a world where God is dead. It will be easy for this apostate to move about where the supernatural is mocked. Fortunately, I am a caretaker of the wisdom of our Fathers. Perhaps we can use this information to our own advantage." Looking up suddenly, his eyes clamped onto Gheorghe's gaze. "What did Inspector Baboescu say his goal was this time?"

"Radu said that his Master was going to drive out the Communists."

"What? That doesn't make sense," Father Petre waved his hand dismissively. "This apostate surely has told Inspector Baboescu what he most wanted to hear. There is no reason for him to bother with governments and their follies. There must be more to his return. What could he want?" He returned to the tome. "Ah!"

"What is it?"

"He has been gone for many generations and now returns to his homeland. He must have been able to move freely without hindrance."

"If that is true, why does he stay in Borş?"

"Yes, why would he linger in such a small, insignificant place? Wherever he went last, he must have been forced from there. He cannot freely travel in the daylight, so how is it that he moves freely?"

"He travels at night and avoids government checkpoints?" Gheorghe offered.

"Of course, of course. But he still must rest during the day. This is when he is the most vulnerable. He knows this as well. He must have a resting place here in Borş. We must find his coffin and destroy it while he sleeps."

"Are you suggesting we hunt down the Master?"

Father Petre's eyes rolled, "Gheorghe, you are as thick as this floor!" He rubbed the back of his neck as he continued, "I am not suggesting it. I am demanding it. This is our duty to God."

"What if he has more than one coffin? How will we even find him? Where do we start?"

Father Petre put his nose back into the book. His face sagged and he fell back into his chair heavily, drooping suddenly. "I don't know. I don't know how we will do this, but we must." His eyes became bright again and he looked at Gheorghe excitedly. "What do they want from you?"

"Radu did not say specifically. He said his Master could help me avenge my mother."

Father Petre held his chin thoughtfully and did not speak for some time.

"Yes, ever since the Garden, promises to take what rightfully belongs to God and place it in the hands of men has been a great temptation. It makes sense that being a militiaman, you would long to see justice done. How much more a wrong done to your mother? Obviously, he is trying to exploit you at your weakest point. You have been hurt and he is appealing to this side of your nature. It is a powerful temptation to seek punishment on those who have committed wrongs against us, to take justice into our own hands. Vengeance belongs to God alone. He settles all accounts." He looked at Gheorghe. "Do you know what happens when you take revenge on another?"

Gheorghe waited for his answer.

"You dig two graves. One for your enemy and the other for yourself."

"I do not want to kill anyone! I just want to live in peace," Gheorghe said.

"He will try to tell you that you killing your enemies will bring you peace."

"So then let me stay here so that I will never have the chance to be tempted."

Father Petre shook his head slowly.

"No, this is your challenge. I cannot remove this temptation; every man must face their own. Once you have overcome your desires, you will have nothing to fear from evil. This is your moment, Gheorghe. With our success will come much good. Do you still have the crucifix I gave you?"

"You are sending me to my death, Father. It is you who will dig my grave."

"No, you will return to me alive and when you do, we will defeat this evil together. Leave me now! I must prepare for my destiny, and so must you. I will learn how to destroy this apostate, once and for all."

Gheorghe could not help but feel angry at the old man. He said nothing more and left the church to return to Oradea, grinding his teeth and feeling sick to his stomach. Father Petre and Codreanu both wanted him to face the Master. One wanted him to be a martyr; the other a hero but he wanted just to be left alone.

The Master Visits

The sun was already low in the sky. The setting summer sun gave the sky a magenta and tangerine glow; the type of sky Gheorghe would normally stop and admire. However, the waning hours gave him an urgency which prohibited him from a relaxing walk home. His heart pounded and breathing tried to keep up its labored work as he stood pacing at the bus station. Standing in the open with the sun closing to the horizon, he felt his surroundings closing in around him. He looked to the east and saw the first evening star emerging from the dark bruised eastern sky. The bus mercifully arrived and Gheorghe inserted himself in the middle of the riders entering the bus. He relaxed as he used the people as a buffer from any unwanted contact. He squirmed through the scrum of riders to get to the back of the bus. He needed his back unexposed so he could focus on any approach from the front. He gave a morbid chuckle. *How would this help? This is pathetic,* he thought.

The long summer shadows stretched across the courtyard of his apartment block as he streaked toward his apartment. The tiled corridor deflected the sounds as they ricocheted off the walls. His footfalls reverberated through the oddly quiet lobby. He knocked on his door and Dobrescu opened it for him. Gheorghe sat in the only chair feeling exhaustion overtake him. The narrow rectangular windows lining the ceiling signaled the end of the day by extinguishing the last rays of sunlight.

"That Bunicuta is a handful," Dobrescu said with a heaving sigh. "I had to plunge her toilet."

Gheorghe laughed but said nothing more. The muffled sounds of the tenants laughing in the courtyard comforted Gheorghe. It was a sign that all was normal. Over time, the sounds dwindled down to murmurs as they trickled back to their apartments. The lobby burst into a cacophony of sound as the last tenant slammed the metal door of the elevator shut. Bunicuta Alexandrescu's booming voice echoed, "Perhaps the breezes will bring relief tonight."

With the apartment bedded down for the evening, Gheorghe darted out into the hallway and quickly locked the front doors. He collapsed onto his divan. As he lay on his back, the ceiling stretched out like a screen replaying the horror of Tatiana's wretched face snarling and spewing its fury at him. His stomach rolled at what may face him this night.

Dobrescu made a tentative resting place by draping a sheet over Radu's bed. Despite his nervousness, the young man was asleep in minutes, snoring quietly with his notebook open on his lap.

With a body twined with agitation, Gheorghe's body began to convulse and shudder under the psychological strain of his predicament. He shivered as if he were abandoned on an icy Siberian steppe. Before him the ambitions of petty men in the Securitate and behind him secret desires an ancient evil closed in on him. He burst into tears. The outburst of emotion expended his remaining energy and he collapsed into a deep sleep. Gheorghe bolted up from his sleep panicked as if he had realized he had left his post unattended. There was a sigh of relief seeing his room was as he had left it.

He refreshed himself with a splash of water to the face and circled his tiny apartment hoping for the sunrise. The dread of his visitor had slowed time as every excruciating minute passed. He checked to make sure Dobrescu was still asleep, moving quietly to keep it so.

Suddenly there was the distinct sound of slow and deliberate footfalls in the lobby. They stopped and paused as if loitering in a museum. The steps came closer to Gheorghe's door. He had not heard the locked doors open so no one had entered through the lobby doors. The steps stopped in front of his door. The metallic knock on the door seized Gheorghe's heart. He looked at Dobrescu, still asleep.

"Yes?" Gheorghe squeaked at the closed door.

"Mr. Ianculescu, may I speak with you?"

Gheorghe slightly opened the door. In the dimly lit corridor, there was a finely dressed man in a black suit. There was no snarling, monstrous visage. Gheorghe opened the door. Before him stood a pale-skinned man with an aquiline nose and large eyebrows. He stood erect with a refined and aristocratic manner. His complexion was waxen and shiny.

"Good evening," he said through red lips.

"Good evening," Gheorghe's gaze transfixed on his eyes and suddenly a sensation of drunkenness overcame him. A sense of dominion pressed down upon his mind as if someone or something was attempting entry into his head and he was powerless to stop the invasion.

Gheorghe threw out his hand to greet him.

The man stared derisively at the outstretched hand. "May I come in?"

His request seemed reasonable, after all, he was not the gruesome monster Gheorghe had anticipated. He severed his gaze and turned to show him into his apartment when he caught his reflection in the glass of his mother's china cabinet. Behind his reflection, the doorframe was empty. He wheeled around to face the man. "I'm sorry, but it is late and I have a busy day planned tomorrow."

The visitor's face exploded into a venomous snarl. "Do you think you speak to a peasant?"

Gheorghe jumped at the sudden eruption of anger. He gave a weak smile and slammed the door. He leaned against the door to listen. Two steps echoed through the lobby and suddenly stopped. Gheorghe held his breath as he focused his ears to the lobby. No other sound was made and all fell silent.

A wave of relief came over him. Was that all it took? A simple, *I'm sorry* and a closed door? *That was too easy,* Gheorghe laughed at the simplicity of it all. He survived another night. He fell back onto the divan.

As soon as his eyes closed again, the divan beneath Gheorghe became softer, melting away beneath his weight like soft sand. The damp smell of earth crept into his nostrils. He opened his eyes again and found that he was no longer in his flat. Greeting him was the arcing embrace of his grandfather's oak tree sprawled out above him, leafless but loaded with small green buds like verdant promises. It was spring again and he was lying beneath the tree among a scattering of fallen acorns.

The soft earth and the distance from his concrete housing complex reassured him. This was a familiar place, only nature was here with Gheorghe now. He felt innervated as if the energy of youth was returned to him, but he did not move from his bed beneath the tree. The sky glowed down upon him from between the many branches and he closed his eyes again to feel the warmth basking on his forehead and cheeks.

It is still beautiful, isn't it?

Gheorghe sat upright and found that Camelia stood beside him. Her luminous eyes sparkled down on him in the gauzy sunlight. He had not seen her in over 20 years, but those eyes told him it was truly her.

Camelia, what are you doing here?

I live here, silly boy, she giggled as she skipped down the hill and ducked under the wooden fence into the field. Her laughter sounded far away.

A smile emerged from his face as he slowly followed her into the field.

Why do you always sit under that tree? She teased.

My grandfather kept it standing so that we'd always have it. Our neighbors say it is the largest tree in all of Crisana, Gheorghe responded. *Why do you always run away?* He asked in the same tone she had used. He approached her in the field.

Because you can never catch me! She took off running again, headed for the hill and the tree atop it.

Gheorghe grabbed hold of her blouse, but she slipped from his grasp, the fabric of her clothing ethereal and without weight. Her laughter brushed against his ears like the wind against the stalks of wheat in the field, tickling and swaying Gheorghe indescribably. He chased after her, letting the playful feelings of youth overtake him.

She reached the hill and disappeared behind the tree.

Gheorghe did a lap around the great oak tree's trunk but could not find her. With a smile still on his face, he lay down again to wait for her. The sun glimmered through his eyelids for this brief moment of serenity until it began to fade. The light was still present, but it no longer felt warm to Gheorghe. Maybe Camelia was at the farmhouse now. Was it time to turn down the land for the night? Hesitant to open his eyes, Gheorghe squirmed deeper into the loamy soil beneath him to recapture the dreamy feelings of well-being from moments ago. The soil was still damp but no longer welcoming.

Now the light of the sun was fading too. Gheorghe opened his eyes and saw the fiery orb retreating into the West, moving faster than he had ever seen it before. But when it reached the horizon, it paused, frozen at the point of greatest distance from him. He surveyed the land, unable to locate the farmhouse where his family lived. He stood with some difficulty, the acorns shifting beneath his feet.

Just as he gained his footing, a chill descended upon his shoulders like a blanket of falling snow. Gheorghe began to walk towards the wooden fence at the border of his grandfather's farming plot but was stopped suddenly when he discovered the source of the cold. Above him, a black wall of shade was advancing on the sun from the opposite side of the sky. The sun still stood in place on the horizon; this was not night.

The dense curtain of darkness unfurled across the sky above him like a rich tapestry. It had wings and the sinewy movements of a living creature but the translucency and impermanence of a shadow. The shadow was shapeless but as it neared the sun, its form became clearer. A reptilian head emerged from its swirling bulk. It was a dragon.

The shadow moved without noise, streaking across the sky with the silent gravity of a tidal wave. The sun still did not move though collision was imminent. Gheorghe ran to the wooden fence and began to yell and scream at the sun, trying to move it with his voice and his violent motions. It was indifferent.

As the dragon neared, its fanged mouth opened wide, wider than its wingspan and swallowed the sun in its shadowy maw. The rest of its smoke-like body continued its momentum and collapsed around its ensnared prey. The sun was vanquished, replaced with a billowing, convulsing orb of darkness that fought to contain itself.

The sky above Gheorghe was dim now, a shade of gray that was unlike any twilight of reality. He stopped yelling but could not take his eyes off the sun and the dragon, fighting with each other to reach some sort of stability. The surface of the orb began to smooth over, no longer bucked at from within. Now it began to dip below the horizon as if a predator was taking up the normal routines of its prey.

Night fell and a magnanimous purple swept across the sky as if to herald a heavenly resolution. Dozens of stars emerged, embedded in the night like incorruptible gemstones, twinkling indifferently as if all was normal again. The air around Gheorghe constricted tight around him, clinging to him with an even colder bite than before. He spotted the moon, now assured that he had lived through darker nights.

He took a few steps in aimless directions because he was uncertain of what he sought and which way was the proper course to it. He was still alone. The ground beneath his feet crunched like broken glass. A fine layer of frost had appeared. The temperature was continuously dropping. Gheorghe returned to the base of the oak tree and picked up an acorn to examine it. It too was encrusted with a thin layer of ice.

An explosion of sound like cannon-fire came from the West and Gheorghe instinctively ducked for cover at the roots of the tree. He turned to face the horizon again. The darkness was spreading across the sky with more speed and force than the sun had previously, drowning out the purple hue with thousands of infinitesimal black tentacles. It grew like ivy and smothered the night beneath its sinister foliage. This was the ancient evil that destroyed his family, and now it had taken the sun.

Gheorghe began to cry, feeling cold and alone. He kneeled at the base of the tree, nestled in its roots and clinging to its bark. He felt the warmth. Gheorghe lay down again beneath the tree, looking up into the abysmal darkness and found the stars still shining. There was one star directly above him between the branches that seemed to glow with the same warmth like the sun. His tears ceased.

A loud noise like a bone snapping disrupted his calm. The force of the sound moved the ground beneath him and he felt his entire body convulse with the tremors. He did not move. The star that spoke to him was growing. Gheorghe squinted. It was moving closer. A shrill whistle like falling artillery fire began to crescendo. Gheorghe quickly scrambled to his feet and tumbled down the small hill on which the oak tree was situated. He was no more than a few yards away when the falling star flashed to the ground and blinded him with iridescence. He uncovered his eyes after the flare.

The tree was cleaved in half and flames erupted from the wood. Heat licked Gheorghe's bewildered face across the distance. There was his mother, standing before the flaming tree in her red dress and gold bangles that were her favorite. She shined with golden hues, the flames dancing in the golden reflections of her jewelry. She smiled. *Gheorghe,* she beckoned. Her voice rekindled a forgotten youthful energy.

Gheorghe walked closer to the mirage, drawn by the heat and youthful remembrance. As he neared, she drifted backward without steps and pointed to the moon. He followed her gaze and the tentacles were wrapping themselves around the moon, slowly and methodically like a boa constrictor. At the top of the coil, the dragon's head reared open again and descended around the shadowy whole of its body and the moon. The sound of cracking bones came again and the moon was gone.

His mother was no longer pointing at the moon. Gheorghe approached her again and she didn't retreat. He put his hand on her shoulder, finding it to be only damp fabric and bone. He turned her around, faced by an eyeless, emaciated corpse. Her jaw unhinged and she let out a long moan.

Enough! A booming voice clapped from above and Gheorghe's mother turned to dust in his hands. A dark cloud hung in the sky where the moon used to be and the figure of a man descended from it, plummeting like another falling star. Before hitting the ground, two great wings unfurled and fanned a gust of wind at the earth to slow the man. He landed gracefully and the force from his wings snuffed out the flaming tree instantly. It was the man who had visited the apartment, still wearing the same black suit. Panic electrified Gheorghe and he froze in place and fell to his knees. He silently dropped to the ground hoping to go undetected.

The man surveyed the smoldering landscape. *There is nothing to compare to the beauty of Romania. Wouldn't you agree, Gheorghe?* the man said affectedly. *I see you have a love for our homeland,* he flashed his teeth playfully. The wings folded onto his back and melded into his form, disappearing from sight.

Where is my mother? Gheorghe asked.

The man laughed. *I do not know. There are things which are hidden from me. Radu tells me you speak fondly of her. She must have been very dear to you.* He stopped and scrutinized Gheorghe as if he were an exhibit in a museum.

Gheorghe squirmed under his gaze.

Yes, I see it clearly. There is a stasis between one's fear and the villainy of men. For you, it reveals itself as regret. However, I'm sure you did everything in your power to save her. A mocking smile appeared on his face.

Gheorghe could not escape the shame. A dullness enveloped his heart and a hollowness wormed through his chest. Tears began streaming down his face. *It is no use. I can't bring her back. True, yet we can ensure those responsible are held accountable for their actions. I can bring peace to you.*

Gheorghe lay on a carpet of frozen acorns gazing into the darkness. The man circled him without a word. The sound of acorns being crushed under foot hemmed him in. Gheorghe fought the temptation to look. A cold, dead, empty silence enticed Gheorghe to glance toward his feet. Above him, the man's velvety silhouette against the overcast night sky stood vigil at his feet.

It was ill-bred to turn me away from your flat tonight, he lifted him to his feet with an effortless movement.

Gheorghe stood on his feet but was off-balance. So this was the Master of which Radu spoke. He examined the spot where the hand clamped around his arm, but his vision blurred as if he were drunk. There did not seem to be any danger and quiet had returned to the darkened farmland.

Such a beautiful tree as this could only have grown in Transylvanian soil. You come from an honorable family line, Gheorghe. The blood of the Roma flows through you. Was not your mother a gypsy?

Yes.

The gypsies were a great support to me in the past. They have been held in derision by many and yet they remain a strong and proud people. You have no reason to be ashamed of your ancestors. Throughout the centuries, they have been my hands and feet as the sun runs its course. Small-minded men have taken them from us, haven't they Gheorghe? Our soil and our blood were stolen for the purposes of others. You see what they have done, he pointed a marble white finger at the scorched tree.

You are responsible for that destruction. Gheorghe cringed at his own bluntness.

The Master laughed.

For over 300 years, I have thrived among the ignorance and hatred of man. Mortals have perfected the art of destruction. When I lived in London, I relied on solicitors to veil my movements. Once I found it necessary to leave London, the coffins which your kindred established for me throughout Europe made it possible to move unhindered. The wars of man have helped me flourish without the avarice of solicitors. I moved in the shadows among the debauched and lazy. They swarmed like locusts stripping each other and feeding on the blood and toil of the weak. It is fascinating to witness moral decay; really quite sad."

He led Gheorghe to the top of the hill where the tree once stood. He motioned to the horizon. Gheorghe followed his spindly hand and saw stretched before him a vast valley dotted with distant fires and smoldering ruins.

Mortals are quite competent in the ways of destruction. Their wars are a testament to that. The Székely were great warriors, but we used our strength to crush the infidels; We never used our strength to wantonly crush another. Though I am of noble birth and you are merely a boor, we both understand the superiority of our blood lines. I have no exclusive claim on destruction and death. On the contrary, I have been inspired by the depths a mortal will go in the ruin of his fellow man. Wars have weakened all mankind, but I remain powerful. The evil that destroyed your family was not mine.

You know nothing about my family, Gheorghe said.

I know more about you than you think, Gheorghe. Your friends and family have been taken from you. Now, darkness is your only companion.

The words were said softly and into the woods away from Gheorghe, but they pierced his heart like an arrow. Doughy snowflakes began to fall from the sky. Gheorghe looked up and found that the blackness had become total.

But it doesn't have to be that way, Gheorghe. Your family has always participated in my legacy. The gypsies from your mother's lineage were protected under my wings for their service to me.

I already serve too many monsters.

I know the monsters of which you speak. Do you find it curious that someone with your family legacy would be promoted to the Securitate? Codreanu seems to be up to some mischief. He stood and waited for a response.

The comment pierced Gheorghe as he realized its validity; he said nothing.

Why do you not speak? Does Codreanu's attempts of building his dossier surprise you? He smiled again, the fangs gleaming like diamonds. *Codreanu sees silence as a virtue of fools; He thinks you most virtuous.* He gave a broad smile. *He takes your silence and deference as weakness, but I know better. He will not be an obstacle for you after you receive my power. There are many reasons to punish that simpleton and I can arrange that satisfaction.*

Gheorghe dared not speak, recognizing that this man's connection with Radu put him at a severe disadvantage. His past was an open book to him.

The Master laughed, taking Gheorghe's silence as progress.

Walk with me, Gheorghe.

Gheorghe approached the slim man, losing some of his apprehensions and feeling the first itches of curiosity in his mind. He looked at the oak tree, charred and deformed to a grotesque specter of its former self. They walked together along the fence and Gheorghe felt enveloped in numbness. He could no longer feel the cold, but snow continued falling. They were heading towards the woods at the edge of the field, but Gheorghe was not nervous to leave the open field. There was nothing here for him.

I've returned so I can reclaim what is rightfully mine, the Master mused. *There is no one alive who can stop me. Do you think you can?* He smiled, his obscene confidence making the question rhetorical. They continued for several paces in silence, penetrating the tree line and entering a different section of farmland. *Our people were once proud, but they have become bent and crooked under the weight of the hammer and sickle.*

At his words, men materialized in the snow-covered fields, hacking at phantom crops that were not visible to Gheorghe.

The persistent upheavals across our land have brought many hardships to our people. When my family ruled these lands, we were strong and forthright; we were a noble family. Those who rule over you now use puppetry and deceit to exploit our blood and soil. Isn't that right, Gheorghe? The man's dark eyes met Gheorghe's.

Gheorghe was compelled to nod, feeling as though a marionette string was moving his head. The numbness was soothing, but he was beginning to feel as though he were no longer in control of his own feet. They continued past the fields, walking along a broad dirt road. There were many fields flanked on either side of them, but his guide pointed ahead.

Codreanu knows what lies at the end of the road he is forcing you to walk, but do you? Your life is disappearing with each step you take for him. Your father went to the end of this road and never came back.

Gheorghe saw a distant figure up ahead, walking away from them.

He was a traitor, Gheorghe said.

Ah, but what he did was for the greater good of Romania. Was it not? He took death into his bosom; He took an oath to embrace death and to dispense death. Perhaps you should do likewise, the man responded.

They were gaining on the figure ahead of them. He wore the green shirt uniform of the Iron Guard and maintained a strict military march. Gheorghe began to get nervous; he had not seen his father in over ten years. The road was becoming smoother and the snow had stopped falling. The plots of farmland on either side of them were becoming fewer.

Now they were abreast with the soldier. Gheorghe held his breath.

The soldier turned and saluted Gheorghe's guide. It was Gheorghe's father. His face was as it had been on that hot September day in 1939, the same distracting nose, but his unblinking eyes were gray like fog, instead of the steel blue that Gheorghe shared. His marching abruptly stopped, slowly turning to him his dead face melted into an uncharacteristic face of compassion. *Gheorghe?* He whispered.

His tenderness disarmed Gheorghe. *Father?*

He looked past Gheorghe. His eyes darted frantically, desperately looking for someone or something. *Have you seen your mother?*

Gheorghe turned to follow his father's gaze. He found himself in a narrow courtyard hemmed in on all sides by terraces. A frigid wind whistled through the courtyard. Gheorghe turned to his father to find he was alone. He felt his throat thicken as he fought back the urge to cry. The numbness had returned. He gasped as he glanced up at the terraces to find them filled with people with yellow armbands with brown inverted triangles. Some were fashionably dressed while others were dressed in rags. All stood vigil over the courtyard as they silently stared down at Gheorghe. Their mute vigil magnified their presence and became claustrophobic. On the far end of the courtyard, Gheorghe's mother lay crumpled on the wet cement. He tried to run to her, but a paralysis kept him in place.

Gheorghe heard his voice from behind him. *Why is your mother at Ullmann Palace?*

Tears suddenly streamed from his eyes and his shoulders began to heave from the once forgotten feelings of helplessness.

A gruff voice snarled, *Gheorghe, stop your sniveling. You are just like your mother.*

A flash of anger seized Gheorghe. He wanted to lash out but restrained himself; His father's brutal temper kept Gheorghe at bay.

A condescending voice called out, *I tried to save her, Gheorghe.*

How?

Once I married her, I tried to keep her away from her family but her mind was poisoned. As much as I tried to keep that vile pack of dogs away, his gaze drilled through Gheorghe and a sadistic smile cracked his stony face, *I came to realize she was the one who was a vile dog.* A subtle laugh simmered through his lips.

Gheorghe tried to run, but his steps were leaden as if steel coils fettered his legs. The courtyard walls swelled until he lay in the bottom of a dry well. He struggled and found himself sinking into a mire. The viscous soil grabbed him and began pulling him down. His paralyzed limbs finally wretched away from the ground. Warm, sticky blood cover his hands. *Father, Please help me!*

His voice echoed down the well, *You are weak, just like your mother. You disgust me.*

Gheorghe felt a current of rage course through his body as his vision clouded over. *No more tricks!*

Very well, The Master laughed as he vanished.

Gheorghe was immediately assaulted by the cold. The numbness wore off and like a drunk waking from his blackout, Gheorghe didn't know how he got to his present location. The well had vanished, replaced with a cobblestone road hemmed with sidewalks and storefronts. Cars bounced noisily across the bricks of the road and people streamed by Gheorghe on either side, brushing against him with heavy coats and thick furs. Gay laughter streamed from their mouths and they shouted in German. Many people stopped to admire the gaudy trinkets and fancy hats in storefront windows, but Gheorghe was somehow invisible.

Gheorghe discovered his father ahead of him, marching down the sidewalk. People cleared a path for his long, officious steps and Gheorghe ran to catch up with him. Just as he neared, his father entered a large building at the end of the block where the road ended. Gheorghe followed him inside.

The entry hall was a long, ornate room with rich red wallpaper and mahogany furniture. Gilded chandeliers dangled from the ceiling with ornate crystal arrangements and the gas lamps on the wall sent long shadows down the narrow room. The light danced on the top of furniture and the carpet, lingering on the glossy surface of frost. There was an open door at the back of the hall, spilling voices and light into the entry hall. Gheorghe inched forward down the frozen red hall, uncertain of what to expect.

When he crossed the threshold into the room, his mind was flooded with delicious smells. The room was much larger than the entry hall and hosted a huge party of guests. They were all seated around a long table, set with intricate place settings and silverware.

The Master was seated at the head of the table, laughing gregariously with a pale-skinned woman in a red dress with a deep plunging neckline. He noticed Gheorghe and waved, beckoning to an empty seat next to him.

Gheorghe did as he was told. He gasped from the coldness of his chair, but also upon the discovery of his table mates. Codreanu was sitting just two seats away chatting with Radu. Gheorghe's father was sitting next to Shalberov. Tatiana had one side of the table all to herself with the school children that Gheorghe had staked. Interspersed with the notable people were several young maidens, similarly complexioned with pale skin and dark red dresses.

We have been awaiting your arrival, the Master said.

What is this? Gheorghe asked.

It's my gift to you, should you accept. All of your enemies in one place joined together to share their bounties with you. They've all taken from you, so now it is time for them to repay you with a feast to your honor and life. With this, the man raised a silver goblet that brimmed with a red drink. The guests around the table mimicked his motion.

Gheorghe could not prevent his mouth from watering. He had not yet seen a morsel of food because the table was lined with covered silver platters, but the smells emanating from the dishes snaked into his nostrils. He checked his own glass and took a sip. It tasted like wine but slid down his tongue with viscous resistance.

I understand your opposition, Gheorghe. Perhaps these impulses are foreign or even repulsive to you. Believe me, the first impulse to act on your thoughts of revenge will always be as fragile as the thread of a spider, He paused to ensure Gheorghe was listening. *But with time, eventually, it becomes as hardened steel.* The

Master smiled. His teeth were red. *Servants!* He yelled. *Unveil our feast. The guest of honor has arrived.*

A cadre of faceless servants wearing black lifted the silver lids off the many platters in unison. One tray remained covered in front of Gheorghe.

The smells vanished and Gheorghe was greeted by a sickening sight. On each tray was piled a number of human body parts. They were not gruesome or butchered, but finely roasted and cooked to completion like any other meal. The guests around the table dug in heartily, reaching for arms and thighs and shoulders to put on their plates. Gheorghe watched as his enemies gorged themselves on the flesh with the dignity and class of sophisticated socialites. He began to get sick.

How did you expect me to entice them to our celebration? The host smirked. *We can repay them for treating you and your family like chattel. But first, you must fulfill your duty to your rightful master. Once you have fulfilled your service to me, your enemies will sleep with their fathers.*

A servant approached the only covered dish remaining on the table. When the lid was lifted, Gheorghe stood immediately. His face stared back at him with unseeing gray eyes. The guests smacked their lips and stripped bones with their teeth. He felt their teeth all over him, eating him alive.

The time has come for you to make your decision. Why do you vacillate? You are already a sacrifice, but whose purpose will you serve? All that awaits you is death and I am its Master. Serve me and feast upon your enemies, or serve your enemies and they will feast upon you.

Gheorghe looked into the eyes of his decapitated head. Revenge would not bring back his mother, his father, his friends, Camelia. Even if he eliminated his foes, there would be no one to bury him.

Suddenly, a surge of white light enveloped Gheorghe. The banquet hall was absorbed and faded from view. *Gheorghe,* a gravelly voice whispered. He turned to see Father Petre. *You will dig your own grave.*

Gheorghe woke up in a cold sweat, his divan soaked in perspiration. He sighed with the realization that all was a dream. The air bit into his skin as billows of steam gave shape to his breath. A velvety layer of frost covered the entire apartment; a glaze of ice floated on the surface of a drinking glass. He sat up from the divan as the sun rose in the east.

Dobrescu had crumpled into a ball on Radu's mattress, crinkling the pages of his open notebook into disorder. He continued to sleep peacefully with no idea of the events of the night.

The reassurance of the day was clouded by the troubling dream. The details of the dream faded with time. The plausibility of dreams becomes absurd with the passage of time. However, the Master's presence protruded from his dream as a rock in the snow. As the details of the dream melted, all that was left was this man. Every detail, every word hung in his mind. This was no mere dream.

Pawns, Knights, and Bishops

Gheorghe rose from the divan and began pacing throughout the apartment. The apartment felt small; he paced its narrow paths as if he were looking for a route of escape. His mind raced as he tried to make sense of the dream. Moving quietly and carefully, he let Dobrescu sleep through the dawn. The chill of the evening was quickly diminishing, but a chill of dread kept Gheorghe shaking. The warm orange rays of sunrise helped soothe Gheorghe as he moved about the apartment. As the time passed, he watched as the velvety frost melted bleeding into the fabric of the furniture; the iced over water glass was now beaded with condensation. Whatever force had visited him the night before was no longer present and this reassured Gheorghe though his thoughts of the dream would not stop.

Father Petre was right. There was no way that Gheorghe could shirk the challenges that hung above his head. If he did not act, Codreanu would find some way to advance his career with Gheorghe's blood; it had happened to his friends and Gheorghe was next. His was no supernatural force, just a little man with ambition and paranoia too large for his own head. Even if Codreanu couldn't pin him, the Master would. Two sides of a vise were closing in around him; one side pursuing his prized Dragon and the other some mysterious cherished item. Both, driven to get what they desired, were propelled by a certitude that they would prevail. Gheorghe realized that he was the instrument they both wanted to use for their own ends. This was not a time for passivity; he was cornered and had no choice but to act. *How do I get out of this vise?*

If Codreanu is so eager to capture his Dragon then I'm more than happy to introduce him personally, he thought.

Gheorghe stopped his pacing as his pained face drained from his face. His eyes widened and a look of surprise flashed on his face. *Wait, both are confident they will get what they want, arrogant in their ability,* he thought. He began weighing all the variables in his equation. He knew what the constants were in his equation: Codreanu and his Dragon were both driven to obtain their prize. *Perhaps, I could use their desires against the other.* Now, his pacing through the apartment was an attempt to catalog the variables he needed to solve this deadly equation. *I will only get one chance and the execution has to be flawless. I can't make any mistakes,* he thought. His heart raced as a subdued excitement took control. He felt rejuvenated with the possibility, however slight, of a resolution.

Gheorghe decided to prepare breakfast for himself and his unwelcomed roommate. Cooking calmed him further and he began to map out what needed to be done.

"Is that breakfast?" Dobrescu called sleepily from the divan.

The question startled Gheorghe as it ripped him from his thoughts. "Yes, It will be ready in a few minutes."

"Wait! Is it morning already?" Dobrescu bolted from the sheets. His hair stood upright on one side from his pillow and added to the appearance of his shock. "What happened? Did I miss the leader's visit?" He began to pace suddenly, flipping through the crumpled pages of his notebook and trying to flatten them. Finding that he had not taken notes in his sleep, he threw the notebook down. "The Captain is going to kill me!"

Gheorghe was now at the point of no return. If he was going to set his plan in motion, now was the time. "Relax, it was best that you fell asleep. Have a seat," Gheorghe pointed to the small table with the frying pan. "You were sleeping like a rock."

Dobrescu slowed down and sat at the table. Receiving orders seemed to calm him.

"So, nothing happened?" He laughed to himself. "I guess you were right all along about Radu."

Gheorghe brushed crumbs off two plates and dished out the eggs. He ripped two large pieces of bread from a loaf bringing the modest breakfast to the table.

"No, but he sent a messenger. When he saw you, he was furious. He was expecting me to be alone. He wanted to kill you, but I assured him you were asleep," he said as he sat with Dobrescu.

"Thank you but Codreanu was expecting me to take notes. If he finds out, I was sleeping..." Dobrescu trailed off thinking of the consequences.

"I don't want you to worry about that. As far as I am concerned, you were awake the whole time. Just let me do the talking."

Dobrescu gave a relieved sigh. "What did he want?"

"Well," Gheorghe started slowly, "There is a hidden weapons cache that he wants me to retrieve for the rebels in Borş."

Dobrescu gave a huge smile. "Really? This is great news! Where did he say it was located?"

"I do not know. He was paranoid and insisted on leaving. I pressed him on it and he said Radu knows the location."

"Oh-," Dobrescu's excitement shattered. He tapped his fork on the table and gave a faint sigh. "Well, at least, we have something to report to comrade Codreanu." He started to rise from the table.

"Wait," Gheorghe said, pointing to breakfast, "Let's have some breakfast first."

Dobrescu was happy to do as told. He dug into his food with uninhibited eagerness. "These are delicious; they remind me of my mother's cooking."

"Were you raised on a farm?"

"Yes, a small farm north of Luduș."

"What was it like on your farm?" Gheorghe asked.

"Very much like any other tenant farm," Dobrescu answered through a mouthful. "We grew wheat and toiled all year to barely feed ourselves. I did not want to follow my family into farming, but there are few options for a peasant. I was happy to join the army. Meeting Captain Codreanu changed my life; he has shown me there are many noble things to be done for our country. Once we can bring stability to the country, we can start bringing the people up from the poverty which oppresses them."

Gheorghe gave him a blank nod wondering if the young man really believed his own words. "I grew up on a farm too. I've been dreaming about it recently," Gheorghe said to his plate. He began to pick through his eggs unenthusiastically. His nerves would not allow his stomach to settle.

Dobrescu looked up from his empty plate, reading the emotion in Gheorghe. "What was your farm like? For some reason, I can only imagine you as a police officer," he said with a smile.

"It was beautiful. My grandfather owned it for many years, He had an oak tree which was known throughout the region. I have been dreaming of my grandfather's farm for weeks now. I have not been there since I was a young man." He gave a soft sigh as memories of Camelia hijacked his thoughts. "It was a simpler time."

"Do you still family there?"

"I don't know. All I have are the faces in my dreams. I see the people that I love, all the faces from my childhood." He whispered in a bruised tone of remembrance, "They're all gone now."

"I've read the files on your father and brother. They were expelled from the police for being members of the Răzbunători. You cannot miss them."

"No, they were never able to convert me to their death cult. They aspired to glorious deaths, thinking life after death would be sweeter because of their sacrifices. I believe in life before death. We did not agree on anything."

As Gheorghe struggled with the crusty bread, Dobrescu squirmed in his seat. The apartment clicked and creaked in the awkward silence. Dobrescu looked up from his plate.

"Did you leave when the war started?"

"No, It has been over 20 years now. Our family moved; once I finished my army service, my father helped get me hired on with the police. I have been doing this ever since." He became self-conscious about his transparency, raking his fork through his food. "I don't mean to bore you." He feigned a smile. "If you want to know more about my past, you should ask Codreanu."

Dobrescu laughed. "I don't know why the captain doesn't trust you, Inspector. I find you to be a very trustworthy man."

"Codreanu does not trust me because I've seen his rise to power. That's why he watches me so closely. I know where all the skeletons are buried; I am his last loose end. You can tell him he has nothing to fear from me. Obviously, He has a high regard for your loyalty."

"Yes, he has been good to me. Aren't you happy with your promotion to the Securitate?" Dobrescu asked. "You were vetted for many weeks before Shalberov approved you."

"I never asked for the position but refusing it would have been suicide. Climbing the ranks has never been my ambition."

"Surely, you want to be rewarded for your work?"

"I do as I'm told to avoid trouble." With Dobrescu relaxed, Gheorghe went fishing. "Haven't you seen my files?"

Dobrescu met Gheorghe's eyes with a boyish smile as if a burden was lifted from his shoulders. "You're right, the Captain asked me to dig into your past. It is as if he wants me to find some deep secret of yours, some unspeakable crime. I know you better than ever now and there has been nothing that I can find to support his suspicions. Why don't you eat?" Dobrescu vigorously chewed the stale bread. "The eggs were very good, thank you."

Dobrescu's candor prickled up the hair on the back of Gheorghe's neck. Gheorghe's defenses bolted up. He looked down at his plate and began forcing the food into his mouth. The eggs were cold and the bread was hard. Dobrescu spoke of his trust of Gheorghe, yet the boy was ordered to find evidence to discredit him. There was no trust possible between them as long as he followed orders, which seemed to be the meaning of his life. The young man was unaware of his corruption by Codreanu's promises of power and reputation. There was no one Gheorghe could trust among Codreanu's ranks.

Gheorghe plunged himself deep into his thoughts. Dobrescu picked through the remnants of his breakfast. He gave Gheorghe a few nervous side-glances. "What's wrong, Inspector?"

"Nothing, we should report in with Codreanu," Gheorghe looked at his watch and stood to dress.

Dobrescu nodded and went to the mirror to fix his hair and straighten his uniform.

They departed and rode the bus to City Hall in silence. Gheorghe was deep in thought and kept his eyes glued to the streets outside the bus. He ignored the many inquisitive looks of his young partner, thinking far ahead of the present. But as they neared the station, he could not shake the image of Camelia in the field from his mind. He remembered what he said to Dobrescu, *I believe in life before death.* He found new resolve.

The bus sputtered to a stop and the men shouldered their way through the crowded aisle. Some people tried to move out of their way, but others stubbornly offered stiff shoulders to them. Gheorghe led the way into the City Hall and reported directly to Codreanu's office. The door was locked and the lights were off; they were early. They sat in two stiff chairs in the hallway to wait.

"Let me do all the talking," Gheorghe ordered. Dobrescu nodded, turning a shade of red.

After a long wait, Gheorghe turned at the sound of loud laughter down the hallway.

Codreanu arrived, trailed by a young and energetic cadre. Their boots clicked down the hallway as their bombastic banter rolled down the hallway like thunder. Codreanu spoke without turning and the men behind him jostled each other for a better position to hear and be heard by the Chief Inspector. The loudest laughter came from the men on the fringe. When he saw the duo waiting outside his office, Codreanu stiffened. With a wave of his hand, he sent his followers scurrying back the way they came. Strolling to his office, he did not address the two men and pulled an ornate key-ring from his breast pocket to open his door.

Gheorghe's loathing simmered within him while he waited to be addressed. He could not fathom how he had remained quiet for so many years under this treatment.

Codreanu entered his office, leaving the door open behind him and turning on the lights. After a few more minutes, he called the waiting men into his office. He was comfortably seated behind his desk, drinking a large mug of tea.

"Good morning, Inspectors." Codreanu blew the steam off his tea with short breaths. "Inspector Dobrescu, please report on the meeting with our Dragon," he said, slurping from his cup.

"The leader wants me to retrieve a weapons cache for a royalist's rebel cell in Borş," Gheorghe cut in.

Codreanu cast an evaluative glance at Dobrescu. "Is this true, Inspector Dobrescu?"

Dobrescu nodded quickly, his face redder than ever. He looked down at his feet.

A wide smile spread across Codreanu's face. The excitement radiating from his eyes urged Gheorghe to continue.

"This also confirms what the priest told me yesterday. According to him, there has been talk in the village of the Order of the Dragon. Many of the villagers are upset with the upcoming farm collectivization and are talking of rebellion. Some wives have come to the priest, asking how they can calm their husbands from this foolish uprising. They are the lazy and insolent villagers who refuse to accept the farming improvements of the Republic. One woman implied the rebels are waiting for a shipment of weapons to mobilize their small force. This shipment was promised by the leader though the priest was uncertain where, when, or how it will be delivered."

Codreanu was brought to the edge of his seat. "Excellent, we may have our Dragon's head on a pike sooner than I thought."

Dobrescu stared at Gheorghe with wide, dissenting eyes. "You didn't-"

Gheorghe tumbled out, "There is one obstacle, however; before we could learn the location of the cache, He fled."

Codreanu's face froze and flamed with silent anger. His jaw pulsated with a force which could crush gravel.

Dobrescu intercepted his fury and barked out, "He said Radu knew its whereabouts." He flashed Gheorghe an innocuous smile.

Codreanu's erupted, "I am losing my patience with this whole affair! I want-," he tripped over his words, "I need this resolved. How do you propose we proceed?"

"I can use my connection with Radu to find the location of this shipment. If we get the exact time and location, we can wipe out this rebellion in one clean sweep. We can catch the leader himself. It appears that he takes a very central role in recruitment."

Codreanu squinted at Gheorghe. He stood from his seat and faced the window on the back wall of his office with his hands clutched behind his back. After a few moments, he walked to the front of his desk and leaned back against it with his arms crossed.

"How will you get Radu to reveal this information?"

"He already assumes that I am part of the Order. I will use this to our advantage."

"There is something you should know, Gheorghe," a devious smile spread across Codreanu's face. "I took the liberty of transferring our little rebel to Piteşti prison. I had hoped to avoid his participation in the program but I think you will be most impressed with the results of his re-education. After their stay, even the most brazen fascists eventually sing the praises of Stalin."

"Then it will be even easier to get the information from him," Gheorghe said.

"True, once he dispenses of his previous convictions, you should find him more compliant. This is the goal of Piteşti and I have seen it work with unbelievable success. Yet, there is no way for him to be in contact with the leader now. You will be wasting your time if you visit him."

"But comrade, according to the Master, Radu knows the location of the cache. I think it is clear he was able to withstand comrade Bălan's inquires."

"Yes, but you have shown that there are many more leads to be found in Borş. I think it would be wiser to interrogate the villagers there. Maybe your priest has more information than he gave you." Codreanu's smile grew. He paced back and forth in front of his desk, excited at the prospect of a new direction. "Yes, yes, you have done very well for the Securitate, Gheorghe. We are getting very close to the conclusion of our rat hunt."

Gheorghe was losing control of the situation.

"If I can get any information from Radu, I will use it to gain the confidence of the villagers in Borş. The priest didn't know much about the Order, nor did the women that informed him. If I can show the villagers I know the leader as well as Radu, I can convince them of the weapons cache and lead them right into your hands. Then you can interrogate each and every one of them at your leisure. If we move on this too fast, the leader will go deeper into hiding before we can get him out in the open. The villagers already trust me for my work on the child abductions."

Codreanu went back to his window and was quiet for some time. When he spoke again, he was still facing the window. "Very well, Gheorghe. You may visit Radu to get closer to the source. I will inform the officials in Piteşti of your arrival today." He came around to the front of his desk. "But Inspector Dobrescu will pay a visit to your priest to see how much more he can say about these villagers and the Order."

"Yes, comrade," Dobrescu shouted.

"Good. Then it is decided. I expect both of your reports first thing tomorrow morning."

Gheorghe nodded, his heart sinking heavily into his chest. He had not intended to endanger Father Petre. But these were the risks of taking action. Now, he needed to move fast.

"You are dismissed," Codreanu said. As they both made for the door, he called out again. "Inspector Dobrescu, stay behind. We need to talk."

Gheorghe left the office and hurried down the hall. He took a bus to the train depot and boarded the first train to Piteşti, counting the minutes on his watch as if they were his last.

Making and Breaking Allegiances

The train was empty except for Gheorghe. The ride was quiet, and Gheorghe stared out his window, happy to have the time in his head. He drifted to sleep a few times, awakened sporadically by flashes of his encounter with Tatiana and the children in Borș. Their voices and the sounds of the shattering glass became synonymous, ringing in his ears. He stared distantly at the smokestacks of oil refineries that smeared the skyline with puffs of black smog. The train arrived at the Pitești train depot. The groaning and hissing of the train ricocheted throughout the train station. The platform was devoid of people. A few uniformed men leaning against the wall glowered and spoke under their breath. Other than a scattered few, the station was deserted. With so few at the station, Gheorghe thought he may have arrived early. Gheorghe checked his watch. He was on time.

An official from the Securitate greeted him as he disembarked, showing Gheorghe to the backseat of a government vehicle. As they pulled away, the driver's hulking shoulders rose from the car seat. As he drove, his head remained fixed. All Gheorghe could see were his eyes framed in the rearview mirror. Occasionally his eyes would dart to the mirror to analyze Gheorghe. Gheorghe began to squirm under his sporadic gaze. He turned to greet a gray landscape of industrial sprawl. He kept his stare on the dreary landscape. The car jolted him from his thoughts as it bottomed out on a bridge spanning the greenish-blue waters of the Argeș River. He flashed his eyes forward to see his driver staring at him once more.

"Have you ever been to Pitești before Inspector?"

"No, but I have heard of it."

"What have you heard?"

"That it has successfully re-educated many prisoners."

The driver's eyes returned to the road. The accompanying silence clawed at Gheorghe.

"I hope my errand is not a pretense for my own imprisonment." He winced at his own the comment.

The driver gave a disapproving head shake and returned his eyes to Gheorghe. "You should not make such jokes."

"Is it as bad, as they say?"

"Worse."

Gheorghe worked up a weak smile. "It cannot be worse than what I have seen in Oradea."

The driver broke his gaze and continued driving. The piercing silence returned.

"What do the locals think?"

"They think what they are told to think; it was built to house common criminals. Our re-education efforts are not as well-known because we do not want the prisoners becoming martyrs."

The prison was encircled by a massive, wrought-iron fence. Affixed to the fence was a bland sign:

CENTER FOR STUDENT RE-EDUCATION

After making it through a security checkpoint, the driver slowly approached the building and dropped him off at the entrance. As he exited the car, the driver leaned over. "You need to ask for the warden, Lieutenant Dumitrescu. He should be able to help you."

The four-story building was the drab white color of mortar, with thin pairs of windows lining its front. Such a banal building did not seem capable of housing anything sinister though there were no clues as to what Gheorghe would encounter from its appearance. He steeled himself and entered through the main doors. Standing in a well-lit hallway, he scanned the ground floor to his left and right. An immaculately dressed guard standing outside a doorway quickly noticed him and approached.

"State your business," the guard said.

He pulled out his badge. "I am Inspector Gheorghe Ianculescu from Oradea. I am investigating a royalist terrorist group in Borş, and one of your prisoners may have pertinent information. I was told to report to Lieutenant Dumitrescu."

The guard maintained his stony expression as he looked at the identification. "Wait here," he commanded. He returned to the doorway and disappeared into the room.

Gheorghe looked at the olive green linoleum tiles beneath his feet; this did not seem so different from their holding station in Oradea.

The guard returned; this time escorted by another officer. The man was older but well-groomed. His uniform was tucked in and sharply pressed along the pants and shoulders. He held his hands behind his back, and his gait was proud. His strut seemed to match their very strict dress code.

"Greetings, comrade! I am Lieutenant Dumitrescu, the warden of Piteşti," he smiled, a wry expression that tucked up only on one side. "I must say, I am slightly confused by the nature of your visit; this is a very unusual request. Once a prisoner has been selected to participate in our re-education program, all contact with the outside is restricted."

"This is an ongoing investigation of an active royalist terrorist group, and his information could be instrumental in neutralizing a current threat," Gheorghe responded.

"Ah, a political threat," his smile broadened. "I will need to get the approval of comrade Iţicovici. Please, follow me." He turned and began to walk down the hallway.

Gheorghe followed, brushing past the first guard and feeling cold eyes on the back of his head as he passed. He cast a glance into the office from where the warden had emerged seeing a handful of guards standing , while others sat at desks scribbling away at piles of paper. Along the back wall, there was a large rack of wooden clubs though many were missing from their slots. He caught up to the warden quickly, moving deeper into the building.

"Are all the prisoners held in the upper floors?" Gheorghe asked.

The warden laughed. He twirled a cudgel around his wrist by its strap.

"No, none at all. The upper floors are our barracks for the guards and a few doctors. I am taking you to the second floor to the administrative offices. If your orders are as you say," he cast a sideway glance at Gheorghe, "you must get approval from the head political investigator."

They continued in silence.

As they proceeded down the hallway, Gheorghe noticed that the windows were shuttered along the first floor. There were fewer doors. They passed a staircase that descended into darkness, the window above it offering a stark contrast to the pitch black of the underground level. A horrid stench wafted past Gheorghe's nose as they passed. They continued a few more paces to a stairway opposite the first that led upwards.

On the second floor, sunlight streamed in through the thin windows and illuminated the green tiles. They quickly arrived at a large office on the west side of the building. The closed wooden door had red letters emblazoned on the glass:

HEAD POLITICAL INVESTIGATOR

MARINA IŢICOVICI.

The warden rapped on the frame and opened the door without waiting. They entered a well-furnished room and were greeted by a man behind a metal desk. He was punching furiously into a typewriter. The shades behind him were drawn, and a wisp of smoke crawled upwards from a full ashtray on his desk.

He squinted through a curtain of swirling smoke. "What is it, Dumitrescu?"

"We have a visitor from Oradea. He says he is investigating a political plot involving one of our prisoners."

"What? Which prisoner?" He pulled off his reading glasses and looked at Gheorghe with beady eyes. "It is not policy to allow contact with prisoners once they are accepted into our program."

"I understand comrade, but this is of utmost importance. I have gained Baboescu's trust, and he has vital information about an ongoing investigation."

"Who ordered you to Piteşti?"

"Comrade Codreanu in Oradea, with the full knowledge of Colonel Shalberov."

"Codreanu specifically requested Baboescu be transferred here, isn't that correct?"

"Yes," Gheorghe answered.

"Baboescu is a category four prisoner and has been charged under law 209 with subversive organizing against the security of the state. Codreanu should not take the process of re-education so lightly."

"Perhaps you could call Codreanu and clear it up with him."

Iţicovici glared at Gheorghe. He lifted his cigarette from the tray and took a drag, rubbing the creases his forehead violently with his other hand.

"I don't have time for this today," he said under his breath. "Get out, I will make a phone call."

The warden escorted Gheorghe out the door, and they stood in the hallway facing out the windows. Gheorghe listened through the door, hearing the crank of the phone rotor and Iţicovici's rushed greeting. Iţicovici's voice became much louder then abruptly stopped as if he had been slapped.

Dumitrescu grinned at Gheorghe, "This may take a while."

Gheorghe relaxed as he listened to the verbal pugilism in the next room.

Iţicovici's voice cracked the silence, "It is not just about one prisoner! Unmasking requires all prisoners be degraded to the same level! We cannot show any special attention..." he was cut off. "Yes, yes I know, but –" His voice was no longer audible.

Gheorghe leaned in and whispered, "Captain Codreanu can be obstinate."

Dumitrescu's smile broadened as he crossed his arms, "Well, your captain has never met Inspector Iţicovici." He turned and began walking away. "While these two immovable objects sort out their differences, I will show you the prison." The warden seemed visibly excited, twirling his cudgel again and walking faster towards the staircase to the ground floor.

Gheorghe stood his ground and gave a long deliberate stare. "We should wait here for the Inspector."

"No, I insist. I believe we are doing an excellent job of reforming these bandits," He disappeared down the stairs. Gheorghe had no recourse but to follow. "We must stop at the office at the main floor first so I can equip you properly for your visit," he winked at Gheorghe. He stepped into the office and went to the back wall where the clubs hung, taking one down. He returned to the hallway and offered it to Gheorghe.

Gheorghe stared at it and waved it away, "That will not be necessary."

Dumitrescu's smile drained from his face, "Take it."

Gheorghe's stomach rolled. The sight of it repulsed him.

Dumitrescu's tone flattened, "You never know when you will be called upon to serve the Republic."

He took the cudgel and turned it over in his hand. It was sticky above the handle; the fractured wood was lashed together with leather strips. He kept it at his side, trying to keep it from touching his clothes. He followed the warden again, who turned down the darkened staircase and descended at a brisk pace.

Gheorghe paused at the top of the stairs, overwhelmed by another gust of putridity. His guide was quickly invisible below the ground, so he hurried behind to avoid getting lost.

Once he was passed the first landing, all natural light disappeared, and only a few small bulbs illuminated the hallway. The floor had changed from tile to roughly poured concrete. The smell grew stronger as he got deeper, rushing past him like a strong wind. It was a mix of human waste and something like vinegar; he could not place the second smell but refused to use his imagination. At the bottom of the stairs, the hallway no longer resembled that of a finished building. The walls were scraped away crudely and seemed to come much closer in than those on the first floor. Gheorghe's breath became short from the combination of closeness and the smell.

Dumitrescu was very far ahead of him, stopped at a cell door. He swung it open, and the loud hinges squealed through the tight space. He turned to Gheorghe and beamed a smile, flashing bright teeth and waving him closer.

"This is one of the classrooms for our students."

Gheorghe walked up. The door was rusted a dark brown. He looked into the room. The bulb behind him shined weakly across the threshold, and he could see almost nothing in the darkness. He stepped in to look closer, feeling the dampness in the air and smelling the metallic scent of blood. There was nothing in the room save for a few rags and a small bed frame. Somewhere down the hallway, he heard a distant shriek that made him jump. He stepped out of the small cell and feigned an appreciation for the warden's joke.

"Come; let's visit some of our bandits." Dumitrescu slammed the door shut. "This facility is for the most stubborn offenders. Some, like Baboescu, are here for actively organizing revolt against the Republic. Others are here for their weak approval of the People's Republic."

"Weak approval?" Gheorghe asked.

"Our prisoners are the ones who have influence over the minds and hearts of the people: College students, who spread their bourgeoisie filth to naïve people and Priests, who poison their minds from clear thinking. We are protecting the Republic from an entire generation of dissidents."

They were going deeper into the basement, and it was apparent they were approaching the source of the smell that was making Gheorghe ill.

"What do they study?" Gheorghe asked. "There was nothing in that cell."

"There were some who thought we should re-educate through persuasion, limiting it to lectures and brochures. Believe me; their minds have been too twisted by the academy and the church to be persuaded by reason and logic. There are other forms of persuasion which are employed to bring them back from their contaminated reasoning."

Gheorghe nodded, hoping he would not find Father Petre here and biting his tongue.

As they approached the next cell along the hallway, Gheorghe could hear a strange noise coming from behind the door. Like a tide of voices, whispers and moans ebbed from behind the thick metal door.

Dumitrescu unlocked the door and swung it open, gesturing with his hand for Gheorghe to enter.

Gheorghe stepped in but recoiled immediately. In the darkness, he saw a mass of life on the floor that he could not identify. The moaning became clear, rising from a train of naked bodies at Gheorghe's feet. He could not see where one man ended, and another began; some prisoners were riding others like horses. The crawling men shuffled on their hands and knees around a tight circuit between four beds on either wall while their passengers clung to them. In the center of this parade was a pair of guards, beating the slowest crawlers and their passengers alike with the same clubs that Gheorghe held in his hand. The crawling men hung their heads below their shoulders, faceless with exhaustion. A crawler collapsed into the new space created by the open doorway and Gheorghe jumped back out of the way of the pair. They were both covered in excrement and hideously swollen bruises.

Dumitrescu pounced upon both the crawler and his passenger, beating them all over their bodies. He screamed at them, ordering the passenger to switch with the crawler. The man on top quickly assumed a crawling position and draped the other lifeless body over his back to stop the beating. They reentered the circle of crawling men and disappeared into the darkness at the back of the cell. There was a small window at the back of the cell, letting in only enough light to illuminate the ceiling of the room and the guards standing above all the prisoners.

Satisfied, Dumitrescu straightened his uniform and wiped a few beads of sweat from his forehead. He nodded to the guards within the cell and shut the door again.

"Shall we move on?" he sauntered down the bare hallway. "I like to tell our students that even if they are made of granite, they will not be able to resist completely." He stopped and drew Gheorghe's attention to a fracture in the cement wall, tracing his fingers on the walls to illustrate. "You see; even the thickest wall, once it has a crack, can be destroyed. All resistance will erode with patience and sufficient force."

Swinging open the door revealed another cell of similar proportions to the first. This room was filled with many more prisoners than the first. Again, Gheorghe could not see where each ended, and the next began. They were taking turns falling backward onto the floor and onto each other without any effort to brace for the impact. He watched as a man the size of a fence post willingly fell backward onto the concrete floor, landing headfirst as if he were dead. Another prisoner made the same motion but fell directly onto the first man. Gheorghe watched in horror as this routine was repeated by six, then seven prisoners and the first man disappeared into a pile of bony limbs.

There was a guard standing on the metal bed frame at the side of the room, supervising these deadfalls. Once all the prisoners were lying atop each other, he stepped across their bodies like a bridge of corpses, crushing his boots into ribs and faces indiscriminately to get to the bed frame on the other side. There were groans and screams, mostly from the men on top. There were no noises from those on the bottom.

Gheorghe heard a sickening crack of bone and flinched, turning away from the sea of frail bodies inside the cell. He caught Dumitrescu watching him with a smile.

"What is the problem, comrade?"

"The smell," Gheorghe lied.

He laughed. "I don't notice it anymore. Besides, enemies of the people have no right to cleanliness. It is a reminder of the filth they spew in our Republic." He slammed the door shut.

The bare cement walls curved into the ceiling. This huge fossilized burrow extended past where the bare light bulbs eked out their faint glow. All the halls, all the stairs seemed to lead to this one hallway; now, the prison itself seemed to be shrinking the further they walked down the hall.

"Lieutenant Dumitrescu!" a voice bellowed from the top of the stairs, "Inspector Iţicovici says that our visitor may proceed with his interrogation of the bandit."

Dumitrescu turned to Gheorghe. "Huh," he shrugged with a grin.

They arrived at a cell at the end of the hallway. Dumitrescu pulled a large key ring from his side and unlocked the door, stepping aside. Gheorghe slinked into the inky darkness of Radu's windowless cell. His footfalls reverberated the length of the cell as a strong fecal smell bellowed from the darkness.

"Radu?" Gheorghe called out. The room was small, and his voice bounced back at him immediately.

As Gheorghe stepped in, the door slammed shut behind. The explosive noise of the metal door startled Gheorghe and he spun around in the pitch black. He turned back to face the way he came but the dark was so complete that he had to reach out with his hands to confirm the metal door's existence. He felt along the inside of it for a handle. Nothing. His heart was racing. He turned to face into the cell again.

"Radu?"

There was no response. Was this Codreanu's plan to remove him? He walked right into this prison and out of existence. He started to bang on the metal door with his club. The blows of the club rang out filling the cell with frantic rusted clangs. He stopped only when he heard a soft noise inside the cell that did not come from him.

It was a low guttural sound percolating through the darkness. Gheorghe turned toward it, squinting into the darkness. His eyes were adjusting. The sound was inhuman, morphing into a growl. Two small flames ignited on the far side of the cell; their vermilion glow blinked as they slowly approached Gheorghe. Gheorghe felt his heart in his throat, and he struggled to breathe. He gripped his club tightly with two hands, still hoping that he was trapped with the man that had once been his best friend.

"Radu?" he called out more desperately. The two eyes were coming closer.

The dark form lunged toward Gheorghe. The ferocity caused Gheorghe to stumble backward against the metal door. He lost his balance and slid down the wall, getting the wind knocked out of him as he met the hard concrete floor. The caged beast mounted him, clutching his shoulders with a sharp grip. Gheorghe looked up, swinging the club wildly and trying to see his attacker. He saw a face.

It was Radu. An untamed fury crackled through Radu's face. His eyes burned with an unnatural red glow that swirled deep within his eyes. Their eyes met, but no recognition passed over Radu's face.

"Radu! It is me, Gheorghe!" Gheorghe shrieked. He held up his club to fend Radu off.

Radu bared his teeth to reveal the mouth of a wolf. He pinned Gheorghe with a supernatural strength and bore down on his neck, dripping with saliva.

The door flew open and flooded the room with the weak electric light of the hallway. Dumitrescu crashed onto Radu with his cudgel. The illuminated door frame and the savage blows of the cudgel forced Radu to retreat into the shadows. Radu's silhouette leaned against the wall of the bare concrete cell. His head turned toward Gheorghe, and the fire diminished from his eyes.

Dumitrescu grabbed Gheorghe by the shoulder. "Are you Okay?"

"Yes, yes," Gheorghe stood and gathered himself. "I am fine. Please, leave the door open."

Dumitrescu eyed Radu at the back of the cell and nodded.

Radu squatted against the wall in silence. He stared at his hands as if he were reading an invisible book. He clenched his fists and looked toward Gheorghe. A raspy voice cut the silence, "Hello, old friend."

Gheorghe crept closer as his vision adjusted to the light again. The skin around Radu's mouth had become wrinkled, and his eyes were sunken as if he had aged several years in a single month. His pale complexion revealed dark green veins beneath his skin. Combined with the splotchy stains on the prison uniform he wore, his appearance was ominously drained of life.

"Radu, you look terrible."

He coughed out a laugh. "Thank you, Gheorghe." Radu's eyes grew wide as they adjusted to the new light in the room. "It won't be much longer until I join my Master." He drew a deep breath and flattened his back against the wall. "It is humorous. They placed me in here thinking it would break me, but I am growing stronger. The darkness strengthens me. They want to make slaves of us, Gheorghe." He moved to a corner where the light did not land. "I remember your father use to say: 'He who is willing to die never need fear being a slave.' Do you remember that?"

"Yes, I remember."

"I understand what he meant now. Gheorghe, fear of death paralyzes you. If you only understood what gift death brings-," Radu abruptly stopped and gazed at a dark corner of the cell. "Master tells me he met you."

Gheorghe could not help but look over his shoulder. There was nothing in the corner.

"That's why I am here. I'm ready to help the Order."

Radu's gaze returned from the corner and lit with renewed zeal.

"Yes! Yes! Excellent!" He stood and began to pace the room. His posture had become more crooked than Gheorghe remembered, and his feet dragged noisily.

"You must commune with the Master. Offer up your blood to him. Give it freely, and he will open doors that are closed to the living. He did for me. Yes! Gheorghe, this is fantastic news!"

"There is bad news, Radu."

Radu stopped pacing.

"I believe the Master is in danger."

Radu laughed.

"You will understand the foolishness of that statement after you share your blood with him. He will visit you again tonight, and you will never know fear again."

"He cannot come to my apartment. Codreanu has Dobrescu shadowing me; now I am under constant surveillance. They will capture me; they will capture the Master. They are searching for his base and targeting anyone that is affiliated with him. They know about Borş."

"You are not listening!" Radu chafed. "It makes no difference who knows our plans, Gheorghe. The Master is more powerful than anyone in the Securitate. He does not answer to anyone and neither will you."

"But Radu, he has given you power but you have been in prison for weeks. If I am to be of any use, I can't end up here like a trapped rat. We can accomplish more without Codreanu breathing down our neck. I've been promoted to the Securitate so I can be a great use to the Master."

"I'm not powerless!" Radu scrambled to the corner of his cell.

"True, but you are useless," Gheorghe snapped. "I can be of greater use if I can move freely during the day. Isn't that what he wants? For me to be his hands and feet during the day? You can help the Master by helping me contact him; that's all."

Radu pulled his legs up to his chest and rocked himself slowly. His face was scrunched into a frantic grimace, searching the dark corners of his cell for confirmation.

"Maybe you are right, my friend. What do you propose?" Radu asked.

"There is something the Master needs me to do. I want to arrange a meeting with the Master; somewhere we won't be seen. Even now, the guard listens to us and will report everything to his supervisors."

"Very well," Radu said. He let go of his legs and sat in a meditative position. The tension in his body dissipated and he turned away from the light in the doorway.

Gheorghe was watching with his breath held, worried that the Master might arrive in the next moments. He studied Radu's face, hoping that this change was just for show.

Radu's eyes were open but unfocused. The sunken pits around them seemed to grow darker, and the whites of his eyes shrunk as if they were receding into his head. He gasped suddenly. His eyes rocketed back in his head, revealing the milky red veins behind them. A guttural groan began pouring from his throat, a long, low tone. His head began to shake, and the groan became louder and more pained. The green veins under his skin were bulging to the surface as if to answer a beckoning call.

Gheorghe took several steps back, approaching the cell door. Images of Tatiana were flashing in front of his eyes as he watched Radu. He felt his blood pumping faster through his body.

And then it was over. Radu's eyes returned to normal.

"You can meet the Master tomorrow night, where you last saw Tatiana," Radu said with a new edge of exhaustion in his voice. "I hope that didn't frighten you," he smiled.

"Is that his only instructions?" Gheorghe asked.

"He says not to worry about your other friends anymore," Radu answered coolly, "The priest too."

A sudden coldness pierced Gheorghe. "Father Petre?"

"Yes, he hides behind his crucifix but it will not protect him forever," Radu's lips curled in disgust, "If he does not stop his meddling, Master will call on you to neutralize him."

Gheorghe tried to deflect his shock with a voice of indifference, "What has the old man done?"

"We do not question Master. We obey. If he says the priest dies, he dies."

"I understand. Thank you, Radu. Thank you for helping me."

"See, I am still of use!" Radu laughed.

Gheorghe nodded. "So long, old friend."

"We will see each other soon!" Radu flashed his dirty smile.

Gheorghe left the cell and waited for Dumitrescu to lock up behind him. From outside, Gheorghe could dimly see the movements of his friend shuffling between the walls of his darkened cell. What had become of his longtime friend? As they ascended the stairs, Gheorghe bounded ahead of Dumitrescu trying to escape. Dumitrescu noticed his quickened pace and slowed to a crawl. Through clenched teeth, Gheorghe intoned, "I need to be getting back to Oradea."

He flashed a quick, cunning smile. "Yes, yes; of course."

Gheorghe was led down the hallway to the central guard station, where he was signed out. Inspector Iţicovici stood waiting for Gheorghe. "Did you get the information you needed, Inspector?"

Gheorghe gave a practiced nonchalant tone, "Yes, thank you for your assistance."

Iţicovici's venomous eyes glared at Gheorghe. "I do not need to stress the importance of discretion concerning your visit, comrade. What you saw here did not happen. These prisoners no longer exist. Do not pity them; they will be happier with their new lives. You must understand."

"I understand." Gheorghe blurted, trying to escape the lobby.

"Comrade Ianculescu," Iţicovici called out, "Chief Inspector Codreanu told me of your investigation," A smile lurked across his weathered face. "Tell Father Petre that Chief Inspector Marina Iţicovici sends his regards."

Iţicovici's words stabbed into Gheorghe's stomach. He gave an unthinking nod and sputtered out, "I will."

A Chain of Lies

Back at City Hall, Gheorghe fidgeted as he waited outside Codreanu's office. His mind raced as he worked out the calculus of his circumstances. The equation looked unsolvable. His tapping foot did not speed up the torturous cadence of the clock on the wall. *I have to get to Father Petre to warn him*, he thought. Gheorghe's impulse to run to Borş was frustrated by Codreanu's games. *Slow down. Remember Codreanu plays the main role in your plan,* he brooded in the over-stuffed chair. His breathing became heavier and louder at the thought of the unknown future that lie ahead. *Well, at least, I have a plan*, he tried convincing himself. *The more I know what the expectations are and if I can have some control of them, I always have a chance*, he thought. Yet, the variables in his equation gnawed through his mind. *I can't wait anymore,* He bolted from his chair and knocked on Codreanu's door entering without waiting. He no longer had the patience to suffer the pretenses of his superior. He found Codreanu seated at his desk, reading a thick docket of papers. Gheorghe stood at attention.

"Reporting in from Piteşti, comrade."

Codreanu, surprised by Gheorghe's sudden entrance, strove to maintain his detachment. After a brief glance, his gaze returned to the papers before him.

"How is our friend doing?"

"Radu is a shadow of his former self. He is barely recognizable now."

One corner Codreanu's mouth lifted into a smirk. He still kept his focus on the pages, though he was taking great pleasure in pressing Gheorghe's buttons.

"Has he abandoned the Order yet?"

"No comrade, he continues to believe that his leader will rescue him."

"Interesting," Codreanu looked up now. "It amazes me how hope can be so tenacious and enduring in the face of despair. I underestimated Radu. He would be the last person I expected to hold onto hope in the face of the anguish we have provided him," Codreanu drawled on. "I always saw him as a weak and silly man, don't you agree?" Codreanu mused with a smile.

Gheorghe felt a tempest of rage swirling in his chest. He swallowed heavily, trying to keep the words from spilling out of his mouth. He could not afford to give Codreanu the satisfaction.

"Radu certainly had his eccentricities. But I was able to get vital information regarding the Master of the Order. Since he still considers me a friend of the Order it was easy to obtain."

"Very good, Gheorghe. But despite your assertions, I always find it necessary to confirm everything you say."

"Comrade?" Gheorghe's heartbeat picked up speed, driving heat and blood to his cheeks. Gheorghe's thoughts flew to Father Petre. Dobrescu may have uncovered Gheorghe's duplicity after questioning Father Petre.

"Never mind, never mind," Codreanu chuckled and waved his hand reveling in his cleverness. "Give me your report."

Gheorghe collected himself, breathing deeply and hoping the sweat on his forehead was not obvious from across the desk. This was supposed to be the easy part of his plan.

"Radu has informed me that the leader of the Order wants to meet me in Borş tomorrow night. He will be providing details on the size, location and delivery of a weapons cache being provided for the rebellion."

"This better than we anticipated-" Codreanu's face lit up with a satisfied smile; his words were laced with a subdued exhilaration, "So this is what our Dragon is up to."

Codreanu's enthusiasm encouraged Gheorghe to continue, "The meeting will occur on the outskirts of the village."

He catapulted from his desk circling to the front. He looked more closely at Gheorghe, squinting up at his face. "Dobrescu has confirmed your initial report from Borş. He met with your priest, who restated the facts of your report on the activities of the Order of the Dragon."

Gheorghe's face went limp. "He did?"

"Yes," Codreanu gave a long calculating gaze. "Does that surprise you?"

'Well, yes-,' he sputtered. A tentative smile grew as he comprehended the news. "It took a lot to gain his trust. Dobrescu works quickly."

"Yes," Codreanu gave a skeptical stare. "I would have liked Dobrescu to press the old man for further assurances, but he claimed that the priest was verging on senility. It was wise of you to visit Radu with such haste before his treasonous history is erased from his mind."

"Thank you, comrade, but your leadership has been crucial in this whole affair." Gheorghe winced at the obvious ingratiation.

Codreanu retreated back to his chair with a satisfied smile. He devoured Gheorghe's pandering. "Gheorghe, I have always seen greatness in you." He settled back in his chair with uncharacteristic casualness. "It is a greatness I can help you cultivate." He leaned forward with a rehearsed, cloying smile.

Gheorghe saw the venom in his smile. "It would be an honor, comrade. With your permission, I'll attend the meeting of the Order tomorrow night in Borş."

"Yes, of course. I need you to keep pursuing this leader. Your ability to communicate with him and predict his movements have been essential to our progress. Without you on the case, I would not be so close to capturing him," He smiled but his cold demeanor lingered.

"Thank you, comrade." Codreanu's compliments made him more uneasy than any of his threats. No matter how restrained his effusiveness, it presaged dark intentions.

"Good, so you will go to Borş tomorrow evening. It will be best for you and Dobrescu to continue working separately. We wouldn't want him to blow your cover with the rebels and our Dragon at the meeting tomorrow."

"Very good, comrade."

"Once you have discovered the location of the weapons cache, I want you to lead the rebels into my hands." He stood and walked to the window with his arms clenched tightly behind his back. The light from outside landed on his upturned face, gleaming off his oily bald spot. "Tell them whatever you have to; promise more weapons, an ambush on our forces or a plot to free some political prisoners. Once you have gained their confidence, you must bring the rebels and their leader to Borş. There is an abandoned warehouse south of the village that will provide us a tactical advantage. We must wipe them out in one sweep. I will be waiting there with a squadron of soldiers. I will ask Shalberov to commit some troops as well. Let them see what happens when they bite the hand that feeds them."

"How will you know when I am bringing them?"

"I expect your update in two days' time. Do not delay after your meeting with the leader. If we cannot bring the leader of the Order to Borş, someone must be held responsible." He stopped to give a challenging stare. "You are dismissed."

He left City Hall and boarded the bus. He settled into his seat, and a wave of exhaustion swept over him. He struggled to keep his eyes open as his mind swam with a dizzying lethargy. The day's travels had finally taken their toll on him. During the day, he fought to fill his waking hours with enough activity to take his mind off his fatigue. With the half empty bus and the grumble of the engine, he found himself drifting off to sleep. A sudden stop jolted him awake. His thoughts returned to Codreanu's words of praise. *Grandpa always put his livestock at ease just before he slit their throats*, he observed, *I don't expect anything less from Codreanu.*

CRSO

He arrived home to an unlocked door, and Dobrescu draped over the divan reading over entries in his notebook. "Good evening, Inspector!" Dobrescu chimed.

His voice stopped Gheorghe cold in the doorway. "What are you doing here?"

"Hasn't Captain told you?" Dobrescu stammered as his face went flush, "I will be staying indefinitely."

"No, I thought it was temporary." Gheorghe surveyed the apartment; it was rearranged with noticeable improvements where Radu had taken up residence. Dobrescu had settled in, uncluttering the space for himself. Several pieces of furniture had been shuffled further into corners.

"I am sorry for the inconvenience, comrade."

"It is fine," a fleeting smile evaporated from his face. "You are just following orders."

The abrupt silence made Dobrescu squirm; he kept a sheepish grasp on his notebook. "Uh-," he squeaked, trying to fill the soundless vacuum.

Gheorghe pitied Codreanu's pawn; he patted him on the shoulder extinguishing the awkwardness. "Tell me about your interview with Father Petre. Did he give you any more information about the rebellion?"

Dobrescu's face softened with a smile. "Well, I have to be honest; I found him very eccentric."

"How?"

"He kept talking about superstitions about vampires visiting in the night stealing people's souls. I suppose it is not surprising a man of the cloth believes in such fairy tales."

"He did mention that...," Gheorghe deflected, "But he did not seem obsessed with it."

"Well, he certainly is now. Apparently he has been exploring caves and ruins around the village looking for coffins. I don't know how you managed to make any sense out of him. He's as insane as Radu!"

"Does Chief Inspector Codreanu know all this?"

"Oh yes, I told him all about it; we had a good laugh."

Gheorghe was not amused. He was uncertain how to behave around Dobrescu now.

"Did the priest corroborate my report?"

"No, he wouldn't confirm anything you told me. I couldn't get him to talk about anything else besides his vampire hunt. The Captain said he wanted to follow your initial report."

"Really? But wasn't the entire purpose of your visit to confirm my report?"

"Yes, it seems odd but I guess the Chief Inspector trusts your report. The priest seems to have gone completely insane."

"Perhaps," Gheorghe muttered to himself. He plunged into a stiff armchair that groaned under the sudden weight. He fixed his gaze on nothing in particular. He wanted to be alone so he could talk himself through his dilemma, but his doe-eyed roommate prohibited any self-talk. Gheorghe discovered himself fidgeting and turned to see Dobrescu staring at him.

"Inspector, I think you are over-analyzing Chief Inspector Codreanu's intentions. We are all on the same side; we're all working toward the same goal. I've been putting in a good word where it's convenient. He did offer you a promotion, you know. "

Gheorghe had an admixture of admiration and pity for Dobrescu. He admired and pitied his trusting simplicity; Codreanu was misleading and deceiving him yet he could not see it happening.

"All promotions are revocable. I've got to deliver his Dragon first," Gheorghe stretched his legs out and gave a weary sigh, "I'm sorry you wasted your time with the priest. I tried to tell you not to go."

"Given your report, we had to see what else he knew. Did you get any more information out of Radu?"

"Yes, I'm heading back to Borş to meet with the leader of the Order. Radu assured me he would come. He is very paranoid and does not trust many people."

"I guess that is how he was able to go so long without being detected."

"Yes, it is hard to know who to trust." A somber smile emerged from Gheorghe's face, *That is my first truthful statement in a long time.*

"All in a day's work, right Inspector?" Dobrescu unfolded a newspaper and began reading.

Gheorghe envied the young man's nonchalance.

Night descended on Oradea, and as much as he longed for it, Gheorghe dared not sleep. The night would not yield any rest to Gheorghe. Gheorghe's imagination used the creeping silence as the backdrop for imagined demonic visitations. Every creak, every pop in the night sent a current of panic through Gheorghe. Then, in the dark, he struggled to find his elusive rest. He feared his dreams were no longer safe from the Master. The sun greeted him on the distant horizon, poking its rays into his room from above the rooftops. He rose before Dobrescu and snuck out.

Oradea was beginning to wake from its slumber. As Gheorghe reached the train station, the sun was high in the sky. He stood on the platform as workers began their daily routines around the depot. The bustle of laborers around him assured him that he was among the living. Yet, his insomnia had taken a toll on him and the warmth of the sun poured over him. While the morning light melted into his skin, he began to drift off on his feet. The growing swell of people with the accompanying noise was powerless to arrest the creeping stupor that enveloped Gheorghe. A shrill steam whistle sounded from a departing train. Through bleary eyes, Gheorghe saw black smoke roll from the undercarriage of the train and rise over the train transforming into a dragon. It continued its ascent only stopping when it detected Gheorghe. The gaping maw of the black dragon closed around him; he awoke with a start. Finding that life continued around him, he sighed with as much relief as resignation. His train arrived, and he boarded without hesitation.

Arriving in Borş, he immediately went to the village church. Gheorghe picked his way through market stalls and overloaded carts. The sun had retreated behind mild cloud cover but Gheorghe sweat from the urgency of his mission. He arrived at the church and walked inside. The cool air landed on his damp skin and chilled him.

"Father!" Gheorghe's voice resounded throughout the church. Only silence responded. The stagnant air revealed a neglected nave with faint incense drifting through Gheorghe's nose. He walked through the aisles scanning the dark corners of the nave. He edged toward the side library where Father Petre kept his desk. He was not there.

⊗⊗

In the dank, a chill overcame Gheorghe. His thoughts returned to the veiled threat at Piteşti. "I'm too late," he whispered to the darkness. *I should have come yesterday,* he thought.

Gheorghe panicked, not anticipating Father Petre would be gone. He turned and ran to the narthex when a cacophony of small bells spilled onto the floor breaking the silence. Gheorghe stopped and turned toward the sound. Behind the altar Gheorghe heard frantic shuffling; the sound subsided as he approached the altar. Behind the altar, the sacristy door lay open. Gheorghe peeked through the cracked door. The vestments and the sacred vessels lay on the stone floor; a faint weeping filtered from the darkened room.

"Father?" The crying stopped. "Father Petre?"

Father Petre emerged from the shadows. His bleary eyes sank to the floor when he saw Gheorghe. "Oh, Gheorghe," his knobby, withered hands covered his furrowed face. " I have failed again."

Gheorghe knelt to bring him to his feet. "What are you talking about?"

All vitality was drained from his face. He stood with an aged vertigo. "I should have known that an old man is no match for the evil we are facing."

"What happened?"

"Two of my parishioners have died," he heaved a heavy sigh.

"Do you think our Dragon was responsible?"

"Yes," his tear glazed eyes seized Gheorghe's gaze, "he told me himself."

Gheorghe's heart sank. "What?"

"He approached me in the market. He taunted me saying I would be next if I did not stop my meddling."

"He walked up to you in broad daylight? I thought he only moved at night."

"The vile creature was sated with blood. I believe, for him to be able to move about during the day, we are dealing with the Prince of vampires."

"So, we are not safe during the day either?"

"Not completely, he has the strength of a mortal during the day. However, I fear he may know we are working together. I believe we may both be in great danger."

"Father, you are right. I saw Radu; he mentioned you. You must be getting close to his Master's lair."

"I am very close. I believe that is why he so brazenly approached me. I only need enough time to get to his coffin, but he is now alerted to my movements."

"The Master wants to meet me tonight. He-,"

Father Petre's eyes flashed to life. "What? You are meeting him tonight? Why?"

"I'm not sure. He wants to meet me at the graveyard."

A broad smile emerged from his face. "I have been despairing how I could ever elude him," He held Gheorghe by the shoulders, "but you have shown me the way. You can buy me time tonight. Tonight, we fulfill our divine purpose."

"Father-,"

"Gheorghe, listen to me." His determined gaze caught Gheorghe by surprise. "You witnessed the evil personally. You have seen it's corrupting influence on the innocent. You have seen it twist the mind and heart of your friend."

145

"Yes,-"

"Doesn't it anger you? Does it not call for action? I have been mired in despair and inaction. There is much evil at work in this land; of all the evil that surrounds us, this is the one thing we can do something about."

"I don't-,"

"Don't succumb to fear and complacency. Augustine said, 'Hope has two beautiful daughters: Anger and Courage: Anger that things are not as they ought to be and Courage to make them as they ought to be.'

"Father, I am not a hero,"

"I don't need you to be a hero, Gheorghe. I need you to have hope, enough hope to be willing to do something."

Gheorghe gave a deep sigh. "If I had my way all this would go away; I just want to live in peace-,"

Father Petre burst into laughter, "-and I would have the prophet Elijah carry me away on a fiery chariot, but it isn't going to happen; is it, Gheorghe?"

Gheorghe felt his face go flush and looked to the ground. "No."

"You have seen much evil and yet you live. You have been given a great responsibility. Together we can defeat this evil. Come with me to the altar, we still have time to prepare and pray," He grabbed Gheorghe by the arm and led him back to the altar.

Face to Face with Death

Gheorghe rose from the altar taking a final blessing from Father Petre. Several hours had passed and now the sun was setting through the stained glass windows

"Father, I need a crucifix."

"Yes, of course," he shuffled to his office returning with a small crucifix. "Keep it hidden for as long as you can. You must keep him preoccupied."

Since Gheorghe's return, the resolve had returned to Father Petre's face. It brought Gheorghe peace knowing that Father Petre walked the same path. They both had their own set of challenges. Father Petre had become strangely distant during their preparations. A foreboding silence lingered between them as they stood in the darkening church.

After an awkward silence, Gheorghe blurted, "Are you afraid to die, Father?"

A bright smile emerged. "No, I have been preparing for this day all my life. As any sane person should."

"Oh, I thought perhaps," he stopped, searching for his words.

"What?" Father Petre probed.

"Well, you were crying in the closet. I thought-,"

"-that I was dreading my own death?" He gave a vigorous shake of his head. "No; no; no, Death is just the grim porter to the door to the Blessed Presence. I was grieving my inability to protect my flock, but you were an answer to my prayers, Inspector!"

With nothing left to prepare, Gheorghe shook the priest's hand and shared a long goodbye in a glance. Neither man was able to speak their farewells. On the way out the door, he took an unlit oil lamp from a sconce on the wall to light his way.

CRED

The village outside the church was settling into a serene evening. Fires for dinner crackled in the hearths of many different buildings, streaking the amber sky with gray dregs of smoke. As Gheorghe walked along the roads before the houses, he heard the sounds of family life and smelled the aromas of home cooked meals.

As he entered the adjoining countryside, a profound peace settled over Gheorghe. The salmon pink sky of the retiring sun cast long shadows in front of Gheorghe. Father Petre's convictions were now his own. He was convinced, whether he lived or died, he was doing the right thing. By the time he arrived at the graveyard, he was relaxed and lucid. The firs lining the plots swayed in a gentle breeze, lulling a weary Gheorghe to sleep. Gheorghe stopped at a modest grave and sat beside the aged headstone. With a sudden jerk of his head, Gheorghe realized he needed to keep moving to stay alert.

The advancing night sky overcame the remaining light; the once glowing clouds were now drained of their color leaving dark gray husks. As Gheorghe rose to his feet, the only noises accompanying him were the crunching twigs beneath his feet. Under the cover of foliage, the last remnants of the sun had disappeared completely from the sky. The lamp in his hand swung like a will-o-wisp, casting lonely rays of light onto the gravestones. The shadows made knee-high goblins along the path before Gheorghe. His eyes darted between the dark shapes, waiting for the one that would advance on him. Reading the names on the headstones, he proceeded to the place he remembered was Tatiana's grave. The bravery that had swelled up earlier evaporated and previous aspirations swallowed up in a vat of inky blackness. He stopped at a gravestone and bent down to check the name. He had arrived. The turned soil on Tatiana's grave had returned to a state of rest with young grass shoots poking up. Her ceremonial fir branch was still heaped on top of the gravestone. A chill went down his spine and he turned, greeted only by darkness at the edge of his lantern's reach. The cacophonic silence paralyzed Gheorghe, magnifying every insignificant sound.

He pointed the lamp to his right, then to his left. He was still alone. The stars emerged in patches, flitting in and out behind a thick curtain of clouds. The moon was out but only exposed a small sliver, illuminating very little on the dark landscape. While he was watching the moon, the clouds closed around it, swallowing the tiny portion of light it exuded.

A stiff wind blew past him from the right, so strong it knocked him off his balance. The glass door on the front of the lantern swung open and the flame flickered hard to the side but remained lit. Gheorghe fumbled with the latch on it. His heart pounded at the threat of total darkness. He secured the latch protecting the lantern's flame again. The wind blew once more from his left, this time snuffing out his light without opening the lantern's door. Gheorghe stood in total darkness with a throbbing heart leaping into his throat.

His eyes adjusted slowly, but his ears perked. The wind died down again and the loud rustle it generated in the grass and trees was replaced by his panicked breathing. The darkness was tamed as he blinked. He found short headstones in front of him and the pale trunks of trees in the distance. He wheeled around, fearing that there was more that he could not see encroaching on him. Still nothing. Then a sound, faint and distant. It was a rumble in his ear, distant at first, but it grew in intensity. Perhaps the silence was getting to him. Gheorghe moved to a crouch to listen more closely. His eyes continued to adjust, finding the deep verdant green on the leaves atop the trunks and the dusty gray of the dirt road. The rumbling drew close, approaching from behind. Gheorghe froze realizing the rumbling was growling. His breathing raced to keep pace with his heart beat. He drew in deep breaths to keep himself from swooning. Gaining the courage, he turned with apprehensive curiosity. Beyond Tatiana's grave stood the silhouette of a massive wolf. A low growl rolled from its mouth. Gheorghe snapped backward. Perhaps by ignoring it, it would go away. As Gheorghe realized the ludicrousness of the thought, the growling ceased. The silence returned.

"Gheorghe," a long, groaning whisper sounded from behind him.

He spun to face the voice. The silhouette of a slender man stood where the wolf once stood. The wind brushed his face as the dark figure converged on him. Gheorghe, transfixed on the approaching form, was unable to register his fear as a dream-like stupor overcame him.

The Dragon from his dream, the devourer of the sun and the moon, approached him. Two faint red eyes glared out at him, coming closer. The Master emerged from the blackened night. He stood three feet from Gheorghe, his pale skin exuding an internal luminescence. He did not give off light, yet his face could be seen distinctly in the darkness. He appeared older than their first meeting. His once taut face had given way to deep fissures; his raven hair was now ivory. He scrutinized Gheorghe with aristocratic contempt.

"Good evening, Gheorghe," the Master drawled, his white teeth emerging from his dark smile. He reached out his hand and clamped down on Gheorghe's shoulder. "We have much to discuss," he drew Gheorghe in closer as if he weighed nothing. Gheorghe resisted but lost his footing beneath him when he was lifted off the ground.

The Master drew Gheorghe in closer. His eyes gleamed with an intense luster. With his free hand, he gripped tightly around Gheorghe's throat. His fingertips laced perfectly around Gheorghe's jugular, bottling his pulse in his head with a painful throbbing. He pulled Gheorghe's face in close, his teeth out and his nostrils flared. He forcefully turned Gheorghe's head with his finger and fixated on Gheorghe's throbbing neck.

Gheorghe tried to speak but found his throat clamped shut by the grip around it.

"I find your association with the priest troubling," the Master hissed. "You have a peculiar way of showing your loyalty, Gheorghe. The priest seeks to thwart me and I will not abide with any treachery. You must demonstrate your fealty to me," His teeth came close to Gheorghe's skin. His breath was cold smelling like rot and decay. He let go of Gheorghe's throat and let him fall. "Your gypsy blood has saved you thus far."

Gheorghe crumpled to the ground, coughing and sputtering to refill his lungs. The blood left his head and he became lightheaded for a moment. His blurry vision registered the sight of the Master with his hands behind his back peering down with scorn. Gheorghe touched his neck and felt small, sticky puncture wounds where the Master's nails had dug into his flesh.

Listen closely, Gheorghe, the Master said. His voice became large and disembodied again like the gust that had knocked Gheorghe down. It seemed not to come from him, but from an external source like a message streaming into his mind. It bounced around him like a reverberation within his head, *Radu tells me you are ready to serve me.*

With a gasp, Gheorghe blurted, "Yes, Master."

The Master stared down on Gheorghe unmoved by his confession of loyalty.

"I have reservations about your sincerity. There are labors which you must undertake for me. Why should I entrust them to you?"

"You have shown me everything that has been taken from me. With your help, Master, I will repay those who have robbed me of the things I love."

A slow smile came to the Master's face. "Yes, very noble Gheorghe."

He knelt and picked up Gheorghe's overturned lantern. He toyed with it, turning it over in his hands and latching it shut again.

Gheorghe said nothing, holding his hand over the scratches on his neck.

"My orders are simple, but you must follow them precisely. Do not stray from my instructions for I cannot waste any more time. Radu prattled himself to uselessness. Do you understand?"

"Yes Master," Gheorghe said.

"You must replenish my stores of ancestral soil from my manor in Transylvania. The location of my castle has long been known to the locals, but I am forced to remain in hiding until I have regained my mobility. You must not bring attention to your activities."

"Where is your castle?"

"My estate lies to the east in the Carpathian Mountains through the Tihuța Pass. You must pass through the city of Bistrița. There is a junction about three leagues from the beginning of the pass that leads up into the mountains. It is a steep path, graded with large flagstones. It has lost all markings since my reign, but you will know it by the split in the rock formation that demarcates it."

"How will I know which dirt to gather? Could I gather dirt from Bistrița?"

"No," the Master bristled. "I am bound to the land of my ancestors. The dirt I require is from the chapel graveyard on my manor grounds. Even in the sleep of death, my lineage cannot intermingle with peasant chattel. I cannot rest in the soil of the peasantry. If you bring me anything other than what I require, you will reap a bitter harvest."

"I understand, Master," Gheorghe bowed deferentially.

"My coffins once laced the entire continent, but the wars of men have destroyed them. Your people labored many years placing them throughout Europe. However, we must begin again. If I am to move freely once more, my coffins must cover the continent as they did in the past."

"Yes, Master. I will bring the dirt back to Borș; I know of an abandoned warehouse. I will see if I can enlist some help. After we return, they will be at your disposal. Does this please you, Master?"

"Yes," the Master said in a creaking, throaty voice. He had been pacing while recounting Gheorghe's tasks but had stopped with his back to Gheorghe while listening. The Master did not speak anymore. Turned away from Gheorghe, the Master's pale skin was no longer visible and his outline was obscured by the night because of his white hair and dark suit.

The silence made Gheorghe uncomfortable. It had been easy to listen to the Master, but now his behavior made it uncertain what his next move would be. Gheorghe squinted to keep his outline focused in his vision. His silhouette dissolved into a thick mist. The impenetrable mist drifted toward Gheorghe. Gheorghe stepped towards the nearest gravestone, seeking it out for some kind of protection. He glanced over his shoulder to estimate a dash to the graveyard gate. When he looked back, the mist had dissipated.

A sudden chill exploded over Gheorghe's skin and he ran. He ran as fast as he could, dashing through the darkness towards the gate. He heard laughter above him. An instant later, a blunt force crashed into his back and flattened him to the ground. His cheek scraped painfully against the cracked dirt and dry grass. He felt something cold brush against his ear, leaning in close to him.

"Why do you run, Gheorghe? If you truly desire revenge over your enemies, you should not fear me. I have in my hands, the power to fulfill your desires. You are on the threshold of obtaining all you wish; tonight, you begin your passage to my realm." The Master whispered in Gheorghe's ear. "Once you have joined me, your enemies will beg for mercy."

Gheorghe began to squirm, fighting to get his limbs free. An immense weight pinned him firmly down, not the weight of a man but that of a merciless wall of gravity pressing him deep into the ground. He could feel the Master's face drawing close to his neck, so close that rancid spittle dripped from his mouth onto him. Gheorghe twisted his neck as far away as possible, but the Master's tongue pressed eagerly into the scrapes on his neck. The Master flipped Gheorghe so he lay supine on the ground. A hazy lethargy returned as the Master closed in on Gheorghe's neck. Gheorghe eyed his approach with detached resignation; his vision started dissolving into a milky void. The Master's ghoulish grin signaled Gheorghe's defeat.

The Master's gaze jolted to the horizon and his grin wrenched from his face. His focus went to a distant horizon. His mouth agape, he gasped a breathy tone, "No!"

In a gust of wind, the oppressive weight was gone. In a screeching assent, the Master flapped large shadowy appendages and blotted out the starlight above Gheorghe. His shape became garbled in the darkness and shrank quickly as it throttled into the distance.

The listless fog lifted from Gheorghe's mind; he caught his breath. He wiped his sleeve along the side of his neck but could not shake the smell of the Master's rancid breath. He patted himself down, wondering if Father Petre's crucifix had wormed its way from his pocket into view. It lay secured in his breast pocket. Despite this, Gheorghe knew the priest had somehow saved him. Gheorghe looked up to see the starlit sky split through the clouds. Father Petre had succeeded.

Orders from the Top

A soft murmur prodded Gheorghe from a dreamless sleep. He pried his eyes open, finding a chorus of eyes examining him.

"Have you seen Father Petre?", a voice whispered.

Gheorghe heaved himself upright, finding himself sitting on the front pew of the church. His eyes recoiled from the morning sun filtering through the smoke glazed windows. "What?", he fumbled in response.

"Father Petre," the voice pleaded, "He is late for morning matins."

"No, no-" He said, rubbing his eyes to adjust to the light, "I have not seen him."

When the villagers responded with unconvinced stares, an elderly lady emerged. Gheorghe squirmed under her puzzled stare. "What?", His question reverberated throughout the sanctuary. A flush swept across his cheeks as the echo of his voice faded from the darkened room.

"Son, are you feeling well?", she creaked.

"Yes," gathering his wits, he bolted to his feet. "I am just..." his voice trailed off as his mind struggled for words, "...late. I am late and need to return to Oradea."

Gheorghe emerged from the church finding the sun had risen above the rooftops. The mid-morning sun produced a nervous flutter in Gheorghe's stomach as he realized Codreanu waited for his report. *I am late,* he confirmed to himself.

ೞೞ

He proceeded through the hallways, giving out brief greetings and exuding deceptive politeness. He knocked on the door and waited to be called in. A brief grunt sounded through the door and he entered.

Codreanu, seated at his desk, scribbled furiously on a piece of paper. He said nothing as he finished writing without acknowledging Gheorghe.

Dobrescu stood in the corner, stiff and mute as a statue; His eyes were fixed squarely on the space in front of him. Gheorghe tried to make eye contact but remained unacknowledged.

"Good morning, Dobrescu."

Dobrescu broke his mute vigil darting a quick glance. A brief smile fluttered across his face which retreated as he resumed an uncharacteristic stony disposition.

Gheorghe inched closer to the desk to see what Codreanu was scribbling but could not make it out. There was official Securitate letterhead and it seemed to be a letter to some high ranking official. He was writing with illegible haste.

Codreanu noticed Gheorghe standing close to his desk and stopped writing. "You are late," he growled with an icy voice as his eyes rose to meet Gheorghe, "Why are you..." A look of disgust formed on his face, "What the hell happened to you?"

Gheorghe caught a glimpse of himself in a side mirror. Dried blood streaked down his throat and coagulated behind his torn shirt; his suit looked to have been unraveled from the axle of a tractor. In Gheorghe's haste to return from Borş, he was oblivious to his appearance. His omission crashed around himself as he tried to explain his appearance. "I...,"

Codreanu leaned in waiting for his response. "Inspector, Is everything Okay? Have you made contact with the leader of the Order?"

"Yes comrade, yes everything is fine. I had a run in with his bodyguards; it was a misunderstanding, it has been resolved," Gheorghe, surprised by his own lucidity, continued, "The weapons delivery is on schedule. It has already arrived at their outpost, but they need help distributing the arms. I told them I could use my contacts within the Militia to safely transport the weapons. They need me to get militiamen to look the other way. It was actually easy to get them to see how I could be of use to them."

"That's very good, Inspector. I knew I was right to trust your ability for deception. Where are the weapons now?"

"They are being held outside of Bistrița."

"Bistrița? To the East? Is this their main base of activity? I thought they were based in Borș," Codreanu stood, pacing excitedly behind his padded armchair.

"They have several factions throughout Romania, but their most active cell is around Bistrița. Their ranks are spreading throughout the Republic, but Bucharest is their biggest prize. I have told them that I can secure them passage for their weapons across the country. Bistrița is just where the cache is stashed. I suspect they are old weapons from the war. They have been sitting on them for a long time, so they were more than eager for my help. We have them eating from our hands, comrade," Gheorghe said with a slight smile.

Codreanu's eyes sparkled as child-like giggles flickered from his throat. "What do you think the rebels' next move will be?" He settled down, gripping the back of his chair and locking intensely on Gheorghe.

Gheorghe continued reeling him in, "I have convinced them to send their top fighters with me to train the new recruits in Borş. The only thing left to do is go out to Bistriţa with a transport that the Militia will know to ignore. I will bring the weapons, the rebels, and the leader of the Order into our corral, all at once."

Codreanu smiled, his thin lips stretched wide across his face.

"You've done very well, Gheorghe. We will move forward with your plan."

"I am more than happy to assist the Republic, comrade. I will need crates for transporting the cache. From their description, I believe five would suffice."

"Yes, of course. I will have Dobrescu contact the quartermaster to outfit you for your mission."

"Thank you, comrade. If it is agreeable to you, while Dobrescu makes all the arrangements, I would like to get cleaned up. Once I have refreshed myself, Dobrescu and I can leave."

Though Dobrescu's face was set in stone, it flushed a deep crimson. He kept his eyes straight forward, glued to the side wall of the office.

"That won't be possible," Codreanu said, his smile fading.

"I thought, since he is my partner, he would naturally be part of the operation. We have an excellent working relationship."

Dobrescu cast his eyes to the floor, his lips pressing firmer together.

"My answer is no," Codreanu went rigid, "Do not question my personnel assignments, Inspector. Do you understand?"

"Yes, comrade."

"I am assigning you a squad to assist you with the transport from Bistriţa," Codreanu turned away and stared out the window. "You should not be responsible for this great task alone. I cannot risk failure at such a crucial juncture of the plan. If they turn on you, there will be no one to protect you. Let me give you protection," he said, facing Gheorghe with his wry smile returning to his face.

"Again, thank you, comrade. I think that is a wise course of action. Who will be joining me?"

"Militiaman Arcos, militiaman Comaneci, and Inspector Korzha," Codreanu read from a page.

A chill overtook Gheorghe; he glanced over to Dobrescu to gauge his reaction. Conscious of Gheorghe's gaze, he refused to look at him. "Militiaman Comaneci and Inspector Korzha are in custody on suspicion of treason. I thought they were awaiting trial. Has their status changed?"

"Since we are currently understaffed, I have decided to allow them this opportunity to redeem themselves," Codreanu dropped into his chair. "I am sure they would love to be a service to the Republic."

"Militiaman Arcos assaulted his commanding officer a few months ago during a disagreement. Do think we should have such a volatile person on this mission?"

"Again," Codreanu's tone deepened, "Being short-handed requires me to assign men I normally would overlook."

Gheorghe shot a look at Dobrescu that was not returned though the crimson flush had deepened on the young man's face.

"I am finished with you," Codreanu droned, slamming a folder shut to punctuate the finality of the conversation, "When do you leave?"

"As soon as I am dismissed and have briefed my team," Gheorghe said.

"The truck will be waiting for you in the armory, along with your new team. Radio ahead once you have loaded the shipment and are in route to Borş," Codreanu said.

Gheorghe exited the office giving an obligatory salute.

"Inspector," Codreanu called out, "Get cleaned up. It reflects poorly on this office when you look like shit. When you look like shit, I look like shit. Understand?"

Gheorghe seethed behind a faint smile, "Of course, comrade."

CSEO

Gheorghe made his way to the armory. It was attached to their loading dock, where many of the militia vehicles were parked. With the resources now available, Gheorghe was ready to move as fast as possible. The drive to Bistriţa was over five hours. He walked through a well-lit hallway at the bottom of the staircase and entered the locker room.

He found all three of his squad members circled around a small wooden table, sitting in folding chairs and playing cards. There was a large bottle of vodka between them and several dirty glasses littered around it. The room reeked of alcohol-tinged body odor. As Gheorghe entered the room, they gave him gloomy stares.

"Good afternoon, comrades," He announced with a cheerful voice, "I am Inspector Ianculescu; you have been assigned to assist me on an important case."

The three men's silent stares betrayed their skepticism. One grabbed the bottle from the table and clasped it close to his chest. "Codreanu's misfits are going on an important mission?" he pondered quietly.

"Ah, shit," another spit out, "We are dead men."

"Not necessarily," Gheorghe interjected, "Codreanu said a successful mission could redeem you."

They glowered at Gheorghe with unblinking eyes. "And you believe him?"

"Yes," Gheorghe lied.

"Then you are a dead man, too."

"Please, comrades. Put the bottle down, we have work to do," Gheorghe chided.

"Chief Inspector Codreanu does not easily forgive the past. I'm not lifting a damn finger until I know why I've suddenly been forgiven."

"Comaneci, The Inspector doesn't know any more than us," the man stood, holding out his hand to greet Gheorghe. "I'm Inspector Korzha; this is militiaman Comaneci and militiaman Arcos. We just got the order a little while ago. What is our assignment?"

"We are picking up a weapons shipment in Bistrița and bringing it back here. I want to get there by nightfall. That leaves us very little time, so if you wouldn't mind, let's not dally here in the barracks. You can relax again once we are on the road," Gheorghe said. He stood aside and waited while the three men fixed their uniforms and rinsed out their mouths. When they were ready, he led the way to the loading dock, where a rusted green cargo truck was idling in wait for them.

"Comaneci! Arcos! Get in the back." Korzha barked. The grumbling pair scaled the open rear gate. Korzha turned to Gheorghe, "Let me drive Inspector; It looks like you could use some rest."

The kindness of Korzha's offer struck Gheorghe. His small, kind gesture contrasted with the hostile world Gheorghe found himself inhabiting. He welcomed the kindness. "Thank you."

The truck pulled out through the barbed wire gate, which slid closed again behind him. Getting onto the highway, Korzha mashed the pedal to the floor, pushing the truck to its top speed.

In the bouncing and vibrations, the alcohol lulled Comaneci and Arcos to sleep. Their limp bodies bobbed and jerked in time with the truck. Gheorghe drew deep breaths, distending his cheeks as he exhaled. His attempts at relaxation only brought the attention of Korzha.

"Inspector, are you well?"

"Yes, I am fine," glancing at his watch, "We are just on a tight schedule."

"Don't worry Inspector, we will get there in plenty of time; you relax."

Gheorghe wanted to believe Korzha. Korzha seemed confident and competent. Why was he the recipient of Codreanu's wrath? The answer came immediately; he was confident and competent. Codreanu was threatened by Korzha's competence and dealt with him the only way he knew how. Gheorghe decided to allow himself the thought that Korzha knew everything would be fine. Just hearing someone say the words: "You relax." Put Gheorghe at ease. He sank into the seat as the stiff seat springs creaked in protest.

∞

The Romanian countryside revealed itself as they made their way from Oradea. The squat, rolling hills with their patchwork of fields and forests put Gheorghe further at ease. The sun settled on his face and his eyelids sank under its warmth. The sun strobed under his closed lids lulling him to sleep. Soon, he was in a deep sleep, oblivious of his surroundings.

Gheorghe was jolted awake by the sudden stillness of the truck. He was greeted by the clucking of the idling truck. He bolted up. A long queue of cars, trucks and farm equipment snaked around a grassy bend in the road.

"Where are we? What's wrong?"

"We are in Dej; it looks like the bridge is out over the Someş River. I sent Arcos to investigate."

Gheorghe scanned the growing crowd that migrated past the bend in the road. Some would emerge calling out to others to come see the spectacle.

Arcos surfaced from the crowd shaking his head. "This does not look promising," Korzha announced. Arcos hopped onto the runner of the truck propping his elbows in the window. "We won't be going this way; the damn bridge collapsed."

Gheorghe scrubbed his hands over his face. He heaved a deep sigh and threw his hands up. "How is that possible!" he exploded.

His outburst startled his companions. Without pause, Arcos quipped, "Russian quality construction."

"Watch what you say, militiaman," Korzha interjected. The dejected Arcos withdrew from the window, "You figure it out; I will be in the back."

Gheorghe and Korzha sat in the truck serenaded by the idling truck. "Well," Korzha sighed, "We can head back south; I know another way."

Gheorghe tracked the sun; it had long since cracked overhead. The shadows began stretching to the east. "This really puts us behind schedule-," Gheorghe glowered at the snarled traffic ahead, "-but we have no other choice."

Korzha ground the truck into reverse and headed south.

The delay set Gheorghe on edge, robbing him of sleep. The cargo truck rolled off the highway and down a country road. The dust kicked up on either side of them, obscuring the trees and undergrowth around the road. On occasion, the road passed through a scenic overpass, revealing verdant hillsides rolling off into the distance. They approached Bistriţa; Korzha parked near the roundabout at the center of the town. Gheorghe peered through the window, scanning the surrounding buildings. He dipped his chin to his chest and gave a sheepish glance to Korzha, "Have you ever been to Bistriţa?"

"Once or twice as a child, why?"

"I was given partial information. I was told the locals could direct me to the location we are looking for."

Korzha joined Gheorghe in his search. "Why don't you stay here and I will see what I can find." He jumped from the cab and started down the sidewalk. Gheorghe watched as Korzha navigated through the streets. Korzha appeared to possess a native nobleness which Gheorghe admired. He found him so completely likable; he debated if he should tell him of the great burden he carried. Gheorghe ached for someone to be forthright with him. When Gheorghe wrote the script in his head, his explanation sounded insane. He waited for his return.

Korzha popped his head in the driver's side window, "I think I may have found someone who can help."

"Who?"

"There is a barkeep at an inn down this way," he pointed straight ahead, "to the left."

"Very good, thank you Korzha."

Gheorghe was greeted by a churning, gray cloud wall which had swallowed the southern sky. A faint southern wind brushed against his face. He craned his head to look to the south. "Looks like we are going to get some rain," Korzha offered.

Gheorghe muttered, "Yes," and made his way toward the inn. Arcos and Comaneci poured out of the truck behind him. Comaneci landed flat-footed on the ground giving a satisfying stretch; every joint popped and snapped as he reached to the sky. "Where are we?" he said through a yawn.

Arcos thumped him on the arm, "Bistriţa, you idiot."

Comaneci gave thick, heavy blinks as he adjusted to the light. "Already? That was fast."

Arcos thumped him once more, "You idiot; you slept the whole way."

Comaneci dismissed Arcos' comments with a grin, "That is one of the side effects of vodka. When do we eat? I'm hungry."

Korzha, following behind Gheorghe, turned to Comaneci, "Is hunger another side effect?" Comaneci gave a satisfied smile and fell into line.

Gheorghe saw a local leave from the inn, the noise of a large crowd burping out the open door behind him. The building had an aging placard with peeling gold paint. Comaneci seeing the sign laughed under his breath, "If they want to be good Bolsheviks, they need to change their sign." He elbowed Gheorghe to look. Gheorghe glanced up to read the faded letters:

Coroana de Aur

Voices in the Dark

The Inn stood set slightly back from the street. It was an older establishment. The newer buildings surrounded it squeezing the Inn like a vise. The lower part of the inn was made of stone of varying sizes; the entrance was framed by two clusters of windows. The upper floor had dark wooden framed windows set into fading plaster. The front door gave out a creaking groan as it opened. The walls, oozing a stale odor, displayed dozens of grainy black and white photographs and ancient documents in fat, ornate Cyrillic script.

Korzha grabbed his elbow and pointed with his gaze, "Down there, Inspector. The barkeep should be able to help." In a sunken room to the left was the bar. As Gheorghe descended the short steps, the others lingered in the main foyer examining the artifacts on the wall.

Comaneci blurted out, "See what they have to eat."

Comaneci's request reminded him that he had not eaten. The realization released a wave of hunger pangs which left an emptiness in its wake. With the exception of one drunken reveler, the barroom became hushed as Gheorghe approached the bar. He approached the barkeep, not bothering to take a seat.

"Good afternoon, I am Inspector Gheorghe Ianculescu with the Securitate. I am looking for someone who can take us to the Tihuţa Pass."

The barkeep leaned away from Gheorghe, his eyes narrowing, "Why?"

"Well, really about 14 kilometers north of the pass. I am looking for a particular spot-"

The color drained from the barkeep's weathered face, "You mean the old Hungarian outpost?"

Gheorghe blankly stared. "Umm," the barkeep's response caught him off-guard, "There were Hungarians stationed near here?"

"Yes, after the annexation of Transylvania in 1940, a Hungarian unit built an outpost on the ruins of an ancient castle. They chose it for the views of the surrounding countryside-,"

"Yes, yes," Gheorghe interrupted, "an ancient castle. That is what I'm looking for."

The barkeep's eyes darted over Gheorghe's shoulder his tone diminishing, "...but, they abandoned it because of the three sisters."

Gheorghe paused and continued, "Who are the three sisters?"

An abrupt, whiskey-soaked voice trumpeted, "Don't listen to that old man, Inspector. Those Hungarians were incompetent drunks. They abandoned that post to search for more țuică. If you want, I can take you there."

Gheorghe wheeled around and approached a man glazed with sweat and body odor. Gheorghe thought a drive in the country and physical exertion may help sober the man up. "Very good, find two friends and three shovels. I will make it worth your while. Meet us back here in twenty minutes."

Little specks of rain dotted Gheorghe's face as he exited the inn. The sidewalk and road were glazed with rain. He paused in the doorway and craned his head to the sky. The sky was pregnant with fat, charcoal clouds. Gheorghe shook his head in disgust, "Rain."

Korzha poked his head over Gheorghe's shoulder joining his gaze, "Does this cause a problem for us, Inspector?"

He gave a quick sigh, "It can't; we are going to have to work through the weather regardless."

CRSO

After the work crew had returned, they walked back to the cargo truck. He pulled a large map from the glove compartment and began to chart their trip. Tihuţa Pass was just a few kilometers to the east, making the day's activities easily accomplished. Gheorghe checked his watch. It was almost 16:00; they still had a good five hours before nightfall.

They bounced down country roads with their cargo jostling around with clanks and complaints. As the sky grew angrier, the wind stiffened, filling the trees with a rustling murmur. The landscape's greens, yellows, and browns turned monochromatic by the light filtered through the gray clouds. The swaying hiss of the trees exaggerated the height of the hills with large shadows. The men in the truck bed joked and laughed, pointing out big bumps in the road for Korzha to upset their other passengers. In the distance, Gheorghe could see the road got swallowed up in a valley between two large hills. They were getting close.

When they entered the pass, the wind filtered through the trees on either side bathing the truck in coolness. Gheorghe was sweating yet a chill washed over him. The road continued through the pass and opened up again into a wider space. Ahead of them in the distance, there was a rocky outcropping on a particularly grass-bare hill. The hill was so different than the others that it almost seemed a small mountain compared to the green miniatures around it. As they got closer, Gheorghe realized that the lack of green was not due to natural rock faces, but a manmade formation on top of the hill. The mountain's jagged slopes were actually the fractured remains of battlements, the black stone of a castle faded with the passage of time.

"That is our destination," he said and pointed out the windshield.

The banter stopped in the truck and the men studied the defunct castle on the horizon.

Gheorghe said nothing, looking for the sun's outline in the sky behind the castle. The charcoal clouds had prematurely darkened the landscape. He blinked a few times, his eyes still as heavy as when he awoke this morning.

The castle gradually came into the foreground until they were so close that it became hidden again atop its hillside vista. Korzha took the truck off the road and drove across the grassy plains to find a convenient ascent for their vehicle. He had nearly circled the entire hill when he found a cobbled path that had fallen into disrepair though the trees lining it still held their formation around it. They approached the castle gradually along this winding road. The trees formed an impenetrable canopy that blocked remaining light from the sun. The truck arrived at a clearing at the top. Before them, a large wooden portcullis had once stood. But now, the molding support timbers jutted out from behind their crumbling stones like ribs protruding from a rotting corpse. This outer wall had been so disfigured by the passage of time that there were several breaches large enough to drive the truck through. Korzha took his foot off the brake and crept into the castle courtyard.

Passing through the wall, the truck mounted several loose stones and crashed loudly into the open space. The engine's revving and suspension's squeaking were the only noise to be heard, bouncing eerily off the distant walls of the courtyard that still stood. Craning his neck to locate the building he sought, Gheorghe peered around the corners of walls and through the fallen roofs of other structures. In the back corner of the courtyard, he saw the pointed peak of a chapel. The rest of the building was obscured behind debris. The peak was eaten away on one side and standing precariously above all the other structures.

"This is the place," Gheorghe announced to Korzha. He pointed to remains of the chapel lychgate. Making a three point turn, Korzha positioned the truck with its back towards the chapel for easy loading and their subsequent exit.

Korzha shut off the engine and took a deep breath. "We're here," he said.

"What? This is it?" Arcos said. "What the hell are we doing here?"

"I thought we were picking up a shipment for the Securitate," Comaneci said.

"This is what we came for," Gheorghe said. He got out of the truck and went around to the back to speak with the workers they had picked up from Bistriţa. "Let's go! We're here!"

Arcos and Comaneci sprang from the back, yet the four men sitting on the empty crates did not move at Gheorghe's instruction.

"You did not tell us this was where we would be working," a scraggly haired man said. "There is a curse here. This will cost you double. Double or nothing. I want my payment upfront."

"Get out!" Arcos yelled from behind Gheorghe. He drew his gun from its holster thrusting the barrel into the cargo hold of the truck.

The men in the back lifted their hands but did not move.

"Don't test me!" Arcos screamed again. He fired once into the air. The shot shattered the quiet echoing around the vacant courtyard.

A swell of rage erupted from Gheorghe, "That is enough, Arcos! Put the gun away!" Korzha snatched the weapon from Arcos.

"Korzha, you touch me again and I will kill you!", Arcos spewed out.

Comaneci intercepted him, grabbing his shoulder, "Take it easy, Arcos. Let's just get this over with."

The men filed out of the truck without hesitation, jumping down onto the patchy grass and broken stonework beneath them. They kept their heads down, but the leader of their group gave Gheorghe a defiant look as he passed.

"Get them started unloading the truck," Gheorghe said to Korzha. "You two, follow me."

Gheorghe walked past the workers. The pathway to the chapel was obscured by debris that had fallen from nearby buildings. He stepped over broken stones and ducked beneath a collapsed pillar. The courtyard was a wide open space with several prominent buildings. Gheorghe recognized the features of a stable, a servant quarters, farm houses and other feudal structures. Chaos had spread between the dilapidated structures and obscured the original paths between buildings. Some of the stones had been repurposed. A prominent fire ring had been constructed out of smaller stones. Scattered amongst them were shattered crates and rusting implements. Gheorghe paused to sift through the debris. The fading stencil said, *Élelmiszer.* Comaneci looked over Gheorghe's shoulder, "Hungarian."

Some of the larger stones had been placed to construct more permanent structures. Other stones were arranged to allow a lookout to ascend to the top of the crumbled battlements. Plant life had sprung up between the cobblestones and structures, making the congestion worse. He shoved a large rock out of the way so the crates could move back to the truck unobstructed. With Comaneci and Arcos in tow, Gheorghe slowly picked his way through the destroyed grounds towards the chapel behind it all.

The crumbling lychgate demarcated the chapel from the main grounds, encircled by a half-wall of stone and mortar that had survived better than the taller buildings and fortifications. Within the chapel grounds, there was a large plot of land dotted with several gravestones and an aging gazebo out to the side of the chapel. The foliage around the space had grown to an incredible density, with vines, weeds, and short trees choking out the details of the manmade structures beneath them. Gheorghe approached the chapel with his eyes glued to the graveyard and the jagged shadow across it. The fragmented edge of the chapel's fallen peak gave a serrated edge to the darkness over the graves.

"Are you sure about this, Ianculescu? There is nothing here that could be of any use to the Securitate. Could it be we are in the wrong place?" Arcos asked.

"This is exactly the right place," Gheorghe said. He approached the headstones in the chapel graveyard. Four graves were clearly distinguishable, with a handful of other unmarked mounds ominously sprinkled around them. The largest headstone had been broken into many pieces though it remained prominently featured out in front of the group. The foliage and greenery that had consumed most of the chapel grounds had not crossed this grave's threshold and not even grass grew on the ground before the graves. Gheorghe kneeled by the large grave, picking up a piece of the headstone and turning it over in search of a name. There were a few letters, but the ancient Cyrillic script had crumbled into a heap; Gheorghe could not make out any words.

Behind him, Comaneci and Arcos watched with hesitancy. They gave each other quizzical looks.

"Our orders are to excavate the dirt from this graveyard. We only need enough to fill our crates most of the way, if they are too full we won't be able to lift them."

"Our orders were to desecrate a graveyard? I knew I should've stayed in the station," Arcos said. "This bullshit is beneath my pay grade."

"What aren't you telling us?" Comaneci said.

"I don't have time to explain," Gheorghe mumbled.

Arcos and Comaneci stood mute, unconvinced. For all his planning, Gheorghe was unprepared to explain their mission. "Listen," he paused searching for words, " You know the Americans have the atomic bomb, right?"

"Sure, everyone knows that," scoffed Arcos.

"Well, we need to take this soil back for testing. Our comrades in Russia think this may be a good source of uranium."

"Ah, hell, this is radioactive?", groaned Comaneci staring at the ground as if he were sinking, "Let's get this over with!"

"The Captain wants the dirt in Borş for testing. If it is radioactive, it cannot be stored in Oradea."

Gheorghe rushed past them, returning to the truck. The crates had been unloaded and the four workers stood around. Gheorghe jumped up into the truck and handed the shovels stored there to Arcos. He jumped out again and gestured for the group to follow him. They were able to take all the crates back to the chapel. One of the workers stopped outside the half-wall of the chapel grounds, unwilling to go further. He called out to the others in a rushed voice, frantic at the sight of it all.

"Move!" Arcos yelled shoving him forward.

He started moving again, entering the chapel grounds and following Gheorghe towards the gravestones. The work party dropped the crates near Comaneci and Korzha, who stood a bit off from the graves.

"Put dirt into the crates," Gheorghe said flatly, "We're done when each of these crates is over half full."

They accepted the shovels but only stared at the tools in their hands.

"This is a cursed placed. The evil will follow us from here if we take from this place," the scraggly headed worker explained. His face was scrunched with a pleading sadness. "We would not have come if we had known this was the task you required. We are already in danger! Please, take us back to town. Please, I beg of you," he threw down his shovel and fell to his knees.

"Shut up, Anton. Let's get paid and be done with it," another worker said. He took his shovel and walked boldly over to the headstones. The entire group watched him. With a decisive stab, he drove the tip of the shovel into the dirt before the largest headstone.

He looked up with a smile and a shrug. "See, Anton? The only evil here is the ones with the guns," he pointed to Arcos with his chin. He began to scoop out hearty chunks of earth from the ground to dump into the nearest empty crate.

The tension in the rest of the group seemed to ease as the sound of dirt rained into the crates. The other workers made their way over to the graves and followed suit though Anton was the last to join. He gave a knowing look to Gheorghe again as he passed.

"There is a reason they won't dig with us," Anton said. "They know the evil is here."

"Listen to your friends, Anton. I am the only thing you should fear," Arcos said with a smile.

Anton spit on the ground in Arcos' direction but continued shoveling.

Gheorghe walked past the digging and examined the other three graves in the chapel yard. Besides a conspicuous lack of plant life, the dirt on top of the three graves was slightly sunken to a uniform depth. He crouched beside one of the graves, unsuccessfully trying to decipher the headstone and pinching some of the dirt between his fingers. Gheorghe recognized the loamy soil as having the same texture as Tatiana's grave.

The time crawled by and the workers dug deeper with each consecutive shovelful. When they had gotten about a foot deep into the ground, they moved to the other graves to dig. Eventually, the ground around the graves had been chewed up like the fields for plowing. The third crate was being filled when Anton screamed and dropped his shovel. He stumbled backward, tripping on the uneven ground and falling over himself. He pointed at the ground where he was digging.

"I saw it move! The dirt moved!" he yelled.

His companions laughed as they leaned on their shovels. "If you want to take a break, why don't you just ask?"

"I think he is going through withdrawals," another concluded.

Gheorghe checked his watch. He estimated about thirty minutes of sunlight. "Men, we are almost finished," he announced.

As the work progressed the distant thunder grew closer and the rain returned. The sky broke open and a shroud of rain covered them. The workers stopped and looked at Gheorghe.

"Why have you stopped?" Gheorghe's inquiry was consumed by a wall of rain and wind. He cupped his hands around his mouth and belted out, "Keep digging!"

A simultaneous flash of lightning and thunder smashed directly overhead, sending the work party scurrying to the protection of the dilapidated gazebo. Gheorghe surrendered to the weather and joined them under the gazebo. Rain poured from the gaping hole of the gazebo, splattering on the legs of the work party. Their misery was complete.

Gheorghe shivered in the rain as the sunlight was strangled out by the storm. The storm outlasted the remaining daylight. When the storm subsided, the roar of wind and rain were replaced with a chorus of frogs. Gheorghe turned to the men, "Okay, Let's finish and go home." They sloshed back into the graveyard. Aton fell behind the others and ran back to Gheorghe. He grabbed his arm.

"Please, Inspector," he whispered through quivering lips, "We should leave. We are in great danger."

Gheorghe patted him on the hand, "I understand your fear. The master of this castle has visited me."

Aton shook his head, "No; no, it isn't him I fear. I have been trying to tell you, but you will not listen. The three sisters watch over these grounds and the Tihuța Pass awaiting their master's return."

Gheorghe's heart sank. He looked past Aton to the three bare graves; the graves' shallow indentations had filled with rainwater and were now smears of mud. Gheorghe darted out of the gazebo.

"We must hurry," he shrilled with his face drained of color

Korzha approached him, "What is wrong, Inspector?"

Gheorghe swept his hand across his brow. He tried to steady his tone, taking a deep breath, "We are working against a deadline. If we need additional lighting, we have lanterns in the truck."

Korzha tapped him on the shoulder, "No worries, Inspector. Working together, we will have this done quickly." Korzha turned to one of the work party, "Mihai," pointing to the truck, "Go get the lanterns."

Mihai dropped his shovel and left to retrieve the lanterns. His friends leaning on their shovels watched him disappear into the shadows. They turned back to Gheorghe, who was scanning the shadows with attentive ears. Aton approached from behind causing him to startle. "Ah," exclaimed one of the workers, "I know what the problem is, Inspector. You have been listening to Aton's stories." He called out to Aton through a smirk, "Aton, you should be ashamed of yourself for scaring our visitors."

Emboldened from the rebuff, Aton emerged from behind Gheorghe. "You can laugh if you like Dorin, but I have seen them with my own eyes." The conviction steadied the tremor in his voice, "I did not believe it either; I thought they were just stories to keep little boys in line. But, when I was nineteen, I saw them on a hunting trip. They almost had me under their spell, but I escaped. It is how I got this-," He peeled up his sleeve to reveal a faded crimson scar.

Dorin dismissed him with a snort, "That is from a drunken fall, Aton," he slowed his cadence, "You are a drunk."

Aton exploded, "I am tired of you!" He surged forward with his shovel ready to lay a blow. Arcos intercepted him, " That is enough old man," he slung him toward graveyard, "Get back to work." The men resumed their work and the crates gradually filled with dirt. Gheorghe and his crew stood idly by, nailing shut the crates as they were filled.

The night sky was blanketed by thick clouds. All natural light was extinguished as the frogs continued their deafening chorus. Korzha fumbled over to Gheorghe, "Where is Mihai? He should be back. I will go check on him."

Gheorghe sensed Aton's gaze. Their eyes gave a knowing glance. Gheorghe suspected that Aton's fears were legitimate. It seemed that all safeguards had been removed; the only safety Gheorghe felt was on the spot where he stood. He dreaded what lay beyond his sight.

"Wait!" he called out to Korzha, "take someone with you."

Korzha and Comaneci disappeared into the darkness. Aton rushed Gheorghe, "Please we must get out of here now!"

"Yes, nail down the cover on the last crate. Once it is loaded, we will leave."

"Inspector!" Gheorghe turned to see a lone lantern swinging into the graveyard.

Korzha and Comaneci approached. "Mihai is gone. He must have left; there is no sign of him."

"Well, let's load this last-," the chorus of frogs fell silent. The sudden silence left a vacuum making all incidental sound muted and distant. A frigid air descended on the graveyard.

Arcos joined the huddle. "What the hell just happened? Look-" he pointed to the warm billows coming from his mouth, "It is freezing."

Gheorghe's heart dropped and he shot out, "Get the last crate loaded, now! Let's go, now!" The men were startled by the outburst. 'Now!"

As they moved toward the final crate, faint voices creeped out the darkness. Gheorghe scanned the darkness for the source of the voices. Across the graveyard stood the collapsed chapel wall revealing the desecrated interior. On the far side of the chapel ruins, shifting shadows moved in front of the outline of broken windows. Gheorghe trained his ears toward the chapel. The voices seemed to be conferring with each other.

Korzha stopped and looked back at Gheorghe, "Did you hear that?" Korzha turned back to face the chapel.

"Yes," Gheorghe barked, "keep moving Korzha."

As the others wrestled to move the crate, Korzha peeled away toward the chapel. "Hello? Who is there?", He called to the darkened ruins. Nothing but faint laughter was the reply.

Gheorghe rushed to Korzha grabbing his arm, "Korzha, let's go back to the truck."

"Okay," he said, turning to leave with Gheorghe. "I thought I heard voices in the chapel."

A high, petrified scream pierced the night air. Gheorghe and Korzha wheeled around to see the form of a woman kneeling in the gazebo. Her long flaxen hair draped over her face. "My baby!", she shrieked, "Where is my baby?" Her mournful plea drew Korzha away from Gheorghe.

"Korzha, come with me!" Gheorghe urged, "We cannot help her."

The woman rose to her feet. The rain clung to her young body, plastering her flowing ivory dress to her body; the saturated dress revealed every curvature. Her flaxen hair framed a face which matched her dress in paleness. She trained her eyes on Korzha and through glistening garnet lips said, "Have you seen my baby?"

"No," Korzha turned to Gheorghe, "I need to help her."

When Korzha turned to face her again, she opened her palms, both dripping with blood. "Help me find my baby." Her mournful face continued to draw Korzha toward the gazebo. Gheorghe grabbed Korzha once more, pleading, "Korzha, please let's go."

Korzha faced Gheorghe with torpid eyes, "No, she needs my help."

In the darkened ruins, hushed pleas whispered, "Yes, come to us." Gheorghe followed the voices to burning emerald eyes obscured in the darkness. Gheorghe grabbed Korzha once more, trying to pry him from her gaze. Two more women drifted from the shadows. Their long coal black hair flowed like extended raven's wings; their flowing white gowns shimmered with a milky luminance. At their appearance, Gheorghe squeezed his eyes shut as Korzha slipped from his grasp. He wheeled around stumbling into a hole; a mire of mud and stone broke Gheorghe's fall. Gheorghe screamed, "Korzha!" but his voice was overruled by their soft pleading. The seductive chorus masked a seething malice which bored into Korzha's sluggish mind. Gheorghe glanced up to see Korzha disappear into the darkened ruins; the three sisters closing ranks behind him.

Gheorghe sloshed to his feet and bolted to the lychgate. He crashed into Comaneci and Arcos as he entered the courtyard. "What the hell happened to you?" Arcos' eyes clung to Gheorghe's mud encased body.

Gheorghe darted past them, "I fell," he looked over his shoulder without stopping, "Let's go."

"Where is Korzha?"

"He is gone," Gheorghe blurted out.

"Gone? Did he leave with Aton and the others? We cannot find anyone."

"Yes," Gheorghe sighed as he mounted the truck, "He left with the others. Let's go; Codreanu is expecting us."

Tying Up Loose Ends

Gheorghe's long, tortuous sleep was punctuated with sudden jolts of awareness. These unwelcome moments were overtaken by his exhaustion and he drifted back to sleep. He vacillated between sleep and semi-consciousness. The truck bounced along a rough patch unequivocally waking him. He found his head drooping onto Arcos' shoulder, who was asleep against the window. He rubbed his eyes and scanned the surroundings outside the truck. The darkened landscape had flattened out; they were approaching Oradea.

"How long have we been on the road?" Gheorghe asked.

Comaneci was driving with one arm out his window, dragging on a cigarette.

"About six hours. We will be in Borș soon. How did you sleep?"

"Horribly," Gheorghe answered as he tried to stretch in place. "How long till the sun comes up?"

"Uh..." Comaneci squinted to read his watch, "About two hours."

"Okay, did you radio into headquarters?"

"I was going wait until we reached the village and started unloading."

He felt as if he had awakened in a free fall. He darted a glance at his own watch. Though they were approaching their destination, he felt a need for action. The urge to do anything surged through him. "Give me the radio," Gheorghe demanded. He took the radio from Comaneci and gathered his thoughts for a moment. He pressed down on the receiver to issue a brief crackle.

"This is Inspector Ianculescu reporting in from Borș, over."

Gheorghe shifted in his seat waiting for a response, but only the hiss and pop of radio silence responded. He repeated with pointed emphasis, "This is Inspector Ianculescu reporting in from Borș, over."

A garbled voice responded, "Headquarters to Ianculescu, go ahead."

"Inform Captain Codreanu the cargo will be unloaded and ready for inventory within the hour, over," Gheorghe said. He waited in tense silence for the response.

"Headquarters to Ianculescu, report received. The Captain will be meeting you shortly, over."

Gheorghe returned the receiver to Comaneci and slumped in his seat. He fixed a blasé stare into the darkness, focused on nothing in particular. He heaved a sigh, knowing all his deceptions were coming to an end. *Father Petre is at peace,* he thought. *He died protecting his people.* Gheorghe probed into the darkness. *What will my death accomplish?* He thought, *If my death could expel the Russians or bring Codreanu to justice, that would be a good death.* Tears brimmed his weary eyes; He imagined his life being swallowed by a raging sea. His life was just a drop in a sea of innumerable souls that preceded him. The voice of the Master invaded his memory, *Death is a road we all walk.* The thought numbed his heart as the darkness of the night crept into his soul. *He is right,* he concluded.

"The Captain is coming himself?" Arcos asked. "I haven't seen him in months and he shows his face to inspect a bunch of radioactive dirt? What is going on here, Ianculescu?"

"It does not matter anymore," Gheorghe droned.

"Well, it must be something important if it wakes up his fat ass this early," Arcos said with a chuckle, "I hope chokes on the damn stuff."

Comaneci joined Arcos laughing at the thought.

"I suspect he'll make a dramatic entrance," Gheorghe's resignation dulled his indignation, "he will be goose-stepping with the cameras rolling."

"You have known the captain a long time haven't you?"

"Oh, yes; I'm the last of the old guard."

"I thought you old-timers stuck together, Inspector," Comaneci smirked.

With a blank face, Gheorghe intoned, "I am a loose end; Codreanu does not like loose ends."

Arcos and Comaneci glanced at each other. The truck fell silent.

"We're here," Comaneci said. He pointed out the windshield ahead of their truck. The headlights were the only light around them, cutting through the dense darkness of the forest. They passed a sign for the village limits and barreled into Borş, their cargo thumping in the cargo bed. The village was abandoned at this hour. Most of the villagers were still in bed, but the smell of lit hearths streamed through the early morning air. The dark smoke was invisible in the waning hours of the night. As they got deeper into the village, Gheorghe noticed a distant glimmer growing larger. He recognized it as coming from the church. As they passed the building, Gheorghe saw a large array of candles spread before the wooden doors. Half were extinguished as the other half struggled to stay lit. The villagers had held a vigil for their missing priest. Gheorghe craned his neck to watch the church as they passed, feeling a twinge of remorse.

"Where's the warehouse?" Comaneci asked.

"Take a left on this road," Gheorghe pointed.

The truck pulled up to an old warehouse standing just outside the village grounds. It was surrounded by underdeveloped farmland on one side and a partially cleared forest on the other.

"What is this place?" Comaneci asked.

"It was an oil refinery during the war," Gheorghe answered. Arcos jumped to open the perimeter gate. As the truck pulled into the crumbling facility, Arcos jumped into the bed of the truck. The last stretch of road leading up to the ruined refinery was lined with a young forest on one side and an abandoned field on the other. The refinery's silhouette loomed at the end of the unkempt road.

A clatter of gunfire erupted from the bed of the truck. "What the hell?" Comaneci slid to a stop. Gheorghe jumped out to investigate. Arcos was peering over the truck bed door into the empty field. Gheorghe followed his gaze into the darkness. "What did you see?"

"There was a huge dog following us in the field," he stopped and turned to Gheorghe, "at least I thought it was a dog; maybe a wolf." His mouth gaped open as he turned his gaze back to the field.

Gheorghe's heart leap into his throat, "A wolf?"

The truck pulled up to the building, shining its headlights through the perforated structure. Long shadows were cast against the back wall of the building and lingered inside it like a monstrous rib cage. There were shattered windows and support girders bending out from the roof like the great structure had given birth. During the war, it had been taken offline by Allied bombing and dozens of lives had been lost. Even the land surrounding it had become untenable and infertile flecked with craters and riddled with large debris from the blast. The foliage surrounding the site was young and weedy, but thick with neglect. The renovation of the refinery was slowed by the amount of undetonated ordnance and eventually halted by Soviet indifference. The building was left to deteriorate after the war. No one came to this part of the village anymore.

"Leave the headlights on," Gheorghe said. "Let's get moving."

Arcos opened the door and hopped out.

Gheorghe followed and went around to the cargo bay. He went to the compartment that held the shovels and found two flashlights and an electric lamp. He chided himself for not thinking to make sure there were enough flashlights before leaving. The darkness was their enemy. He hung the lamp from a hook in the back of the truck and hopped back out of the cargo bay with the flashlights. He walked past Comaneci and gave the other flashlight to Arcos. "This is all we have. Stick together and don't wander off. We can't waste any time."

He climbed back into the cargo bay with Comaneci in tow. Together, they began lifting the first crate out of the truck in the dim light of the lamp swaying above them. They dropped the crate clumsily out the back with a loud crash and the wood rattled but held. The sound seemed to echo around them, bouncing off the encroaching darkness and breaking the silence of the forest. Gheorghe's ears perked to some rustling nearby.

"Did you hear that?" Comaneci asked.

"It's just the wind," Gheorghe said. But then he remembered the wind from his meeting in the graveyard. He started moving faster, throwing the crates out of the back with even less grace.

Comaneci and Arcos stood outside the truck, lifting the dropped cargo. They waddled around to the front of the truck with their load balanced between them. When they walked in front of the headlights, their shadows flew up against the facade of the building like giant scarecrows. When they returned, Arcos pointed his flashlight out into the woods beside their truck.

"I just saw something move," he said.

"Come on, Arcos! Enough of this campfire scare tactics. Shut up and help me finish," Comaneci said with his hands already on the next crate. "I just want to get back my bed."

"It was big," Arcos continued to point his flashlight out into the woods. His hand was hovering over the revolver in his belt. "Wolves are no joke, comrade."

"You think your revolver will stop one?" Comaneci laughed.

Gheorghe scanned within the flashlight's small circle of light. "What did you see?" Gheorghe asked.

"Gleaming eyes. Red, high off the ground. I guess it could have been a bear but I've never seen a bear's eyes like that," Arcos said.

The hairs on the back of Gheorghe's neck stood up. He grabbed the last crate from the truck with Comaneci and threw it onto the ground. He did a quick inventory. All that the Master required was here. *All is ready. Only the loose ends need to be tied up.* Radu's voice sounded in his head, *The Master does not like loose ends.* The same was true of Codreanu. *I am the only loose end left.* He had delivered Codreanu's Dragon and the Master's crates. He had stayed alive by subterfuge, but his ball of yarn was spent. He no longer had leverage over the Master or Codreanu. *This is it. It is over.* The blood drained from his face. The great weight pressing down on him in the graveyard had returned. He jumped down from the cargo hold and took up one side of a crate.

"Let's move!" he yelled. His voice was uncharacteristically loud, even more so in the relative silence of the pitch black forest.

Arcos still stood with his flashlight and gun pointed into the woods, but Comaneci came down and grabbed the other side of the crate. They shuffled around to the front of the truck.

Gheorghe crossed in front of the headlights, seeing his own shadow fly up on the broken wall before him. He froze in place. The Master could be one of these shadows himself.

Comaneci shot him a confused look. "What is it?"

"Nothing. Let's keep moving," Gheorghe said. They brought the crates deeper into the warehouse. They had pulled up to the back where the receiving bay was still in some recognizable form of its previous function. There was no door so they took the crate into the loading area of the derelict refinery, stepping through muddy puddles and over scraps of corrugated metal. The ceiling above them was a patchwork of stars and twisted steel. The roof had been destroyed in many places, leaving the warehouse floor exposed to the elements. Plants even grew in cracks within the foundation. They set down the crate and Gheorghe pulled out his flashlight to inspect the building. It had been emptied of everything worthwhile, but the collateral damage of the war lingered and industrial equipment in all states of disrepair littered the floor and walls. There was a scaffold above them with a fragmented catwalk almost reaching from one side to the other. He pointed his flashlight along the walls, looking for exits. There were holes everywhere, making it nearly impossible to secure the building.

Arcos and Comaneci shuffled past him with another crate.

Gheorghe went back outside for the last crate waiting for Comaneci's eager help. He returned to the truck to retrieve a lamp and brought it back to the crew inside the warehouse. He set it on top of the crates and the men rested in the weak aura of its light. The headlights shined through the broken exterior, creating a sparse patchwork of light beams on the far wall of the warehouse. The room had become eerily illuminated, with irregular shadows taking up more space than the light creating them.

"What now?" Arcos asked.

"We wait," Gheorghe answered. He kept his eyes on the catwalk above them.

The crew shuffled around their small lamp and made themselves comfortable. Comaneci pulled out another cigarette and handed out one to the others. Gheorghe declined, his eyes still scanning the ceiling above them. They lit up, adding two small embers at the end of their faces to the weak glow around them.

"What do you think that animal was outside?" Comaneci asked.

"Maybe it was a bear," Arcos said eagerly. "We used to hunt them in our village."

"You are overconfident, Arcos. A pistol is nothing for a beast of that size," Comaneci said.

"There is nothing that can survive a bullet through the brain. Unless you are brainless like you," Arcos said.

The two laughed, their voices carrying throughout the vacant space.

Gheorghe remained quiet. He was trying not to frighten them, but he could not help but to scan their surroundings with his flashlight. The men remained propped up on the crates, disinterested in the warehouse. Gheorghe's light hovered over the many openings in the building around them, disappearing into the distance where there was no wall to contain it. During one of these circular sweeps, he thought he saw the flashlights beam reflect back on something bright. He paused and returned the light to the spot. There was nothing; the edges of a shattered window gleaming back at him. In his imagination, every reflective glimmer was the Master's eyes watching him.

The wind blew through the building's gaps, creating a strange whistle. The beams from the headlights were interrupted for a moment and no one seemed to notice except Gheorghe. Their conversation continued its lightheartedness and Gheorghe walked back outside to inspect the truck. He would rather meet with the Master alone. His crew did not need to know the danger they were in, this was his burden alone. Stepping outside, the wind whipped him like a cool lash. He had unknowingly broken out in a sweat and the night air chilled him to the bone. He pointed his flashlight to the patch of trees where the men had spotted movement but saw nothing. He returned inside the warehouse. His crew was still laughing around their dim lamp, smoking short cigarettes and getting louder in their boredom. Gheorghe inspected the ceiling once more, finding the catwalk empty and the stars still gleaming unobstructed in the holes of the roof. He sat on the floor to calm himself, leaning his back against one of the crates. There were four stacked near each other and a fifth away from the group, the first that had been unloaded. Gheorghe noticed that the top of the crate was lifted. He bolted to his feet, pointing the flashlight. Someone was still standing there, concealed behind the lid.

"Show yourself!" Gheorghe yelled. The conversation around him ceased instantly. He pointed his flashlight at the crate's lid, its circle shaking in his grip.

The lid lowered slowly. The cone of light streamed around it, but nothing was behind it. When the lid was shut completely, Gheorghe could not fathom what he was seeing. The beam was landing on something because it did not extend to the back wall of the building, but the shape was so dark that it seemed to swallow the brightness. The surface teemed with a curtain of throbbing smoke with opaque ringlets snaking out, The cloud parted at the top and a pallid face emerged, bright white in the flashlight's glare.

"You are late; yet you have done well, Gheorghe," the Master's voice was unnervingly smooth. His appearance had withered since Gheorghe had last seen him. There were hundreds of wrinkles across his face and his crimson eyes were bulging from his pale skin, much larger in proportion to the rest of his face than before. In his weakened state, he looked closer to his true, demonic form.

The crew jumped to their feet, drawing weapons and crying out in alarm.

Arcos pointed his flashlight and pistol at the Master.

"Who are you?" he demanded.

The Master's withering gaze landed on Arcos with all the power of a coiled spring ready to release its malicious energy. The shadowy figure of the Master erupted into a torrent of dark, shapeless movement and dispersed before their eyes. The beams of the flashlights now landed on a wrecked conveyor belt along the back of the refinery.

"What the hell was that?" Comaneci demanded as he crouched behind a crate with his gun drawn.

Gheorghe said nothing. He returned their incredulous stares with a hardened look. Even if he could, there was no time to explain. He scanned the room again with the flashlight, knowing it was futile. His hand found its way to the side of his neck, covering the scratch marks as if to protect himself. He heard laughter from above them.

"What are you planning, Gheorghe?" The Master's voice resounded from all around them. "I've tasted your blood, I know your fear. You are right; it will not work."

The sound of wind rushed through the building again. The lamp was swept from its place atop a crate and crashed to the floor. The warehouse became dark except for the ominous shadows of the headlights and the two frantic beams of the flashlights slicing through the air in a panic.

"You cannot escape your fate," the Master's voice was suddenly nearby.

Arcos swept his flashlight quickly to the source, pointing it at Gheorghe.

Gheorghe was blinded in the light but heard the gasps from his crew. Behind him, the Master had grown to a monstrous size, reaching his shadowy wings around Gheorghe to totally engulf him.

The blackness of his shape surrounded Gheorghe like a fog of writhing snakes and the light from the flashlight began to fade. Gheorghe inhaled sharply and his stomach dropped as if he had just fallen into an abyss. The darkness was closing around him and a feeling of weightlessness accompanied it. He felt as though he were being lifted off the ground, the chill of death racing up his spine.

Gunshots sounded. Gheorghe heard them distantly at first, but they passed by him with the sound of shredding fabric. The darkness suddenly let him loose and he dropped to his feet, blinded again by the return of the flashlight's beam. He scrambled towards his crew, taking a knee and pointing his flashlight to help them fire. The muzzle flashes from their guns briefly lit up the room around them and bullets dinged off equipment and walls with bright ricochets. The men stopped firing after a moment.

"What in God's name was that?" Comaneci yelled.

"What have you gotten us into?" Arcos screamed.

The light from the headlights disappeared, accompanied by the sound of shattering glass. Arcos pointed his flashlight towards their truck, revealing only the jagged entryway they had used to enter. Two red eyes gleamed from beneath the hood of the truck. The dark shape pulled itself out from beneath the truck.

"The eyes!" Arcos yelled. He began firing wildly at the truck. The bullets clanged noisily off the front of the car, penetrating the hood and popping a tire with an angry hiss. The wind blew through the warehouse again, this time so strong that the men had to shield their eyes from the debris it carried. Arcos began to scream, but his voice was cut off suddenly.

Gheorghe pointed his flashlight in the direction but found nothing where Arcos had stood. The second flashlight rolled across the floor, removed from its previous holder.

Comaneci picked up the flashlight and bolted for the exit.

"Wait!" Gheorghe called.

"Hold your fire!" a voice called through a megaphone from outside. The sound of large spotlights shuttering open echoed from outside the warehouse and new patches of light shined through another broken wall of the refinery.

"Help! Help!" Comaneci shouted outside. His cries were cut short by the dull thud of machine gun fire. An eerie silence descended on the warehouse and not even the wind moved.

Gheorghe threw his pistol to the side, knowing it would be useless against either of his enemies. He pointed his flashlight at their cargo truck, then back up to the ceiling. His heart pounded wildly in his throat, *Where are you*? He continued scanning the warehouse, even when he heard the chorus of boots marching through the loading bay they had used. A squad of six soldiers burst into the building looking down the barrels of their rifles.

The leading soldier spoke into the radio on his shoulder, "Area is secured, over." Outside, the sound of an engine revved to life and the spotlights came closer, illuminating more of the warehouse's ground floor. Without thought, Gheorghe fell to his knees and put his hands behind head. With more light, Gheorghe could see a trail of blood leading out one of the building's holes.

Codreanu appeared behind his squad of soldiers. He wore an immaculate pressed black suit. His face could barely contain the smile which grew on his face. His body pulsed with raw energy. He reined in his smile and announced in a broad voice, "Deputy Chief

Inspector Gheorghe Ianculescu, you are under arrest for treason against the People's Republic of Romania," he turned to the squad, "Arrest him."

Codreanu scanned the perimeter of light within the warehouse. "Where is the rest of your little rebel squad?" A slow smile emerged, reveling in victory. "We have accounted for Comaneci. He died for his rebellion, a fitting end for any traitor. Where are Arcos and Korzha?"

Gheorghe's racing heart seized his breath; he breathed shallow bursts through his nose. Gheorghe pointed with his head toward the trail of blood.

Codreanu followed his gaze to the trail of blood. "We must have injured them," He turned to his squad leader, "Alert the perimeter troops to perform a sweep of the surrounding woods."

"Now for our rebel leader," Codreanu turned to Gheorghe with his hands clasped behind his back. "I knew these rumors would eventually lead me to your crimes, Gheorghe. You may have fooled everyone with your spineless devotion to your job, but I know the resentment that festers inside you. I'm not blind. I saw how you and Radu thumbed your nose at me, making jokes behind my back," Codreanu's acidic gaze demanded Gheorghe's attention, "Look at me," he exploded, "Do I look like a joke to you?"

Gheorghe's eyes flitted up to meet Codreanu. *Does he really want my answer?* He thought.

"Your and Radu's problem was you did not have the respect for authority that is required for members of the Republic," Codreanu smiled.

Two soldiers appeared out of the darkness. "Captain, no sign of any other rebels."

"It does not matter," Codreanu dismissed, "For my purposes, this Dragon will be enough." He gestured with his head towards Gheorghe and two more soldiers stepped forward to put him in handcuffs. They seized his hands from behind his head, wrenching them to the small of his back. Codreanu heard him wince as the handcuffs clicked shut. "I have been saving those handcuffs just for you," A cruel smile emerged, "Do they not fit?" Codreanu strolled to one of the crates and held out his hand. A soldier darted from behind him and placed a crowbar in his palm. Codreanu pried off the top of the box and peered in. "What is this?" He turned to face Gheorghe. His face twisted and went flush. He barreled toward Gheorghe. "Where are the weapons?"

Gheorghe could not speak; he lowered his eyes. *This is not the way it was supposed to end,* he thought, *I wanted to say something clever. Radu would know what to say.* Gheorghe slumped over closing his eyes.

"You sniveling piece of shit," Codreanu drove the butt of his pistol into the back of Gheorghe's head. Gheorghe collapsed under the force of the blow. Gravel and broken glass ground into Gheorghe's face as he slammed into the floor.

Codreanu rushed back to the crates. "Help me with these crates," he barked to a soldier. Together, they pushed one over and dirt cascaded onto the floor of the warehouse. In concert, the crates were opened revealing their contents. Codreanu's neck tensed and corded like a rope about to snap with every successive crate. Codreanu slowly turned back toward Gheorghe, revealing a roiling crimson face. His voice erupted, "Gheorghe!" He stormed back to Gheorghe's sprawling body. Codreanu's shoe crashed into Gheorghe's face. The force flipped Gheorghe onto his back. Codreanu straddled Gheorghe's limp body lifting his head by the knot of his tattered necktie. Gheorghe gurgled as he struggled to breathe.

"You have played your last trick," Codreanu seethed through clenched teeth. He pressed the barrel to Gheorghe's temple. The gun metal seared Gheorghe's skin from a previous discharge. "Your prank will cost you dearly," billows of steam from Codreanu's mouth lit up the air. Gheorghe's neck hair prickled as the temperature plunged. Codreanu's rage insulated him from the sudden change in temperature.

Gheorghe choked, "Dragon..."

Codreanu relaxed his grip. "What did you say?"

Gheorghe snatched a deep breath and exhaled, "Your Dragon is here."

"Chief Inspector," a soldier called, "look," He pointed with his rifle. Codreanu stood looking where the soldier had pointed. A massive gray wolf stood in the distance of the warehouse. Its fur gleamed silver in the spotlights, splashed with red along the forearms and face. It panted heavily, its tongue lolling out eagerly.

"What is this, Gheorghe?" Codreanu asked. He stepped backward. "Fire a warning shot to scare it off," he ordered to one of the soldiers.

The soldier who had spotted the beast fired his rifle at the wall next to it. The wolf did not move.

"Kill it," Codreanu said.

The soldier fired again, but now the wolf was running towards them. He continued firing but could not make contact. The group of men became frantic and all the soldiers began firing. The wolf darted in and out of their line of fire, zigzagging between industrial equipment and into the cover of shadows. As it got closer, its great size became apparent. The men's frenzied firing and yelling swelled into a cacophony terror. The wolf was upon them. The soldiers in the front were bowled over as the wolf leaped into the air and came down hard on one of them. Breaking rank, the rest turned and ran for cover.

In the chaos, Codreanu seized Gheorghe's arm and dragged him behind between two large containment vats. They were tucked between the iron struts of the legwork and Codreanu peeked out from between the bars. "You won't get away with this," he hissed at Gheorghe.

The entire warehouse was flooded with the sound of bullets and the smell of gunpowder. In the flashes of muzzle bursts, Gheorghe could see the wolf darting from body to body. The constant stream of gunfire created a strobe effect as the wolf flashed between the men without interruption. It had already claimed two of Codreanu's squad. The remaining soldiers had backed themselves against the exit in a small semi-circle, firing at anything and everything, shooting into their fallen comrades if only to hit the wolf once. An acrid fog descended as the area filled with gun smoke.

Codreanu rattled out frantic commands, "Flank it," His grasp of the situation unraveled as it fell further into chaos, "Surround it!"

The soldiers ignored him, firing wildly at the wolf. It ducked behind some debris, but they continued firing until their clips were empty. Two rushed forward to drag their fallen comrades back to their fortified semi-circle. The wolf had taken large bites out of their throats and faces.

"We need back-up!" one screamed to Codreanu.

"It's just a wolf! Kill it!" he yelled back. He crawled out from between the two vats and hustled out to the loading dock. "Just kill-," he stopped in his tracks seeing the members of his squad spattered on the warehouse floor. A piercing scream sent Codreanu scurrying back to Gheorghe. As he squeezed into the small hiding space with Gheorghe, he roared, "Call in Shalberov! We need back up, now!"

A voice rose from the wreckage, "We need immediate back-up. Men down! We need all available assets!"

The floodlights coming from outside began to disappear one by one, each heralded by the sound of a popping light bulb. The swathes of light that had been cast on the warehouse walls and floor were erased, replaced with impenetrable darkness. Gheorghe's eyes had adjusted to the light, but now the surroundings were an inky void. He felt Codreanu grab him by the collar and lean heavily into him. His weight crushed him against a metal strut. Gheorghe labored to breathe under the weight of Codreanu. Gheorghe closed his eyes as Codreanu pressed the muzzle of his pistol against his temple. With the click of the hammer, Codreanu whispered, "Join the rest of your family-"

Codreanu fell silent as his weight lifted off Gheorghe's body. He heard gurgling noises above him. When he opened his eyes, he saw Codreanu dangling by his throat from three meters off the ground and kicking his feet helplessly.

The Master was holding him with one arm, floating above the ground in his nearly human form. In the darkness, the Master's bright white skin cast an eerie glow on their immediate surroundings. His face was fuller again and he was smiling his fanged grin, his mouth hanging open with bloodlust.

Codreanu's eyes bulged from his head, staring in disbelief at the face of death.

"Are you...," Codreanu gasped, "The Dragon?"

The Master paused pondering a distant horizon. A slow, jagged smile formed on his face, "You speak of my father. I am his son- Dracula." He tightened his grip around Codreanu's throat. Air hissed from Codreanu's mouth like a gashed tire; he forced out unintelligible noises in an attempt to speak. His legs flailed in vain as the life drained from his body. Dracula flicked him away and he plummeted to the ground with a thump. A few twitches of lingering movement prickled over his lifeless body.

Dracula grabbed Gheorghe by the ankle sliding him out from his hiding place. His dark form towered over him. His swirling red eyes captured Gheorghe's gaze. Attempts to resist were thwarted by a paralysis which seized his body. *Almost had...,* he thought. His thoughts succumbed to the weight of Dracula's stare.

"Captain!" a voice bellowed. Gheorghe felt as if he had been dropped from a great distance. Dracula's dark shadow had disappeared. With his hands cuffed behind his back, He struggled to sit up.

The beams of flashlights grabbed his eyes. "Where is Captain Codreanu?" a faceless voice asked.

"He is over here," Gheorghe blurted, "He has been injured; we need to evacuate him."

"We don't have time," another shaky voice called out, "Colonel Shalberov's reinforcements are on their way." Losing their resolve, they began shuffling backward as a group, stepping towards the exit.

Just as the soldiers made it to the exit, a dark shape descended on them from above. Two of them were pulled into the air with only the light from their flashlights revealing their movement. They were gone before they had time to scream and the flashlights fell to the ground, shattering on the floor. The remaining pair of soldiers began firing at the ceiling, causing a chorus of clangs and pings from the metal roof. The strobe of the machine-guns revealed the monster dropping the two bodies from the catwalk overhead and a sickening crunch followed.

Through the cacophony, a pleading voice screamed, "Shalberov, engage! Engage!"

The two remaining soldiers dropped their weapons and ran.

Dracula descended and lifted Gheorghe to his feet and stood him up before him. Dracula then turned to the crates to finish his inspection as if there had been no interruption. He regarded the overturned crate with some displeasure, but after peering into the others, turned to face Gheorghe with a look of satisfaction.

"Your service to me is complete." With that, Dracula seized him by the neck. His cold grip was like steel and he drew Gheorghe in close to his mouth. With his other hand, he bent Gheorghe's head to the side to reveal the thumping jugular on his neck.

Gheorghe went limp, feeling all the tension leave his body. Codreanu's corpse lay in Gheorghe's line of sight. *I don't want that to be the last thing I see,* he thought. With fading strength, He averted his eyes away from Dracula's gaping maw as it closed in on his neck. His eyes lingered on the ceiling and found a patch of stars. *I am ready,* he thought. The starlight sparkled above him. A sudden gash of light streaked across the sky. Gheorghe recalled the legend that a star falls when a soul passes over. *It's true; my star is falling to earth-*, Gheorghe was wrenched from his stupor as an artillery shell screamed out of the sky and exploded on the warehouse roof. The impact shook the very ground they stood on and the roof came crashing in on them.

A look of surprise flashed across Dracula's eyes though his mouth was still gaping over Gheorghe's neck. His face twisted into a terrifying grimace of rage and anguish. He released Gheorghe and darted towards the ceiling by clawing his way up the wall.

Another whistle sounded off in the distance and from his back, Gheorghe could see Dracula soar into the night through an opening in a shattered skylight. Gheorghe dragged himself backward, tucking himself under the vats just as he saw the roof buckle under a second mortar. The ground shook steadily with a distant rumbling and the refinery began to collapse from all sides. Gheorghe's vision was snuffed out in the downpour of debris and everything went black.

Last Man Standing

Light flickered past Gheorghe's eyes and the weight was suddenly removed from his eyelids. His eyes fluttered open, squinting into a bright overhead light. His vision began to focus and after identifying the incandescent light bulbs above him, he listened to their ambient hum in the silence around him. The quiet was soothing but alien and his heartbeat slowed again. The last thing he remembered was the icy grip around his neck and the screech of artillery. His eyelids became heavy again and they drooped to a close. He drifted off to sleep.

Gheorghe awoke again to a dull pain throughout his body. He opened his eyes and found himself beneath the same white lights as before. He tried lifting himself upright with his arms, but a stabbing pain shot down the back of his leg. He fell back wincing from the effort.

"Let me help you," a voice whispered.

Gheorghe looked to see the kind face of a nurse approaching him. She tenderly lifted him from the shoulders to help prop himself onto the flimsy pillow. The exertion telegraphed searing pain back down Gheorghe's leg. Gheorghe's face cinched in a contortion of pain.

"Just relax; everything will be alright," she soothed.

"Where am I?"

"You are in the hospital in Oradea," she gently rubbed his arm, "There is someone who has been wanting to see you." She pivoted and scurried out of the room.

Who would want to see me? He thought.

propped up on his elbows, he could see the rest of the room. The weight of his torso bore down on his waist and he felt a throbbing pain in his side and hips. Looking down at his body, he found that he was wearing a hospital gown and swaddled in bandages. He gave a faint smile since there were no handcuffs on his wrists. He scanned the room. The room was devoid of flowers, cards, or any other signs of visitation. Distant voices in conference seeped into the bland, antiseptic room.

Radu would have loved it, he thought as he replayed Codreanu's final moments. *Radu-,* he choked back tears. *What should I do about, Radu?* He stared at the ceiling for answers. *He is the Republic's problem now,* he concluded with a smile. Yet, the realization that he lost his only friend brought tears rolling down his cheeks. As he tried to suppress his tears, he winced from the pain of his heaving sighs.

The nurse reentered the room, with Shalberov following close behind. A large smile spread across his face when he saw Gheorghe lying in the hospital bed. He was carrying a small black box in his hands and he came in alone.

Gheorghe began to panic, squirming back against his pillow.

"Comrade, you are fortunate to be alive," Shalberov said.

Gheorghe stopped his fussing, eyeing the Russian officer. There was no hostility.

"What happened?" Gheorghe asked.

Shalberov nodded to the nurse standing nearby.

"Besides some cuts and scrapes, you have a concussion, several bruised ribs, and a fractured hip. Fortunately, the fracture is hairline. We cannot set the fracture so it will need to heal on its own. It will be a slow process, but you should be fine in a few months," the nurse said.

Shalberov drummed his fingers on top of the black box he had brought and stepped closer to the hospital bed. The box was covered in velvet and bore an official Soviet seal on its lid.

"Comrade Ianculescu, on behalf of a grateful nation, I am honored to award you the medal 'For Distinction in the Protection of Public Order' for the bravery and resourcefulness you displayed in uncovering and single-handedly dismantling a major rebel faction," Shalberov said. His voice was loaded with ceremonious tenors, but his eyes bored into Gheorghe's without a shred of sympathy. "Without your dedicated service, the internal security of the Romanian People's Republic would still be under threat. Thank you for your loyalty, comrade." Shalberov flipped open the box to reveal a silver medallion covered in elaborate script.

Gheorghe returned Shalberov's stare, searching for a hint of subterfuge. His thoughts were slow and disconnected. *What was the meaning of this award?* He thought. He remained silent, alternating his stare between the medal and the craters in Shalberov's bulbous nose. He did not take the box from him, still awkwardly trying to lean away from his visitor and the honorary offering.

Shalberov's eyebrows furrowed for a moment, a hint of anger simmered beneath his cool exterior. His upper lip was twitching as if he was fighting to keep it from curling away in disgust. He removed the medal from its box and no longer looked Gheorghe in the face.

"You are an example for all Romanians," Shalberov said towards the floor. He pinned the medal on the top of Gheorghe's hospital gown.

"Where is Codreanu?" Gheorghe asked.

"The treacherous snake and his den of conspirators are dead," he said with a practiced smile. His eyes flashed for a moment, sending Gheorghe an unspoken word of caution. When Gheorghe asked nothing further, Shalberov continued. "Given your achievements and your injuries, I think you have earned some time off to recuperate. I will notify your new supervisor that you will be on leave to recover from your wounds. Once you have returned to health, we will debrief you and determine your next assignment."

Gheorghe did not know what to say, so he stared at the drab medal on his chest.

"I must be going, but we will be in touch, comrade," Shalberov said with a subtle smirk. He was seen out of the room by the attending nurse and the door shut behind them.

A rich, warm silence filled the room. The curtain-less windows streamed in unfiltered morning sunlight. The dull roar of traffic below signaled all was normal. Gheorghe closed his eyes and took a deep, satisfying breath. A great weight lifted and he felt as if he were floating. An unfamiliar feeling came over him. Peace.

He replayed the events in his head. *How?* He thought with a smirk. *I have beat Codreanu at his own game.*

A faint knock on the door brought Gheorghe's thoughts back to the room. Without acknowledgment, the door opened and Dobrescu slid into the room. "Good morning, Deputy Chief Inspector. Or should I say Chief Inspector Ianculescu?" he chuckled.

"Chief Inspector? What are you talking about?"

"Well, I hear rumors that you will be replacing Codreanu," Dobrescu said with a boyish grin.

"Well, I don't-"

"Comrade," Dobrescu blurted, "I want to apologize for my past behavior-"

"There is no need to-" Gheorghe interrupted.

"No, no, I need to say this," Dobrescu countered, "Codreanu put me in an awkward situation. He confided in me his suspicions concerning your involvement with 'The Order of the Dragon' and his plans to entrap you."

"Really?" Gheorghe asked with a gaping mouth.

"Yes, I never realized it was he who was the traitor until Major Shalberov debriefed me yesterday," he squirmed and dropped his eyes to the floor, "I am truly sorry."

"Dobrescu," Gheorghe announced to regain his gaze, "Everything is fine. There is no way you could have known. You were just doing as you were told."

Dobrescu's smile returned. "Well, it looks like you will be rewarded...Chief Inspector."

I have no stomach for this anymore, he thought. "We shall see," he sighed to Dobrescu.

A clumsy silence fell on them. With nothing left to say, Dobrescu cleared his throat, "I need to get back to the station. If you need anything, let me know." He turned to leave.

Gheorghe ripped the medal off his gown. "Dobrescu," He called out, "There is something you can do for me."

Dobrescu turned, "What?"

☙❧

Gheorghe jostled awake in the backseat of Dobrescu's car. Despite the sudden interruption, a smile spread across his face. The summer daylight lingered at these early hours of the evening; and yet, Gheorghe was no longer scared of what the night may bring. Through his convalescence, sleep had progressively become easier as the memories of Dracula and Codreanu faded. He peered through the window. The landscape shed Oradea's sprawl to reveal the country's rolling hills. The further they entered into the countryside, the bumps in the road reminded him had not fully recovered. A dull stabbing pain greeted every hole in the road.

Dobrescu crested a slight hill to reveal a tiny village standing vigil in a patchwork of fields. "Does any of this look familiar?" he called out to Gheorghe.

He rolled down his window and absorbed the sights and sounds. "Yes," he sighed, "We are here."

"Is it as you remember it?" Dobrescu inquired through the rearview mirror.

"Sort of..." he trailed off as he inspected every detail, "Everything looks smaller."

"Anything different?"

"Well, the roads are paved. That is the first thing that sticks out," He tapped him on the shoulder and pointed ahead, "Let's stop at the square and walk around."

Dobrescu rolled into the square. Horses' carts still dominated the village square.

"How long has it been?"

The question stumped Gheorghe. With an unfocused stare, he did the math in his head. "Twenty-five years. No-", he interrupted himself, "Twenty-seven years, to be exact."

Once the car stopped, Gheorghe poured out the back of the car. He creaked to his feet and stiffly lurched through the square. Dobrescu popped out of the car and trotted to catch up with Gheorghe. "Careful," he called out, "you don't want to over-extend yourself." Gheorghe's injuries slowed his pace, but his nostalgia did not protest the sluggish gait. Dobrescu walked next to him as he lumbered through the square. "Look there," Gheorghe pointed, "All these storefronts use to be wooden stalls." The stalls had given way to more permanent structures with bright awnings with metal signage.

Gheorghe stopped to get his bearings. "There was a man who use to..." Gheorghe stopped when he noticed an elderly man following them.

He approached Gheorghe. "Excuse me, son," he said in a whisper, "You look familiar, do I know you?"

Gheorghe smiled. "Maybe, I am Florica's son. Gheorghe."

"Florica..." he pondered.

"Ion's daughter," he clarified.

"Ah," his face beamed with recognition, "Ion! You are Ion Kirpachi's grandson?" He lunged toward Gheorghe, giving him a bear hug. Stabbing pains shot through Gheorghe's ribs. He winced yet did not protest the hug. He clung to Gheorghe like a barnacle, "We thought all the Kirpachi's were gone."

Never thought of my family as being extinct, he mused. Gheorghe peeled himself away from his embrace, "No, not all. I am the last one."

The old man's smile dimmed "Have you been back to your grandfather's place?"

"No, I was hoping to visit it today."

"Well," his voice weakened, "The communists confiscated it and turned it over to the local party officials."

Gheorghe gave a slight smile. "I wouldn't expect anything less from them," he sighed.

"They probably wouldn't mind you visiting," he assured.

Reality began to fray the edges of his idealized memories of his childhood home. The drab collective spirit was beginning to leech into the remotest parts of Romania. *Time to reign in your expectations,* he told himself.

Like a migratory bird, He instinctively followed the road that led to his grandfather's farm. When he stopped to gauge the distance, a stabbing pain shot down his leg. "Mm..." rubbing his hip, he turned to Dobrescu, "I was hoping to walk to the farm. We better use your car."

CRSO

Driving the country road, he saw fields on either side of him laden with a tall crop of wheat. The sun gradually retreated behind the hills in the distance. In a matter of time, he began to recognize the geography around him. The hills, the trees, the old wooden fences, some things had not changed. He found his heart racing again, imagining he may even come across his mother and grandparents at the farm as if he had never left. Once he found the road that led to his family's plot, he tapped Dobrescu on the shoulder, "This is it. Let me out here." Dobrescu pulled to the side and rolled to a stop. With a slam of the door, Gheorghe said, "Wait for me here. I'll be back." He continued up the road, approaching a two-story farmhouse that was nestled between two large tracts of farmland.

The building was different from how he had known it as a child, rather small and off-colored. It had been painted light blue, different from how his family had kept it. A second floor had been added though the overall stature of the house was unchanged. Gheorghe paused, wondering if it was wise to proceed. He scanned his surroundings, realizing that there was nowhere else for him to be. Fate had returned him to his home. As he neared the farmhouse, he recognized the hill behind it. It was the hill from his dreams, the hill that demarcated his grandfather's oak tree from the house.

Gaining momentum, he walked faster than he had all day and climbed the hill with difficulty. Reaching the top with pained breaths and a throbbing ache in his leg, Gheorghe's heart sank at the sight that greeted him. He stood unsteadily on top of the hill, surveying the field that once harbored his grandfather's famous tree and instead found a sprawling collection of chicken houses. The stench of Chicken manure assaulted Gheorghe's nose. The tree was no longer there and Gheorghe let out a long sigh. He set himself down gently on the hillside.

"Gheorghe?" a soft voice called out from behind him.

Gheorghe looked over his shoulder. A woman with silver-streaked black hair tied in a ponytail stood several meters away from him, hesitant to approach. A patina of sadness covered her face. He fumbled to his feet. It was Camelia.

"Camelia, what are you doing here?" he asked.

She laughed at the question. "I live here. Where else would I be?" Her eyes still crinkled at the edges the same way as when they were young. Despite the wrinkles that laced her face, her cheeks still held the ruddy glow of life. Her smile brought him back to his youth.

Gheorghe laughed. "You're right. I'm the one who left," he said. He approached her and they shared a long hug; the years vanished along with the space between them. They stood quietly in their embrace, drinking in each other's presence.

"So, what are you doing here?" Camelia finally asked.

"I came to see the farm again," Gheorghe said with a blush, "and other things."

Camelia looked down bashfully at her apron, twisting at the frayed fabric.

A silence fell between them. Gheorghe, desperate to keep the conversation alive, asked, "How are your brothers doing?"

"They are dead, Gheorghe." A veil of grief settled over her face, "they are all gone." It was as if she just heard the news and burst into tears. Gheorghe held her close once more, fumbling out, "I'm sorry."

She buried her face into Gheorghe's shoulder. With muffled cries, she choked out, "Oh Gheorghe, if you could have seen the things I have seen."

"I know," he murmured. He thought his words sounded trite. *But, I do know*, he concluded. "We have lost so much," he whispered.

She pulled away from Gheorghe. "I'm sorry," she gathered her shawl together, "that was a pitiful welcome." She looked to the ground refusing to look at Gheorghe.

"Camelia," he cradled her chin and gently raised it, "it is okay."

"Well…" her voice faded, "I don't know…." She walked away from Gheorghe and peered down at the sprawl of chicken coops.

"When did they build those?" Gheorghe asked, pointing to the chicken houses.

"Two years ago. Comrade Ceauşescu ordered them built. I was here when they tore down your grandfather's tree. I cried."

Gheorghe returned his gaze to the field. He found himself smiling. He turned to Camelia with his smile in full bloom, "We'll plant a new one."

Alex J. Webster

Epilogue

PROLETARI DIN TOATE TÅRILE, UNIȚI-VÅ!

Scînteia

ORGAN AL COMITETULUI CENTRAL AL PARTIDULUI COMUNIST ROMÂN

| Anul XX | Nr. 50013 | marți 15 august 1950 | 6 PAGINI – 50 BANI |

Royalist Rebellion Thwarted in Borş

Oradea- In the throes of a dark and windy night last Thursday, the brave forces of the Securitate protected the people of Borş from a brazen Royalist uprising. Led by a former Chief Inspector of the Militia headquartered in Oradea, the rebellion had amassed a 50-man force to unseat the local government. The former Captain of the Militia in Oradea, C. Codreanu, was plotting to set fire to government buildings and homes of prominent Communists in a bid to win the support of a small band of rebels in a farming village northeast of Oradea. His traitorous plans had been laid bare days before Thursday, thanks to the unparalleled commitment and unwavering loyalty of an undercover officer of the Securitate. The rebel contagion of disorder and violence in Borş was stopped before it ever had the chance to spread.

The heroic officer, Officer Gheorghe Ianculescu, is being awarded one of the highest honors on the force, the medal for "Distinction in the Protection of Public Order" for outsmarting one of the most conniving and manipulative Militia Captains that The People's Republic of Romania has ever seen. Officer Ianculescu is a decorated veteran of the Second World War and has been serving

219

on the Militia since its inception. Previous to his investigation of his corrupt and traitorous Captain, he rescued over half a dozen school children from a serial kidnapper. Quickly after this success and subsequent promotion to the Securitate, he discovered a far greater crime had been going on under his nose all along.

On Thursday at 12:30 PM, the Securitate positioned its tactical forces outside a shuttered oil refinery which had been severely damaged by allied bombing during the war. As Officer Ianculescu had reported, Codreanu gathered his ragtag group of rebels in the warehouse. Located northeast of Oradea in Romania, Borş has long been an industrious agriculture center that provides the strong foundation for the lives of their urban comrades throughout the Republic. But dissent had been fomenting for weeks among a small group of farmers. They had no means to destabilize the state without Codreanu's assistance. Secluded but close enough to strike at the heart of Oradea, the warehouse in Borş made a perfect place for Codreanu's den of snakes.

Rallying late in the night, the rebel faction set fire to the abandoned warehouse they had been using as a base and began their march to overtake the village. Before the warehouse had even gone up in flames, the Securitate tactical squad was upon the rebels. A firefight raged with the blazing warehouse as a backdrop. The rebels were armed with leftover grenades and semi-automatic weapons that had trickled into the Militia armory from the War and five Securitate officers lost their lives. The Securitate team was outnumbered by nearly 5 to 1 though they held the rebels from advancing. Mortar fire was called in to dispatch the fortifications the rebels had made around their burning base. In almost no time at all, the warehouse crumbled around them like their weak coalition.

The rebels were completely wiped out, including their leader, Inspector Codreanu. The massive blaze of the warehouse caused and consumed many of the casualties of the night's battle. The following morning, the state government leveled the site to protect villagers from the debris and to redevelop the land for future use. With the unparalleled might and effectiveness of the Soviet military behind them, the Securitate and its valuable soldiers have once again proven that the will of the people always wins out over the self-interest of individuals. Long live the Republic!